CELTIC LORE & LEGEND

Meet the Gods, Heroes, Kings, Fairies, Monsters, and Ghosts of Yore

Compiled and Edited By Dr. Bob Curran

A division of The Career Press
Franklin Lakes, NJ

CELTIC LORE & LEGEND
TYPESET BY KATE HENCHES
Cover art by Lisa Hunt; Cover design by Kort Kramer
Interior Images from the Stuart Booth Collection
Printed in the U.S.A. by Book-mart Press

To order this title, please call toll-free 1-800-CAREER-1 (NJ and Canada: 201-848-0310) to order using VISA or MasterCard, or for further information on books from Career Press.

The Career Press, Inc., 3 Tice Road, PO Box 687,
Franklin Lakes, NJ 07417
www.careerpress.com
www.newpagebooks.com

Library of Congress Cataloging-in-Publication Data

Celtic lore & legend : meet the gods, heroes, kings, fairies, monsters, and
  ghosts of yore / compiled and edited by Bob Curran.
     p. cm.
   Includes index.
   ISBN 1-56414-786-X (pbk.)
     1. Mythology, Celtic. 2. Celts—Folklore. I. Title: Celtic lore and legend.
  II. Curran, Bob.

BL900.C44 2005
398.2′089′916--dc22

                                                                    2004063171

Dedication

To Mary,
for her long-suffering and
unstinting support in the
writing of this book;
and to Michael and Jennifer,
for their faith
in their father.

Acknowledgments

I wish to thank Derek Bryce and Llanerch Press for their permission to use their translations of two Breton folktales—"The Ankou" and "The Night Dancers"—and the Stuart Booth Collection for the use of the classic prints in this book. I would also like to thank Michael Pye at New Page Books for his help and encouragement throughout the writing of this book.

Contents

Fictional Tales

Introduction

The Celts, claimed Julius Caesar, wrote very little down. There was a very good reason for this: If written material were to fall into the hands of their enemies, it would disclose their strengths and weaknesses, their problems and uncertainties, their way of looking at the world. It could leave them open for conquest. And so, although they did have a written language, the tradition of the Celts was primarily an oral one. Information, history, and cultural perceptions were passed from generation to generation by word of mouth, building into a corpus of lore and legend that persisted even when the Celtic peoples became more settled.

Amongst the Celts, too, were those who were the custodians of such tradition—the storytellers and poets who were known as Bards and fili. These were the men (and women) who remembered the great kings who had ruled, the mysterious and inexplicable events that had befallen their communities, together with the genealogies of the leading families of the region. These were the people who offered history, tradition, and interpretation all rolled into one through the medium of oral story and tale. They were treated with deference and respect because they were the repositories of the traditions and culture that shaped their societies. In some places where the Celts have settled, this oral tradition continues even today through the medium of the *seanachie*, or local storyteller.

The stories that were passed down from one generation to the next—the *lore* of the community—were those of ancient gods and kings, of great heroes, of awful monsters, of passionate love in the face of adversity. As the centuries passed and one storyteller followed another, details were added or amended to give the tales more imminence, more terror, more splendor, or to fit them into the context in which they were told. Tales, therefore, shifted localities, characters changed, details were added—all crafted and molded by the storyteller's art. Despite changes and modifications, such tales retained the perceptions, traditions, and hopes of the Celtic race.

From time to time, great communal festivals such as the Irish *Ard Feis* or the Welsh *Eisteddfod* were held not only to celebrate the unity, skill, and strength of the Celtic people, but also their storytelling abilities. Here the Bards performed, displaying their imagination and talents to full effect. Although these events were national gatherings often used for the swearing of allegiance to a national ruler, they were not the sole venue at which Celtic stories were celebrated. In local areas, there were smaller gatherings, many of which persisted almost into modern times in rural Ireland as *ceilidh*-houses, or houses in which people from the local community met in order to sing songs, recite poetry, and tell stories. Sadly, with the advent of television and other forms of media, such places have now more or less died out.

Many of the stories told in these venues had a strongly local flavor and concerned aspects that were familiar to the audiences who heard them. They dealt with everyday life: work, romance, relations with neighbors, and the landscape all around. As with the epic legends before them, these stories were passed orally from generation to generation. As new cultural trends began to take precedence amongst the Celtic peoples, many of these old stories appeared to lose their immediacy and significance and were gradually lost to memory. Part of the Celtic tradition had vanished. And the oral tradition continues to vanish today as the last of the old generations die off.

Initially, no attempt was made to write any of these tales down. The Celts themselves were a predominantly oral people with little impetus to formally record any of their tradition. (Julius Caesar seems to suggest they were expressly forbidden to write by their *druids*, or holy men, for fear of such texts falling into the hands of others.) Ironically, it was the dying of the pagan way of life that spawned many of the stories and the coming of the new religion—Christianity—that actually preserved the traditions. It was the monks of the new order who first wrote down some of these ancient tales in order to pad out their holy commentaries and lives of saints and to make their teachings more acceptable to their formerly pagan audiences. The stories they recorded were the epic legends of the former tradition: tales of heroes and mighty fighting men, of sorcery and battles, of monsters and warriors. They were the oral traditions the Bards had proclaimed. These legends were gathered together into collections that formed the basis of the Great Myth Cycles, some of which have been passed down to us today. Although there may originally have been many more, only two of these Cycles survive today: the Irish and the Welsh. Other epics may have devolved into lesser collections, which were remembered by the seanachies—the direct successors of the Bards.

The name *seanachie* is an Irish word that traditionally means "man of lore" (although there were women amongst them, too). This is an excellent name, as it encapsulates what the traditional storyteller was all about. He (or she) was the repository of all the communal wisdom and experience that had percolated down across the years and the one who

9

revealed such wisdom and interpretation through the entertaining medium of stories and remembrances. The "man of lore" offered up interpretations of the landscape round about—sometimes tinged with local history, sometimes with local imagination.

At one time in rural Ireland, nearly every district had its particular seanachie. And areas in other parts of the Celtic world had the same. As mentioned earlier, these storytellers were an integral part of the communities in which they lived. Because of them, the tales had taken on a more homely, localized quality. These were not primarily stories of great gods, kings, and heroes, but rather they were tales of locally known characters, of fairies, of ghosts, and of the supernatural. They were the tales told by the fireside on a dark evening to friends and neighbors who had gathered round. They were stories that bound a community together and also gave it its identity. In effect, they were the means that shaped the society all around, as well as explained and interpreted it to itself.

Despite all of this traditional cohesion, societies began to fragment and split as the years went by and other forms of social interaction took over. Local traditions and tales began to be viewed as being too parochial and as having no relevance to the developing modern world. Television, with its imported culture, began to invade the kitchens where once the local storyteller had reigned supreme. Cinema offered wonders that were said to rival the greatest efforts of the tale-spinners. Gradually, the seanachies and people of lore began to slip away into the shadows as other forms of entertainment came to the forefront. Though there were still some gatherings in the ceilidh-houses of Ireland and other parts of the Celtic world during the 1950s and early 1960s, they had all but died out completely by the 1980s. And with them went the stories and legends.

The tales themselves, however, did not completely die out. Realizing what was happening, some folklorists *did* make an attempt to record for posterity at least some of the old tales and perceptions. Stories were transcribed into both written text and

10

audio format, and so some archives were built up. And, of course, there are written accounts of the great Myth Cycles that were preserved across the ages. But it has to be said that the majority of the old tales were lost as the human repositories of this lore died off.

And yet, the stories themselves did not *quite* die. Because they were so intricately interwoven with the perceptions and experiences of the Celtic peoples, their influence continued to bubble under the surface of Celtic society. They began to drift into the more mainstream art forms. Writers, artists, playwrights, musicians, and poets who had personal roots in the Celtic world were aware of these legends and used them and the themes they suggested in their work. Although these may not have been the tales of great gods and heroes or stories told by the fireside, the modern works owe much to the lore and language of such tales—tales that the Celts had crafted over the centuries and have now found their way into a more modern idiom. The influence, the perception, and the vision were still there. The lore and legend that had underpinned the earlier tales are present in the more modern works and continue to be so to this day.

This book is a celebration of that lore and legend. Its main purposes are to explore the old tales that have come down to us across the years and to see how they have shaped and honed our perceptions about Celtic life. In order to do this, I have followed a chronological structure that has already been laid out. The Mythological Tales section looks at some of the tales that have appeared in the Great Myth Cycles—those tales of heroes and gods. Because, as has already been noted, the Irish and Welsh Cycles are really the only ones that are in existence, many of the stories from them have been overly published in other volumes. This collection seeks out some of the lesser-known tales and presents them for the reader's interest and delight.

The second section, Fireside Tales, contains stories from a later chronological period, although the two sections are not necessarily mutually exclusive. These are the stories that reflect the hopes, ideals, fears, and opinions of the later Celtic people,

11

which were passed on by the seanachies who gathered around the fires in communal kitchens throughout the Celtic world. They are tales of witches, ghosts, fairies, and the like—things that had a distinct imminence to our Celtic forebears.

The final section of the book, Fictional Tales, serves to demonstrate how the ancient stories have influenced more modern writers. Themes that are common in many of these old tales, together with some of their more supernatural aspects, have influenced authors—especially ghost and horror authors—who have in turn placed some of them at the center of their works. Even in some of today's more visual works (graphic novels and films) such as *Slaine* and *Hellboy*, the influence of some of the old Celtic tales is evident. Indeed, *Hellboy*'s creator, Mike Mignola, often seems to borrow directly from Celtic folktale and myth for some of his work. It would therefore be an omission *not* to include such material in this volume.

Within Western culture, the influence of Celtic lore and legend spans a wide and diverse spectrum, ranging from the early Bardic storytellers to modern-day graphic illustrators and filmmakers. The Celtic contribution to the way we think, read, and imagine is incalculable; therefore, it is timely that this book should celebrate that contribution. The selections have been made so that they reflect the breadth and scope of the Celtic vision and perception. They come from a number of differing sources from the countries that made up the western Celtic world: from Ireland, Wales, Scotland, Brittany, and the Isle of Man. By doing so, hopefully this book reflects both the unity and diversity of the Celtic experience. So turn the pages and read on. Behold a world that lies just beyond the edge of your mortal perception—an unseen world that may now be drawing steadily further away from us as the years roll by and new interpretations take hold, but that was once very imminent to our ancient Celtic ancestors: the world of Celtic lore and legend.

Mythological

Tales

Introduction

The first stories amongst the Celtic peoples were oral ones. They were most probably told around the campfires by warriors and old men. As with most stories, they reflected the world these people knew. These were tales of great battles, of the deeds of heroes and kings, and of places with which they were familiar. Some of these stories may have been personal memories, but others had certainly been passed down by word of mouth from one generation to another.

Storytelling was highly valued amongst the Celtic peoples: the stories that came down across the ages gave them their identity and distinctiveness. Professional storytellers and recounters of tales soon began to emerge amongst them. These were the *Bards*, a specific group within Celtic society charged with recording the deeds of kings and men of valor, as well as the remarkable events within their respective communities. These men (and women) enjoyed great status in their society, but with this came the daunting task of remembering and being able to recite the great tales that characterized their communities. Every three years or so, great festivals were held at which reciters recounted their tales and competed with each other in the complexity and vividness of their stories, many of which were in verse in order to aid memory. In Ireland, for instance, such a gathering was known as an Ard Feis. This festival also held political significance in that it combined recitations, feats of strength, and so on, with the swearing of loyalty by all sub-rulers and chieftains to the High King. Today, this tradition is carried on in Wales through the Eisteddfod, or the Gathering of the Bards. In order to outdo each other and to help their own memory, the Bards embellished their tales, adding to the basic structure with elements out of their own imaginations. So, centered around the basic incident of the story itself, the Bards wove a wonderful fantasy that enthralled and excited their listeners.

Such tales were recounted directly from memory—a great feat by any means, considering the length and complexity of the stories and that none of them were written down. This did not occur until much later, as Christianity began to spread across the Celtic world. Monks, the scholars of their day, slowly and systematically began to record some of these old stories in written form. They had probably heard these stories from local storytellers. At first, some of the legends were simply added to pad out more religious texts, such as an addition at the end of the life of a saint. Gradually, however, the monastic scribes began to write down collections of tales. Roughly around the 10th and 11th centuries, some of these anthologies began to circulate throughout the Celtic world, forming, in effect, some of the earliest corpus of legendary lore that we have in the West. These were the Great Myth Cycles: stories of legendary heroes and rulers who made war on each other and who transacted with supernatural entities and races, such as the Sidhe, and of strange places far beyond mortal knowledge.

Only part of this literature survives, and it only remains in fragmentary form. The main remnants of the Myth Cycles are to be found in Ireland and Wales, where such works as the

Tain Bo Cuailnge ("The Cattle Raid of Cooley") and the *Mabinogion* are still extant. However, much of the remaining literature is now lost. For instance, it is thought that Scotland once boasted a rich and vibrant mythological cycle, but that it was largely destroyed during the history of that turbulent country and during the Scottish Reformation. Other isolated fragments of the Myth Cycles appear in places such as Cornwall and the Isle of Man, but these are only small remnants of a once great storytelling tradition.

As we read some of the ancient tales, we must also remember that the monkish clerics who wrote and copied them down were not altogether unbiased. As with the pagan storytellers of old, they shaped the tales to their own perspective, introducing elements of morality and justice that perhaps some of the original stories lacked. And yet the pagan tradition shines through, giving a depth and undoubted antiquity to the tales. These are the earliest fantasies of the Celtic peoples, born in the dawn of their civilization and just as vivid and vibrant as when they were first told around the warrior campfires eons ago.

Cruachan: The Place of the Sidhe

For the early Celts, the land assumed an almost magical significance. They believed they had emerged from the land and that the land was a part of them. It gave them their sustenance and shaped their identity. And it was filled with spirits and forces that continually watched human beings— spirits that might aid or attack them if they so chose. Such forces inhabited rocks, trees, wells, and hills and had existed alongside mankind ever since the foundation of the world. These were the *Sidhe*, the "People of the Mounds," and their dwellings were sometimes characterized by the ancient tumuli and earthworks of former peoples who had lived on the land that the Celts now inhabited.

The Celtic peoples often sought to appease these forces so that they could count upon their goodwill, and so many ancient kings built their forts and strongholds close to the places where the Sidhe might be dwelling. This combined well with their strong sense of place and associated certain chieftains with areas that were magical or had some sort of supernatural connotation. It was hoped that the ancient powers of the site would somehow influence the powers of the chieftain and his clan. Places, therefore, held a special significance in the Celtic mind. These were the places of the fairies, the physical manifestations of those early and dangerous forces.

The following excerpt is taken from Lady Augusta Gregory's *Cuchulain of Muirthemne* (1902). Lady Gregory (1832–1932), a contemporary and friend of W.B. Yeats, was a noted collector of popular and local folktales and stories from the great Irish Myth Cycles. Her stories of Cuchulain, the Hound of Ulster, are amongst the best-collected examples of the ancient myths. The extract cited here tells of the enchanted royal place of Cruachan and the Hill of the Sidhe. The language used is rich in extravagant detail, typical of early Celtic poetic legend, and is an exceptionally fine example of the storyteller's art.

Excerpt From
Cuchulain of Muirthemne

by Lady Augusta Gregory

Now as to Cruachan, the home of Ailell and Maeve it is on the plain of Magh Ai in the province of Connaught.

And this was the way that the plain came by its name. In the time long ago there was a king whose name was Conn that had the Druid power so that when the Sidhe themselves came against him, he was able to defend himself with enchantments as good as their own. And one time he went out against them and broke up their houses and carried away their cattle and then, to hinder them from following after him, he covered the whole province with a deep snow.

The Sidhe went then to consult with Dalach, the king's brother, that had the Druid knowledge even better than himself;

and this is what he told them to do: to kill three hundred white cows with red ears and to spread out their livers on a certain plain. And when they had done this, he made spells on them, and the heat the livers gave out, melted the snow over the whole plain and the whole province and after that the plain was given the name of Magh Ai, the Plain of the Livers.

Ailell was the son of Ross Ruadh, king of Leinster and Maeve was the daughter of Eochaid, king of Ireland and her brothers were the Three Fair Twins that rose up against their father and fought against him at Druim Criadh. And they were beaten in the fight and went back over the Sionnan [Shannon] and they were overtaken and their heads were brought back to their father, and he fretted after them to the end of his life.

Seven sons Ailell and Maeve had and the name of every one of them was Maine. There was Maine Milscothach, like his mother, and Maine Athremail like his father, and Maine Mo Erpert, the Talker and Maine Milscothach, the Honey-Worded, and Maine Andoe the Quick, and Maine Mingor, the Gently Dutiful and Maine Morgar, the Very Dutiful. Their own people they had, and their own place of living.

This now was the appearance of Cruachan, the Royal house of Ailell and of Maeve that some called Cruachan of the Poets; there were seven divisions in the house with couches in them, from the hearth to the wall; a front of bronze to every division, and of red yew with carvings on it; and there were seven strips of bronze from the foundation to the roof of the house. The house was made of oak, and the roof was covered with oak shingles; sixteen windows with glass there were, and shutters of bronze on them, and a bar of bronze across every shutter. There was a raised place in the middle of the house for Ailell and Maeve, with silver fronts and strips of bronze around it, and four brass pillars on it, and a silver rod beside it, the way Ailell and Maeve could strike the middle beam and check their people.

21

And outside the royal house was the dun with the walls about it that was built by Brocc, son of Blar, and the great gate; and it is there the houses were for strangers to be lodged.

And besides this, there was at Cruachan, the Hill of the Sidhe, or as some called it, the Cave of Cruachan. It was there that Midhir brought Etain one time, and it is there that the people of the Sidhe lived; but it is seldom that any living person had the power to see them.

It is out of that hill a flock of white birds came one time, and everything they touched in all Ireland withered up until at last the men of Ulster killed them with their slings. And another time, enchanted pigs came out of the hill, and in every place they trod, neither corn nor grass nor leaf would sprout before the end of seven years and no sort of weapon would wound them. But if they were counted in any place, or if the people so much as tried to count them, they would not stop in that place but they would go on to another. But however often the people of the country tried to count them, no two people could ever make out the one number and one man would call out: "There are three pigs in it," and another "No there are seven" and another that it was eleven were in it, or thirteen and so the count would be lost. One time Maeve and Ailell themselves tried to count them on the plain but when they were doing it, one of the pigs made a leap over Maeve's chariot and she in it. Every one called out: "The pig has gone over you Maeve!"

"It has not," she said, and with that she caught hold of the pig by the shank, but if she did, its skin split open at the head and it made its escape. And it is from that the place was called Magh-mucrimha, the Plain of Swine-counting.

Another time, Fraech, son of Idath, of the men of Connaught, that was the son of Boann's sister Befind from the Sidhe, came to Cruachan. He was the most beautiful of the men of Ireland or of Alban but his life was not long. It was to

The king and queen watch a chess match.

ask Findabair for his wife he came, and before he set out his people said: "Send a message to your mother's people, the way that they will send you the clothing of the Sidhe." So he went to Broann that was in Magh Breagh and he brought away fifty blue cloaks with four black ears on each cloak and a brooch of red gold with each, and pale white shirts with looped beasts of gold around them; and fifty silver shields with edges; and a candle of the king's house in a hand of each of the men, knobs of carbuncle under them, and their points of precious stones. They used to light up the night as if they were the sun's rays.

And he had with him seven trumpeters with gold and silver trumpets, with many coloured clothing, with golden, silken heads of hair, with coloured cloaks; and three harpers with the appearance of a king on each of them; every harper having the white skin of a deer about him and a cloak of white linen, and a harp-bag of the skins of water-dogs.

The watchman saw them from the dun when they had come into the Plain of Cruachan.

"I see a great crowd," he said, "coming towards us. Since Aillel was king and Maeve was queen, there never came and there never will come a grander or more beautiful crowd than this one. It is like if I had my head in a vat of wine, with the breeze that goes over them."

Then Fraech's people let out their hounds, and the hounds found seven deer and seven foxes and seven hares and seven wild boars, and hunted them to Rath Cruachan, and there they were killed on the lawn of the dun.

Then did Ailell and Maeve give them a welcome and they were brought into the house, and while food was being made ready, Maeve sat down to play a game of chess with Fraech. It was a beautiful chessboard they had, all of white bronze, and the chessmen of gold and silver, and a candle of precious stones lighting them.

Then Ailell said, "Let your harpers play for us while the feast is being made ready."

"Let them play indeed," said Fraech.

So the harpers began to play, and it was much that the people of the house did not die with crying and with sadness. And the music they played was "The Three Cries of Uaithne." It was Uaithne, the harp of the Dagda, that first played those cries the time that Broann's were born. The first was a song of sorrow for the hardness of her pains and the second was a song of smiling and joy for the birth of her sons and the third was a sleeping song after the birth.

And with the music of the harpers, and with the light that shone from the precious stones in the house, they did not know that the night was on them, till at last Maeve started up and she said:

"We have done a great deed to keep these young men without food."

"It is more you think of chess-playing than of providing for them," said Ailell: "and now let them stop from the music," he said, "until the food is given out."

Then the food was divided. It was Lothar used to be sitting on the floor of the house, dividing the food with his cleaver, and he not eating himself, and from the time he began dividing the food, never failed under his hand.

After that Fraech was brought into the conversation of the house, and they asked him what it was he wanted.

"A visit to yourselves," said he, but said nothing of Findabair. So they told him he was welcome and he stopped with them for a while and every day they went out hunting and all the people of Connaught used to come and to be looking at them.

But all this time Fraech got no chance of speaking with Findabair, until one morning, he went down to the river for washing and Findabair and her young girls had gone there before him. And he took her hand and said: "Stay here and talk with me, for it is for your sake that I am come and would you go away with me secretly?"

"I will not go secretly," she said, "for I am the daughter of a king and of a queen."

So she went from him, but she left him a ring to remember her by. It was a ring her mother had given her.

Then Fraech went to the conversation-house to Ailell and to Maeve.

"Will you give your daughter to me?" he said.

"We will give her if you will give the marriage portion we ask," said Ailell, "and that is sixty black-grey horses with gold bits, and twelve milch cows and a white red-eared calf with each of them; and you to come with us with all your strength and all your musicians at whatever time we go to war in Ulster."

"I swear by my shield and my sword, I would not give that for Maeve herself," he said; and he went away out of the house.

But Ailell had taken notice of Findabair's ring with Fraech, and he said to Maeve:

"If he brings our daughter away with him, we will lose the help of many of the kings of Ireland. Let us go after him and make an end of him before he has time to harm us."

"That would be a pity," said Maeve, "and it would be a reproach on us."

"It will be no reproach on us, the way I will manage it," said he. And Maeve agreed to it for there was a vexation on her that it was Findabair that Fraech wanted and not herself. So they went into the palace and Ailell said: "Let us go and see the hounds hunting until mid-day." So they did so, and at mid-day they were tired, and they all went to bathe in the river. And Fraech was swimming in the river and Ailell said to him, "Do not come back until you bring me a branch of the rowan tree there beyond, with the beautiful berries." For he knew there was a prophecy that it was in a river that Fraech would get his death.

So he went and broke a branch off the tree and brought it back over the water, and it is beautiful he looked over the black water, his body without fault and his face so nice, and his eyes very grey and the branch with the red berries between the throat and the white face. And he threw the branch to them out of the water.

"It is ripe and beautiful the berries are," said Ailell; "Bring us more of them."

So he went off again to the tree and the water-worm that guarded the tree caught a hold of him.

"Let me have a sword," he called out but there was not a man on the land would dare to give it to him for fear of Ailell and Maeve. But Findabair made a leap to go into the water with a gold knife she had in her hand, but Ailell threw a sharp pointed spear from above, through her plaited hair that held her, but she threw the knife to Fraech and he cut the head off the monster, and brought it with him to the land, but he himself got a deep wound. Then Ailell and Maeve went back to the house.

"It is a great deed that we have done," said Maeve.

"It is a great pity indeed what we have done to the man," said Ailell. "And let a healing-bath be made for him now," he said, "of the marrow of pigs and of a heifer." Fraech was put in the bath then, and pleasant music was played by the trumpeters and a bed was made for him.

Then a sorrowful crying was heard of Cruachan, and they saw three times fifty women with purple gowns with green head-dresses and pins of silver on their wrists, and a messenger went and asked them who it was they were crying for. "For Fraech, son of Idath," they said, "boy darling of the King of the Sidhe of Ireland."

Then Fraech heard their crying and said, "Lift me out of this, for that is the cry of my mother and of the women of Broann." So they lifted him out and the women came round him and brought him away into the Hill of Cruachan.

The next day he came out, and he was whole and sound, and fifty women with him, and they with the appearance of the women of the Sidhe. And at the door of the dun they left him, and they gave out their cry again, so that all the people that heard it could not but feel sorrowful. It is from this the musicians of Ireland learned the sorrowful cry of the women of the Sidhe.

And when he went into the house, the whole household rose up before him and bade him welcome, as if from another world he was come. And there was shame and repentance on Ailell and on Maeve for trying to harm him, and a peace was made, and he went away to his own place.

And it was after that he came to help Ailell and Maeve, and that he got his death in a river as was foretold at the beginning of the war for the Brown Bull of Cuailgne.

And at one time the Hill was robbed by the men of Cruachan and this is the way it happened:

One night at Samhain, Ailell and Maeve were in Cruachan with their whole household and the food was being made ready.

Two prisoners had been hanged by them the day before and Ailell said: "Whoever will put a gad round the foot of wither of the two men on the gallows, will get a prize from me." It was a very dark night and bad things would always appear on that night of Samhain, and every man that went out to try came back very quickly into the house.

"I will go if I get a prize," said Nera, then.

"I will give you this gold-hilted sword," said Ailell.

So Nera went out and he put a gad round the foot of one of the men that had been hanged. Then the man spoke to him.

"It is a good courage you have," he said, "and bring me with you to where I can get a drink for I was very thirsty when I was hanged." So Nera brought him where he could get a drink, and then he put him on the gallows again and went back to Cruachan.

But what he saw was the whole palace as if it was on fire before him and the heads of the people lying on the ground and then he thought he saw an army going into the Hill of Cruachan and he followed after the army.

"There is a man on our track," the last man said.

"The track is the heavier," said the [man] next to him and each said that word to the other from the last to the first. Then they went into the Hill of Cruachan. And they said to their king:

"What shall be done to the man that is come in?"

"Let him come here till I speak with him," said the king. So Nera came and the king asked him who it was had brought him in.

"I came in with your army," said Nera.

"Go to that house beyond," said the king. "There is a woman there that will make you welcome. Tell her it is I, myself, sent you to her. And come every day," he said, "to this house with a load of firing."

So Nera went where he was told and the woman said: "A welcome before you if it is the king sent you." So he stopped there and took the woman for his wife. And every day for three days, he brought a load of firing to the king's house, and on each day he saw a blind man and a lame man on his back coming out of the house before him. They would go on until they were at the brink of the well before the hill.

"Is it there?" the blind man would say.

"It is indeed," the lame man would say. "Let us go away," the lame man would say then.

And at the end of three days, as he thought, Nera asked the woman about this.

"Why do the blind man and the lame man go every day to the well?" he said.

"They go to know is the crown safe that is in the well. It is where the king's crown is kept."

"Why do these two go?" said Nera.

"It is easy to tell that," she said, "they are trusted by the king to visit the crown, and one of them was blinded by him and the other was lamed. And another thing," she said, "go and give a warning to your people to mind themselves next Samhain night, unless they will come and attack the hill, for it is only at Samhain," she said, "the army of the Sidhe can go out, for it is at that time all the hills of the Sidhe of Ireland are opened. But if they will come, I will promise them this, the crown of Briun to be carried off by Ailell and by Maeve."

"How can I give them that message," said Nera, "when I saw the whole dun of Cruachan burned and destroyed and all the people destroyed with it?"

"You did not see that indeed," she said. "It was the host of the Sidhe came and put that appearance before your eyes. And go back to them now," she said, "and you will find them sitting round the same great pot, and the meat not yet taken off the fire."

"How will it be believed that I have gone into the Hill?" said Nera.

"Bring flowers of summer with you," said the woman. So he brought wild garlic with him, and primroses and golden fern.

So he went back to the palace and he found his people round the same great pot, and he told them all that had happened to him, and the sword was given to him, and he stopped with his people to the end of a year.

At the end of the year, Ailell said to Nera: "We are going now against the Hill of the Sidhe, and let you go back," he said, "if you have anything to bring out of it." So he went back to see the woman and she bade him welcome.

"Go now," she said, "and bring a load of firing to the king, for I went in myself every day for the last year with the load on my back, and I said there was sickness on you." So he did that.

Then the men of Connaught and the black host of the exiles of Ulster went into the Hill and robbed it and brought away the crown of Briun, son of Smetra, that was made by the smith of Angus, son of Umor, and that was kept in the well at Cruachan, to save it from the Morrigu. And Nera was left with his people in the hill, and he has not come out till now, and he will not come out till the end of life and time.

Now one time the Morrigu brought away a cow from the Hill of the Cruachan to the Brown Bull of Cuailgne, and after she brought it back its calf was born. And one day it went out of the Hill and bellowed three times. At that time Ailell and Fergus were playing draughts, for it was after Fergus had come as an exile from Ulster because of the death of the sons of Usnach, and they heard the bellowing of the bull-calf in the plain. Then Fergus said:

"I do not like the sound of that calf bellowing. There will be calves without cows," he said, "when the king goes on his march."

But now Ailell's bull, Finbanach, the White-Horned met the calf on the plain of Cruachan, and they fought together, and the calf was beaten and it bellowed.

"What did the calf bellow?" Maeve asked her cow-herd Buaigle.

"I know that, my master Fergus," said Bricriu. "It is the song that you were singing a while ago." On that Fergus turned and struck with his fist at his head, so that five of the chess-men that were in his hand went into Bricriu's head and it was a lasting hurt to him.

"Tell me now Buaigle, what did the calf bellow?" said Maeve.

"It said indeed," said Buaigle, "that if its father, the Brown Bull of Cuailgne would come to fight with the White-Horned, he would not been seen any more in Ai, he would be beaten through the whole plain of Ai on every side." And it is what Maeve said:

"I swear by the gods my people swear by, I will not lie down on feathers or drink red or white ale, till I see those two bulls fighting before my face."

Magical Stones

No picture of the early Celtic landscape would be complete without its stone rings or individual upright-standing stones. In fact, they have come to characterize all that is Celtic about the countryside and have become so entwined with Celtic mythology that it would be neglectful to omit references to them from this selection.

For the early Celts also, these stones were symbolic. Many of them had been left over from the great Ice Age. To the Celtic mind, they spoke of ancient giants who had inhabited the lands before them. The great stones were the dwelling places of fierce spirits who coexisted with the Celtic peoples themselves. They were to be treated with reverence.

It is not clear whether the stone circles that once predominated the Celtic lands are directly attributable to the Celts themselves or to an earlier people. In many instances, they are referred to as 'druid circles,' but it is not certain that this is strictly accurate. They were thought to be places of ritual, not only for the Celts but also for the peoples that came before them. Therefore, they were places of great supernatural power. Certainly the druids, the Celtic holy men, may well have used them for their own purposes, thus adding to the occult significance of these sites.

Possibly the most famous of all these stone circles today is Stonehenge on Salisbury Plain in England, which attracts tourists and visitors from all over the world. It is certainly currently the most impressive of all the great megaliths. But in times more ancient, it must have been only one of a number of such menhirs scattered all through the Celtic world. Stonehenge, of course, was believed to have been magically brought from Ireland (where it was known as the Dance of the Giants) in the days of Vortigern, an early Celtic king. There were other great rings in Scotland, the most famous being the Ring of Kingussie in the Upper Spey Valley at the foot of the Cairngorms, which was supposedly used as a courthouse by the infamous Wolf of Badenoch in the 14th century.

Cornwall, too, was full of stone circles and isolated standing stones. Some of these can still be seen today on the moors and remote hills of the country. The following extract is taken from Robert Hunt's (1807-1887) essay "Romances of the Rocks," written around 1880. It is a clear attempt to provide some sort of "scientific" explanation for the ancient rocks and for the myths and legends (many of great antiquity) that surround them by linking them with extremely ancient and mythological traditions and histories.

Excerpt From "Romances of the Rocks"

by Robert Hunt

It is a common belief among the peasantry over every part of Cornwall, that no human power can remove any of those stones, which have been rendered sacred to them by traditionary romance. Many a time have I been told that certain stones had

34

been removed by day, but that they always returned by night to their original positions and that the parties who had dared to tamper with these sacred stones were punished in some way. When the rash commander of a revenue cutter landed with a party of his men and overturned the Logan Rock, to prove the folly of the prevalent superstition, he did but little service in dispelling an old belief, but proved himself to be a fool for his pains.

I could desire, for the preservation of many of our Celtic remains, that we could impress the educated classes with a similar reverence for the few relics which are left to us of an ancient and a peculiar people of whose history we know so little, and from whose remains we might, by careful study, learn so much. Those poised stones and perforated rocks must be of high antiquity, for we find the Anglo-Saxons making laws to prevent the British people from pursuing their old pagan practices.

The geologist, looking upon the Logan stones and other curiously formed rock masses dismisses at once from his mind, the idea of their having been formed by the hand of man and hastily sets aside the tradition that the Druids ever employed them, or that the old Celt ever regarded them with reverence. There cannot be any doubt but that many large masses of granite are, by atmospheric causes, now passing into the condition required for the formation of the Logan Rock. It is *possible* that in some cases, the "weathering" may have gone on so uniformly around the stone as to poise it so exactly that the thrust of a child will shake a mass many tons in weight.

The result, however, of my own observations, made with much curiosity and considerable care, has been to convince me, that in by far the greatest number of instances the disintegration, though general around the line of a "bed way," or horizontal joint, has gone on rapidly on the side exposed to the beat of the weather, while the opposite extremity has been but slightly worn; consequently the stones have a tendency to be depressed on the sheltered side. With a little labour, man could correct this natural defect, and with a little skill make a poised stone. We have incontrovertible evidence that certain poised stones have been regarded, through long periods of time, as of a sacred character. Whether these stones were used by the Druids, or merely that the ignorant people supposed them to have some particular virtue, I care not. The earliest inhabitants of Cornwall, probably Celts, were possessed with some idea that these stones were connected with the mysteries of existence; and from father to son, for centuries, notwithstanding the introduction of Christianity, these stones have maintained their *sacred character*. Therefore, may we not infer that the leaders of the people availed themselves of this feeling; and finding many rocks of gigantic size, upon which nature had begun the work, completed them and used the mighty moving masses to impress with terror— the principle by which they ruled—the untaught, but poetically constituted minds of the people. Dr. Borlase has been laughed at for finding rock-basins, the works of the Druids in every granitic mass. At the same time those who laugh have failed to examine these rock masses with unprejudiced care and hence they have erred as wildly as did the Cornish antiquary; but in a contrary direction. Hundreds of depressions are being formed by the winds and rains upon the faces of the granite rocks. With these no Druid ever perplexed himself or his people. But there are numerous hollows to be found in large flat rocks which have unmistakeably been formed, if not entirely, partly by the hands of men. The Sacrificing Rock or Carn Brea, is a remarkable example. The longer hollows on the Men-rock in Constantine, several basins in the Logan Rock group and at Carn Boscawen, may be referred to as other examples. With these remarks, I proceed to notice a few of the most remarkable rock-masses with which tradition has associated some tale.

The Logan or Loging Rock

[*Editor's Note*: Hunt states that much study has been given to the name of this rock mass at Trereen Dinas. The poised central stone—the Logan Rock—appears to be unsteady, and Hunt suggests that the name derives from a local Cornish word "to log," meaning to move unsteadily or "roll like a drunk man."]

Modred, in Mason's "Caractacus," addressing Vellinus and Ellidurus says:

Thither youths,
Turn your astonished eyes; behold you huge
And unhewn sphere of living adamant,
Which, poised by magic, rests its central weight,
On yonder pointed rock—from as it seems,
Such is the strange and virtuous property,
It moves obsequious to the gentle touch,
Of him whose breath is pure, but to a traitor,
Though even a giant's prowess, served his arm,
It stands as fixed as Snowdon.

This faithfully preserves the traditionary idea of the purpose to which this very remarkable rock is devoted.

Up to the time when Lieutenant Goldsmith, on the 8th April 1824, slid the rock from its support, to prove the falsehood of Dr. Borlaise's statement, that "it is morally impossible that any lever, or indeed force, however applied in a mechanical way, can remove it from its present position," the Logan rock was believed to cure children who were rocked upon it at certain seasons; but the charm is broken, although the rock is restored.

[*Editor's Note*: The stone was restored to its former site once again by Lieutenant Goldsmith, following a "great excitement" in the locality. A Mr. Davies Gilbert persuaded the Lord of the Admiralty to lend the Lieutenant the required mechanical apparatus in order to return it to its former position.]

Mincamber, Main-Amber, or Ambrose's Stone

A might Logan Stone was poised and blessed by Ambrose Merlin not far from Penzance. [*Editor's Note*: In some parts of Cornwall, the great Arthurian magician Merlin is sometimes given the Christian name Ambrose, presumably to fit in with Christian legend. Certain Cornish "conjurers," or local wise men, also adopted this name. It is not clear from Hunt's account whom he is specifically referring to.] "So great," says Drayton in his "Polyalbion," "that many men's united strength cannot remove it though with one finger may wag it."

Merlin proclaimed that this stone should stand until England had no king; and Scawen tells us:

> Here, too, we may add what wrong another sort of strangers have done to us, especially in the civil wars, and in particular by the destroying of the Mincamber, a famous monument, being a rock of infinite weight, which as a burden was laid upon other great stones, and yet, so equally thereon poised up by nature only. That a little child could instantly move it, but no one man or many, remove it. This natural monument all travellers that came that way desired to behold; but in the time of Oliver's usurpation [*Editor's Note*: The rise of the English Commonwealth under Oliver Cromwell after the execution of King Charles I in 1649], when all monumental things became despicable, one Sherubsall, one of Oliver's heroes, then Governor of Pendennes, by labour and much ado, caused to be undermined and thrown down, to the great grief of the country, but to his own great glory, as he thought; doing it, as he said, with a small cane in his hand. I myself have heard him to boast of this act, being a prisoner under him.
>
> So was Merlin's prophesy fulfilled.

[*Editor's Note*: Hunt takes this as the fulfillment of an ancient prophesy—the execution of the King and the establishment of a Republic under Cromwell as Lord Protector. The above quotation is taken from C. S. Gilbert's "Historical Survey." He also cites Scawen's "Description of the Cornish Language" and Sttukley's "Stonehenge."]

Zennor Coits

C. Taylor Stephens, lately deceased, who was for some time the rural postman of Zennor sought. In his poem, "The Chief of Barat-Anac", to embody in a story some description of the Zennor coits and other rock curiosities.

I employed this man for some weeks to gather up for me all that remained of the legendary lore of Zennor and Morva. He did his work well; and from his knowledge of the people, he learned more from them than any other man could have done. The results of his labours are scattered through these volumes. [*Editor's Note*: Hunt refers to the "Drolls, Traditions and Superstitions of Old Cornwall."]

C. Taylor Stephens wrote me on the subject of the cromlechs as follows:

Superstitious Belief respecting the Quoits

"I was in the neighbourhood of Zennor in 1859, and by accident came across the Zennor cromlech, and was struck with the mode of its construction (not having heard of its existence before), and thinking it bore some resemblance to the Druidical altars I had read of, I inquired of a group of persons who were gathered about the village smithery, whether any one could tell me anything concerning the heap of stones on the top of the hill. One said, 'Tes caal'd the giant's kite, thas all I know. At last, one more thoughtful, and one who, I found out, was considered the wiseacre and oracle of the village, looked up and gave me this important piece of information—

'Them ere rocks were put there afore you and me was boren or thoft ov; but who done it is a puzler to everybody in *Sunnur* (Zennor). I de bleve there put up there wen thes ere world was maade; but wether they was up or no don't very much mattur by hal akounts. Thes I'd knaw, that nobody caant take car em awa'; if anybody was too, they'd be brot there agin. [*Editor's Note*: If the stones were removed from their site, they'd be mysteriously returned before long.] Hees an' ef they was tuked awa wone nite, theys shur to be had rite up top o' th' hill first thing in mornin'. But I can't tell 'ee as much as Passon (Parson) can; if you see he, he'd tel he hal about it"

In one of the notes received from the poet and postman, he gives a curious instance of the many parts a man played in these remote districts but a few years since:

"My venerable grandpapa was well known by all the old people for he was not only a local preacher, but a character, a botanist, a veterinary surgeon, a secretary to a burial and sick benefit society and, moreover, the blacksmith of the neighbourhood".

The Men-an-Tol

Not more than two miles from Penzance stands the celebrated cromlech of Lanyon—often pronounced Lanine. This, like all other cromlechs, marks, no doubt, the resting place of a British chieftain, many of whose followers repose within a short distance of this, the principal monument.

Beyond the village of Lanyon, on a "furry down", stands the Men-an-Tol or the "holed stone". For some purpose—it is vain to speculate on it now—the bardic priesthood employed this stone, and probably the superstition which attaches itself to it may indicate its ancient uses.

If scrofulous children are passed *naked through the Men-an-Tol three times and then drawn on the grass three times against the sun*, it is felt by the faithful that much has been done towards insuring a speedy cure. Even men and women who have been afflicted with spinal diseases, or who have suffered from scrofulous taint, have been drawn through the magic stone, which all declare still retains its ancient virtues.

If two brass pins are carefully laid across each other on the top edge of this stone, any questions put to the rock will be answered by the pins acquiring through some unknown agency, a peculiar motion.

The Crick Stone in Morva

If any one suffering from a "crick in the back" can pass through this forked rock, on the borders of Zennor and Morva, without touching the stone, he is certain of being cured. This is but a substitute for the holed stone, which, it is admitted, has much more virtue than the forked stone.

In various parts of the country there are, amongst the granite masses, rocks which have fallen across each other, leaving small openings, or there are holes, low and narrow, extending under a pile of rocks. In nearly every case of this kind, we find it is popularly stated, that any one suffering from rheumatism or lumbago would be cured if he crawled through the openings. In some cases, nine times are insisted on "to make this charm complete".

Mrs. Bray in her "Traditions of Devonshire", gives several examples of the prevalence of this superstition over the granite district of Dartmoor.

The Dancing Stones, the Hurlers, etc.

In many parts of Cornwall we find, more or less perfect, circles of stones, which the learned ascribe to the Druids. Tradition and the common people, who have faith in all that their fathers have taught them, tell us another tale. These stones are the everlasting marks of the Divine displeasure, being maidens or men, who were changed into stone for some wicked profanation of the Sabbath-day. These monuments of impiety are scattered over the country; they are to be found, indeed, to the extremity of *Old Cornwall*, many of these circles being upon Dartmoor. It is not necessary to name them all. Every purpose will be served if the tourist is directed to those which lie more directly in the route which is usually prescribed. In the parish of Borlan, are the "*Dawns Myin*" or *Men*—the standing stones—commonly called "The Merry Maidens", and near them are two granite pillars named the "Pipers." One Sabbath evening, some of the thoughtless maidens of the neighbouring village. Instead of attending vespers, strayed into the fields, and two evil spirits, assuming the guise of pipers, began to play some dance tunes. The young people yielded to the temptation; and, forgetting the holy day, commenced dancing. The excitement increased with the exercise, and soon the music and the dance became extremely wild; when lo!, a flash of lightning from the clear sky transfixed them all, the tempters and the tempted, and there in stone they stand.

The celebrated circle of nineteen stones—which is seen on the road to Lands End—known as the "Boscawen-un circle" is another example. "The Nine Maids" or "The Virgin Sisters" in Stitithens and other "Nine Maids" or as called in Cornish Naw-Whoors in Colomb-Major parish should also be seen in the hope of impressing the moral lesson they convey yet more strongly on the mind.

The three circles which are seen on the moors, not far from Cheesewring, in the parish of St. Cleer, are also notable examples of the punishment of Sabbath-breaking. These are called the "Hurlers" and they preserve the position in which the several parties stood around in the full excitement of the game of hurling, when, for the crime of profaning the Sabbath, they were changed to stone.

The Nine Maids or Virgin Sisters

Nine "Moor Stones" are set up near the road in the parish of Gwendron or Wendron, to which the above name is given. The perpendicular blocks have obviously been placed with much labour in their present position. Tradition says they indicate the graves of nine sisters. Hals appears to think some nuns are buried there. From one person only I heard the old story of the stones having been matamorphosed maidens. Other groups of stone might be named, as Rosemedery, Tregaseal, Boskednan, Botalleck, Tredinek, and Crowlas, in the west, to which the same story extends, and many others in the eastern parts of the country; but it cannot be necessary.

The Twelve o' Clock Stone

Numbers of people would formerly visit a remarkable Logan stone, near Nancledrea, which had been, by supernatural power, impressed with some peculiar sense at midnight. Although it was quite impossible to move this stone during daylight, or induced by human power at any other time, it would rock like a cradle exactly at midnight. Many a child has been cured of rickets by being placed naked at this hour on the twelve o' clock stone. If, however, the child was "misbegotten", or if it was the offspring of dissolute parents, the stone would not move and consequently no cure could be effected. On the Cuckoo Hill, eastward of Nancledrea, there stood, but a few years since, two piles of rock about eight feet apart, and these were united by a large flat-stone carefully placed upon them— thus forming a doorway which was, my informant told me, "large and high enough to drive a horse and cart through". It was formerly the custom to march in procession through this "doorway" in going to the twelve-o'-clock stone.

The stone-mason has, however, been busy hereabout; and every mass of granite, whether rendered notorious by the Giants or holy by the Druids, if found to be of the size required, has been removed.

Table-Men

The Saxon Kings' Visit to the Land's End

At a short distance from Sennan church, and near the end of a cottage is a block of granite nearly eight feet long and

43

about three feet high. This rock is known as the Table-men or the Table-*main* which appears to signify the stone table. At Bosavern in St. Just, is a somewhat similar stone; and the same story attaches to each.

It is to the effect that some Saxon kings used the stone as a dining table. The number has been variously stated; some traditions fixing on three kings; others on seven. Hals is far more explicit; for, as he says, on the authority of the chronicle of Samuel Daniell, they were:

Ethelbert, 5th king of Kent

Cissa 2nd king of the South Saxons

Kingilis 6th king of the West Saxons

Sebert 3rd king of the East Saxons

Ethelfred 7th king of Northumberers

Penda 5th king of the Mercians

Sigebert 5th king of the East Angles—who all flourished about the year 600.

At a point where the four parishes of Zennor, Morvah, Gulval and Madron meet, is a flat stone with a cross cut in it. The Saxon kings were also said to have dined on this.

The only tradition which is known among the peasantry of Sennan is that Prince Arthur and the kings who aided him against the Danes, in the great battle fought near Vellan-Drucher, dined on the Table-men, after which they defeated the Danes.

The Armed Knight

At low water is to be seen, off the Land's End towards the Scilly Island (probably so called from the abundance of eel or conger fishes caught there, which are called sillys or lillis) for a mile or more, a dangerous strag of ragged rocks, amongst which the Atlantic Sea and the waves of St. George's and the British Channel meeting, make a dreadful bellowing and rumbling noise at half-ebb and half-flood, which let seamen take notice of and avoid them.

Of old there was one of these rocks more notable than the rest, which tradition saith was ninety feet above the flux and reflux of the sea, with an iron spire at the top thereof which was over-turned or thrown down in a violent storm, 1647, and the rock was broken in three pieces. This iron spire, as the additions to Camden's *Britannia* inform us was thought to have been erected by the Romans, or set up as a trophy there by King Athelstan, when he first conquered the Scilley Islands (which was in those parts); but it is not very probable such a piece of iron, in this salt sea and air, without being consumed by rust, would endure so long a time. However, it is or was, certain I am it was commonly called in Cornish An Marogeth Arvowed i.e. the Armed Knight; for what reason I know not, except erected by or in memory of some armed knight; as also Carne-an-peal i.e. the spike, spire or javelin rock. Again, remember silly, lilly is in Cornish and Arrmoric language a conger fish or fishes from whence Scilley Islands is probably denominated. Mr. Blight says this rock is also called *Guela* or *Guelas*—the "rock easily seen".

The Devil's Doorway

In the slate formations behind Polperro is a good example of a *fauit*. The geologist, in the pride of his knowledge, refers to some movement of the solid mass—a rending of the rocks, produced either by the action of some subterranean force lifting the earth-crust, or by a depression of one division of the rocks. The grey-bearded wisdom of our grandfathers led them to a conclusion widely different from this.

The mighty ruler of the realms of darkness who is known to have a special fondness for rides at midnight, "to see how his little ones thrive", ascending from his subterranean country, chose this spot as his point of egress.

As he rose from below in his fiery car, drawn by gigantic jet-black steed, the rocks gave way before him and the rent at Polporro remains this day to convince all unbelievers. Not only this, as his Satanic majesty burst through the slate rocks his horse, delighted with the airs of this upper world, reared in wild triumph, and planting again his hoof upon the ground, made these islands shake as with an earthquake; and he left the deep impression of his burning foot behind. There, any unbeliever may see the hoof-shaped pool, unmistakable evidence of the days gone by.

King Arthur's Stone

In the western part of Cornwall, all the marks of any peculiar kind found on rocks are referred either to the giants or the devil. In the eastern part of the county such markings are almost always attributed to King Arthur. Not far from the Devil's Coit in St. Columb, on the edge of Gossmoor, there is a large stone, upon which are deeply impressed marks, which a little fancy may convert into the marks of four horse-shoes. This is "King Arthur's Stone", and these marks were made by the horse upon which the British king rode when he resided as *Castle Denis*, and hunted on these moors. King Arthur's beds, and chairs, and caves are frequently to be met with. The Giant's Coits are probably remnants of the earliest types of rock mythology Those of Arthur belong to the period when the Britons were so advanced in civilisation as to war under experienced rulers; and those which are appropriated by the devil are evidently instances of priestcraft on the minds of an impressible people.

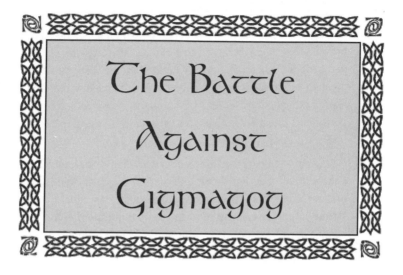

The Battle Against Gigmagog

Giants exercised a fascination for the Celtic mind. The lands of the West in which the Celtic peoples had settled had been formed by volcanoes and ice, and great reminders of this turbulent past were to be seen everywhere. Odd rock formations formed by volcanic activity together with huge boulders carried and deposited by glaciers dotted the landscape, and on these the early Celts gazed with awe. Who had created these? Who had hurled such massive megaliths to the places where they lay? For the Celts there was only one answer. This was the work of giants—monstrous, warlike creatures that had ruled these lands in some previous time. So fundamental was this belief that gradually, legends concerning these beings and their constructions began to appear in both Celtic myth and folktale. The Celts gazed in wonder at geological phenomena such as the Giants Causeway in County Antrim in the north of Ireland, and created wonderful stories of how it had been built by the Irish giant Fion McCumhaill (Finn McCool) as a highway to the West of Scotland that he could cross in order to attack his Scottish counterpart Benandoner.

In most of the tales, the giants are both ferocious and brutish. They were believed to have hurled rocks about and scooped out great clods of earth with abandon, thus creating the standing stones, loughs, and deep hollows that littered the countryside. Apart from one or two who were crafty and artful, most of the titans were dull and stupid and were easily outwitted.

What had become of these monstrous titans? The Celts believed that they had been defeated and exterminated by their forefathers in a series of violent battles. Gradually, stories began to emerge of wars against the giant-kind conducted by ancient kings in the days before history.

Nowhere throughout the Celtic lands were the giants so numerous, so huge, or so fierce than in Cornwall. Celtic legends tell of the confrontation between a wily king (some say it was King Arthur, others say it was another king known as Brute or Brutus who was said to have come from Troy after the siege there) and Cormoran, king of the Cornish giants, at St. Michael's Mount on the southern tip of England. The result of this clash was the defeat of the monster humankind emerging triumphant. With the defeat of Cormoran, the Cornish giants were said to have died out, although there are legends of some living on in later years. The following account concerns the leader of the giant brood here called Gigmagog. The account of the battle against this monster is taken from Robert Hunt's collection "Drolls, Traditions and Superstitions of Old Cornwall" (1881), a veritable storehouse of ancient lore. This is yet another version of the traditional tale of King Brute, the Trojan exile, and Cormoran, which is here presented as fact and in the style of ancient history.

Beseiged by enemies, a warrior defends a citadel.

Excerpt From
"Drolls, Traditions and Superstitions of Old Cornwall"

by Robert Hunt

Who can dare question such an authority as John Milton? In his *"History of Britain, that part especially which is now called England. From the first Traditional beginning continued to the Norman Conquest. Collected out of the ancientest and best authors thereof"* he gives us the story of Brutus and Corineus, "who with the battele Ax which he was wont to manage against the *Tyrrhen Giants* is said to have done marvells. With the adventures of these heroes in *Africa* and in *Aquitania* we have little concern. They suffer severe defeats; and then Brutus, finding his powers much lessn'd and this not the place foretold him, leaves Aquitain, and with an easy course, arriving at Totness in *Dev'nshire* quickly perceives heer to be the pomis'd end of his labours" The following matters interest us more closely:

"The Iland (Island), not yet *Britain* but *Albion* was in a manner, desert and inhospitable, kept only by a remnant of *Giants*, whose excessive Force and Tyrannie had consumed the rest. Them Brutus destroies, and to his people divides the land, which, with some reference to his own name, he thenceforth calls *Britain*. To *Corineus, Cornwall*, as we now call it, fell by lot; the rather by him lik't for that the hugest Giants in the Rocks and Caves were said to lurk there, which kind of Monsters to deal with, was his old exercise.

And heer, with leave bespok'n to recite a grand fable, though dignify'd by our best Poets: While Brutus, on a certain Festival day, solemnly kept on that shoar (shore) where he first landed (*Totness*) was with the People in great jollity and mirth, a crew of these savages breaking in upon them, began on the sudden, another sort of Game than at such a meeting was expected. But at last, by many hands overcome, *Godmegog* (*Gigmagog*), the hugest, in hight twelve cubits, is reserved alive; and with him *Corineus* who desired nothing more, might try his strength, whom in a Wrestle, the Giant,

50

catching aloft, with a terrible Hugg, broke three of his Rib. Nevertheless. Corineus, enraged, heaving him up by main force, and on his shoulders bearing him to the next high rock, threw him headlong, all shattered into the sea, and left his name on the cliff, called ever since *Longodmagog*, which is to say, the Giant's Leap."

The same story has been somewhat differently told, although there is but little variation in the main incidents. When Brutus and Corineus, with their Trojan hosts, landed at Plymouth, three chiefs wisely sent parties into the interior to explore the country and to learn something of the people. At the end of the first day, the soldiers who had been sent out as exploring parties, returned in great terror, pursued by several terrific giants. Brutus and Corineus were not, however, to be terrified by the immense size of their enemies, nor by the horrid noises which they made, hoping to strike terror into the armed hosts. These chieftain rallied their hosts, and marched to meet the giants, hurling their spears and flinging their darts against their huge bodies. The assault was so unexpected that the giants gave way; and eventually fled into the hills of Dartmoor. Gigmagog (Gogmagog), the captain of the giants, who was sadly wounded in the leg, and unable to proceed, hid himself in a bog, but there by the light of the moon, he was found by the Trojan soldiers, bound with strong cords, and carried back to the Hoe of Plymouth where the camp was. His victors treated Gigmagog nobly, and his wounds were speedily healed. Brutus desired to make terms with the giants; and it was at length proposed by Gigmagog to try a fall with the strongest in the host, and that whoever came off the conqueror should be proclaimed the king of Cornwall, and hold possession of all the western lands. Corineus at once accepted the challenge of the monster. Notwithstanding, the giant:

> *"Though bent with woes;*
> *Full eighteen feet in height, he rose;*
> *His hair exposed to sun and wind,*
> *Like wither'd heath, his head entwined"*

51

and that Corineus was but little above the ordinary size of man, the Trojan chief felt sure of a victory. The day for the wrestling was fixed. The huge Gigmagog was allowed to send for the giants, and they assembled on one side of a cleared space on Plymouth Hoe, while the Trojan soldiers occupied the other. All arms were thrown aside; and fronting each other, naked to the waist, stood the most lordly of giants and the most noble of men. The conflict was long, and it appeared for some time doubtful. Brute strength was exerted on one side, and trained skill on the other. At length, Corineus succeeded in grabbing Gigmagog by the girdle, and by regularly repeated impulses, he made the monster undulate, like a tree shaken by a winter storm, until at length, gathering all his strength, the giant was forced to his back on the ground, the earth shaking with his weight, and the air echoing with the thunder of his mighty groan, as the breath was forced from his body by the terrible momentum of his fall. There lay the giant, and there were all the other giants, appalled at the power which they could not understand, but which convinced them that there was something superior to animal strength. Corineus breathed for a minute, then he rushed upon his prostrate foe, and seizing him by the legs, dragged him to the edge of the cliff and precipitated him into the sea. The giant fell on the rocks below, and his body was broken into fragments by the fall; while the

"*Fretted flood,*
Rolled frothy waves of purple blood"

"Gigmagog's (Gogmagog's) Leap" has been preserved near the spot which now presents a fortress to the foes of Britain; and there are those "who say that, at the last digging on the Haw (Hoe), for the foundation of the citadel of Plymouth, the great jaws and teeth therein found were those of Gigmagog."

The Coming of Fionn and the War Against the Norsemen

From roughly the sixth to the 11th centuries, the Celtic peoples of the British Isles were frequently harassed and attacked by warriors from the North. Saxons, Angles, and Jutes formed the first wave, attacking the southern part of England almost as soon as the Roman legions had left, but it was the second wave, whom the Celts called either Fine Gall (white foreigners) and Dubh Gall (black foreigners)— a description that probably referred to their hair coloring, who were most feared. These were the Vikings: fierce raiders and settlers who began their attacks on the Celtic coastline around the eighth century and perhaps even earlier They were sea-borne raiders (the name "Viking" comes from the West Norwegian "vikingr," which later meant "sea warrior"), sweeping down from the countries that now form Scandinavia (Norway, Denmark, Sweden) and from some of the Baltic and Russian countries. Strong, ferocious, and merciless, they sacked Celtic settlements, carrying away booty and slaves and sometimes even seizing lands for themselves. As their attacks increased throughout the ninth and 10th centuries, these hardened warriors often entered the mythology of the Celtic people as fearsome giants and monsters who were thwarted and defeated by the skill and guile of the early Celtic kings.

Two parts of the Celtic world suffered greatly from the Viking raids: Ireland and the west coast of Scotland. In Ireland, the Vikings had established great bases, such as the area that constitutes the present-day city of Dublin, from which they raided deep into surrounding kingdoms. Scotland too, experienced their hostile intentions. Viking kingdoms were established in Argyll (the place of the Eastern Gael) and in the Western Isles, and it is here that some of the ancient mythological tales about them are to be found. Tales of battles against the Norsemen by Scottish rulers sometimes find parallels in later Irish mythology and serve as a connection between the two bodies of legend—both Irish and Scottish.

The following extract is taken from a series of tales orally collected in the early 19th century by the Scottish folklorist J.F. Campbell (1821–1885). Many of these stories come from the Western Highlands and the Western Isles where Norse influence was particularly strong. The following story was recorded from Angus McDonald of Stoneybrodge on the island of South Uist around 1860 and reinforces the connection between Ireland and Scotland. It is also characterized by the almost surreal heroic deeds, which are sometimes to be found in Irish mythology.

Story by Angus McDonald

There was a king on a time in Eirinn, to whom the cess (misfortune and destruction) which the Lochlanners (Norsemen) had laid on Alba (Scotland) and Eireann was grievous. They were coming on his own realm, in harvest and summer, to feed themselves on his goods, and they were brave, strong men, eating and spoiling as much as the Scots and Irish (Albannaich and Eirionnaich; Alban-ians, Eirin-ians) were making ready for another year.

He sent word for a counsellor that he had, and he told him all that was in his thought, that he wanted to find a way to keep the Scandinavians (Lochlainnaich, Lochlian-ians) back. The counsellor said to him that this would not grow with him (be achieved) in a moment, but if he would take his counsel, that it would grow with him in time.

"Marry", she told him "the hundred biggest men and woman in Eirinn to each other; marry that race to each other; marry that second race to each other again; and let the third kindred (ginealach) go to face the Lochlaners".

This was done and when the third kindred came to man's estate, they came over to Albainn and Cumhal was at their head.

It grew with them to rout the Lochlaners, and drive them back. Cumhal made a king of himself in Alba that time with these men, and he would not let Lochlaner or Irelander to Alba but himself. This was a grief to the King of Lochlann [*Editor's Note*: Probably Western Norway. Much of the settlement on the Western coast of Scotland was initially believed to have come from Westfold.] and he made up with the King of Alba that there should be a friendship between them, her and yonder at that time. They settled together, the three kings—the King of Lochlann and the King of Alba, and the King of Eirinn—that they would have a great "*ball*" of dancing and there should be friendship and truce amongst them.

There was a "schame" (plot) between the King of Eirinn and the King of Lochlann to put the King of Scotland (Alba) to death. Cumhal was so mighty that there was no contrivance for putting him to death, unless he was slain with his own sword when he was spoilt with drink, and love making and asleep.

He had his choice of a sweetheart amongst any of the women in the company, and it was the daughter of the King of Lochlann whom he chose.

When they went to rest, there was a man in the company, whose name was Black Arcan, whom they set apart to do the murder when they should be asleep. When they slept, Black Arcan got the sword of Cumhal, and he slew him with it. The murder was done and everything was right. Alba was under the Lochalaners and the Irelanders and the Black Arcan had the sword of Cumhal.

The King of Lochlann left his sister with the King of Eirinn, with an order that if she should have a babe son to slay him but if it were a baby daughter, to keep her alive. A prophet had told that Fionn MacChumhail would come, and the sign for this was a river in Eirinn that no trout could be killed in till Fionn should come. That which came of the fruit of the wedding that was there, was that the daughter of the King of Lochlann bore a son and a daughter to Cumhal. Fionn had no sister but this one and she was the mother of Diarmaid. On the night they were borne, his muime (nurse) fled with the son, and she went to a desert place with him, and she was keeping him there till she raised him as a stalwart and goodly child. [*Editor's Note*: This is a Scottish version of the birth of the celebrated Irish hero Fionn MacCumhail (Finn McCool) one of the foremost Knights of the Fianna in Irish mythology and father of the great Irish Bard and poet Oisin, who was also well known as a hero in the Western Isles.]

She thought it was sorry for her that he should be nameless with her. The thing she did was to go with him to the town, to try if she could find means to give him a name. She saw the school-boys of the town swimming in a fresh water loch.

"Go out together with these", she said to him, "and if thou gettest hold of one, put him under and drown him; and if thou gettest hold of two, put them under and drown them"

He went out on the loch and he began drowning the children, and it happened that one of the bishops of the place was looking on.

"Who", said he, "is that bluff fair son with the eye of a king in his head, who is drowning those school boys?"

"May he steal his name!" said his muime. "Fionn son of Cumhall, son of Finn, son of every eloquence, son of Art, son of Eirinn's high king, and it is my part to take myself away".

Then he came on shore and she snatched him with her.

When the following (those who were pursuing them) were about to catch them, he leapt off his muime's back, and seized her by the two ankles, and he put her about his neck. He went in through a wood with her and when he came out he had but the two shanks. He met with a loch after he came out of the wood, and he threw the two legs out on the loch, and it is Loch nan Lurgan, the lake of the shanks, that the loch was called after this. Two great monsters grew from the shanks of Fionn's muime. That is the kindred that he had with the two monsters of Loch nan Lurgan.

Then he went, and without meat or drink, to the great town. He met Black Arcan, fishing on the river, and a hound in company with him—Bran MacBruidehig (black, or raven, son of little yellow).

"Put out the rod for me", said he to the fisherman, "for I am hungry, to try if thou canst get a trout for me". The trout was laid out to him, and he killed the trout. He then asked the trout from Black Arcan (he asked Arcan to give him the trout).

"Thou art the man!" said Black Arcan; "when thou wouldst ask a trout and that I am fishing for years for the king, and that I am as yet without a trout for him".

He knew that it was Fionn that he had. To put the tale on the short cut, he killed a trout for the king, and for his wife, and for his son and for his daughter, before he gave any to

Fionn. Then he gave him a trout. [*Editor's Note*: This story of the fisherman doling out fish to all and sundry before giving the *hero* or holy man his portion is common in Irish storytelling. It is said that St. Teca of Aanghloo—County Londonderry in the North of Ireland—asked a fisherman on the banks of the River Roe, for the first fish that he caught. The fisherman landed a great fish which he gave to his wife, claiming that he would catch a bigger fish for the saint; he did in fact catch a larger fish which he gave to his own children, promising her would catch an even larger one for the holy man. When he did so, he presented it to a neighbor who was passing by and the saint lost patience and cursed the river so that it always ran red as blood. Similar stories exist on the Inner Hebridean islands of Islay and Jura and elsewhere in the Western Isles.]

"Thou must", said Black Arcan, "broil the trout on the further side of the river, and the fire on this side of it, before thou gettest a bit of it to eat, and thou shalt not have leave to set a stick that is in the wood to broil it". He did not know what he should do. The thing that he fell in with was a mound of sawdust and he set it on fore beyond the river. A wave of the flame came over and it burned a spot on the trout, the thing that was on the crook. [*Editor's Note*: Campbell points out in his notes on the text that the word that is used here in the original Gallic is the same that is used for a shepherd's crook or a bishop's crozier—bachall, generally the staff of a holy man. This may be a later addition to the tale, as the traditional way of roasting fish was probably on some sort of spit.] Then he put his finger on the black spot that came on the trout and it burnt him, and then he put it into his mouth. Then he got knowledge that it was Black Arcan who had slain his father, and unless he should slay Black Arcan in his sleep, that Black Arcan would slay him when he should wake. [*Editor's Note*: This appears to be a version of the Irish legend of the Salmon of Knowledge. Fionn catches the fish and cooks it but burns himself by touching its back and by sucking his finger, grains all the knowledge of the world, making him a formidable hero.] The thing that happened was that he killed the carle (Black Arcan), and then he got a glaive (a polearm, or sword/knife with a long curving blade) and a hound, and the name of the hound was Bran MacBuidheig.

Then he thought that he would not stay any longer in Eirinn, but that he would come to Alba to get the soldiers of his father. He came to the shore in Fairbaine. There he found a great clump of giants, men of stature. He understood that these were the soldiers that his father had and that they were as poor captives by the Lochlaners hunting for them and not getting aught but the remnants of the land's increase for themselves. The Lochlaners took from the arms (had taken their weapons) when war or anything should come, for fear they should rise with the foes. They had one special man for taking their arms, whose name was Ullamh Lamh fhada (Pronounced: oolav lav ada—Oolav Long Hand). He gathered the arms and he took them with him altogether, and it fell out that the sword of Fionn was amongst them. Fionn went after him, asking for his own sword. When they came within sight of the armies of Lochlann, he said:

"*Blood on man and man bloodless,*
Wind over hosts, 'tis pity without the son of Luin"

[*Editor's Note*: In this version of the tale, Fionn's sword seems to have been given a name—common in some Irish mythological tales. The name which he give it is MacLuan— son of Luan. In the couplet, Fionn is therefore referring to his weapon.]

"To what might belong?" said Ulamh lamh fhada.

"It is to a little bit of a knife of a sword that I had" said Fionn. "You took it with you among the rest, and I am the worse for wanting it and you are no better for having it"

"What is the best exploit, thou wouldst do if thou hadst it?"

"I wouldst quell the third part of the hosts that I see before me."

Oolav Longhand laid his hand on the arms. The most likely sword and the best that he found, he gave it to him He seized it and he shook it, and he cast it out of the wooden handle, and said he—

"It is one of the black-edged glaives,
It was not Mac Luan, my blade;
It was no hurt to draw it from sheath,
It would not take the head of a lamb"

Then he said the second time, the same words. He said for the third time:

"Blood on man and bloodless man,
Wind on the people, 'tis pity without the son of Luan."

"What wouldst thou do with it if thou shouldst get it?"
"I would do this, that I would quell utterly all I see."

He threw down the arms altogether on the ground. Then Fionn got his sword and said he then:

"This is the one of thy right hand."

Then he returned to the people he had left. He got the Ord Fiannta of the Finn [*Editor's Note*: This was said to be a great war horn of the Irish Fianna, described as being "a mighty cylinder of brass," which called the Knights to battle. It now seems to have been transposed into Scottish legend. There are however representations of an ancient horn carved into stones in the West of Scotland and it is possible that there were several such horns, both in Scotland and in Ireland.] and he sounded it.

There gathered all that were in the southern end of Alba of the Faiantaichain, to where he was. [*Editor's Note*: The name "Faintaichain" may refer to a group of Dalriadans who may have been in the southwestern area of Scotland. Dalriada was an ancient Celtic maritime kingdom, which stretched from County Antrim in the North of Ireland into the Mull of Kintyre and possibly Argyll as well. The kingdom was comprised mostly of Irish settlers who spread out through Kintyre, Lorn, and the Western Isles. The Irish sector of the kingdom collapsed in the sixth century, mainly, it is thought, due to internal divisions within the country, but the Scottish section continued until the early ninth century. The great Scottish king Cineach MacAlpin (Kenneth MacAlpin) was believed to be descended from a Dalriadan Irish father. Fionn, therefore, might be seen as an Irish leader of nominally Scottish warriors.] He went with these men and they went to attack the Lochlann, and those which he did not kill, he swept them out of Alba.

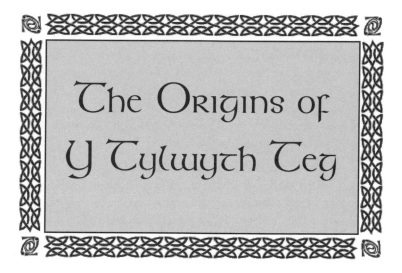

The Origins of Y Tylwyth Teg

From earliest times, Men and the fairy kind seem to have existed side by side. Ancient myths and legends tell how, as the Sidhe (the People of the Mounds), they influenced and aided great heroes in their efforts or else worked against them on behalf of their enemies. Initially, they were probably no more than the embodiment of the elemental forces, which the Celts believed to be in the landscape all around them. Latterly, however, they were considered to be another race not human and were known under a variety of names. For example, as the Tuatha de Danaan (the People of Danu), they were known throughout ancient Ireland as great healers but also were feared as powerful magicians. According to the "Book of Invasions" (a monkish text probably written around the 12th century), they arrived "from the East" (Greece?) in a "golden mist" and partly drove out those who already occupied Ireland. As the slightly more hostile Sluagh in Scotland, they were responsible for creating fierce winds and for hurling stone and rocks at the humans whom they despised

They often appeared, when they allowed the Sons of Adam to see them, as humanoid creatures, sometimes in old legends as beautiful men and girls, golden-skinned and with noble features. Their society, according to tradition, was loosely modeled on Celtic society itself so that the mortals whom they captured could make the transition between the two spheres of existence quite easily.

But where had the fairy kind—the Sidhe, the Sluagh, or whatever local Celts chose to call them—come from? Had they, as some sources suggest, come from the East? Were they all that remained of the ancient gods and goddesses who had once been worshipped throughout the Celtic lands before the coming of Christianity? Or were they really angels who had been banished from Heaven? Were they friendly or utterly and implacably hostile towards Humankind? Down through the centuries, from very ancient to relatively recent times, there have been many explanations for their origin.

One of those who considered the problem from a learned perspective and with regard to the Welsh Tylwth Teg (as the Sidhe were named in Wales) was the folklorist and Classicist Elias Owen, Vicar of Llanyblodwel. Turning his not inconsiderable knowledge to the matter, he began to speculate on the origins of these supernatural beings from earliest, mythological antiquity. His 'Notes on Y Tylwyth Teg' (1895-6) set the Celtic fairies within a wider Classical and mythological context, as the following excerpt shows.

Excerpt From
"Notes on Y Tylwyth Teg"

by Elias Owen

The Fairy tales that abound in the Principality (of Wales) have much in common with like legends in other countries.

This points to a common origin of all such tales. There is a real and unreal, a mythical and material aspect to Fairy Folk-lore. The prevalence, the obscurity and the different versions of the same Fairy tale shows that their origin dates from remote antiquity. The supernatural and the material are strangely blended together in these legends, and this also points to their great age, and intimates that these wild and imaginative Fairy narratives had some historical foundation. If carefully sifted, these legends will yield a fruitful harvest of ancient thoughts and facts connected with a history of a people which, as a race is, perhaps, now extinct, but which has to a certain extent been merged into a stronger and more robust race, by whom they were conquered and dispossessed of much of their land. The conquerors of the Fair Tribe have transmitted to us tales of their timid, unwarlike, but truthful predecessors of the soil, and these tales shew that for a time, both races were the inhabitants of the land, and to a certain extent, by stealth, intermarried.

Fairy tales, much alike in character, are to be heard in many countries, peopled by peoples of the Aryan race [*Editor's Note*: With whom the Celts were believed to have strong connections], and consequently these stories in outline were most probably in existence before the emigration of the families belonging to that race. It is not improbable that the emigrants would carry with them, into all countries whithersoever they went, their ancestral legends, and they would have no difficulty in supplying these interesting stories with a home in their new country. If that supposition be correct, we must look for the origin of Fairy Mythology in the cradle of the Ayrian people, and not in any part of the world inhabited by the descendants of that great race.

But it is not improbable that incidents in the process of colonisation would repeat themselves, or under special circumstances, vary, and thus we should have similar and different variations of the same historical event in all countries once inhabited by a diminutive race, which was overcome by a more powerful people.

In Wales, Fairy legends have such peculiarities that they seem to be historical fragments of by-gone days. And apparently, they refer to a race which immediately preceded the Celt in the occupation of the country, and with which the Celt, to a limited degree, amalgamated.

Names Given to the Fairies

The Fairies have, in Wales, at least three common and distinctive names, as well as others that are not nowadays used.

The first and most general name given to the Fairies is "*Y Tylwyth Teg*" or the Fair Tribe, as an expressive and descriptive term. They are spoken of as people, and not as myths or goblins, and they are said to be a fair or handsome race.

Another common name for the Fairies is *Bendyth y Mamau* or "A Mother's Blessing". In Doctor Owen Pughe's Dictionary, they are called "*Benditth eu Mamau*" or, "*Their* Mother's Blessing". The first is the more common expression, at least in North Wales. It is a singularly strange expression, and difficult to explain. Perhaps it hints at Fairy origin on the mother's side of certain fortunate people.

The third name given to the Fairies is "*Ellyll*", an elf, a demon, a goblin. This conveys these beings to the land of spirits, and makes them resemble the oriental Genii, and Shakespeare's sportive elves. It agrees, likewise, with the modern popular creed respecting goblins and their doings.

Davydd ab Gwilym in a description of a mountain mist in which he was once enveloped says:

"*Yr ydoedd ym mbob gobant
Ellyllon mingeimiou gant*"

"There were in every hollow,
A hundred wrymouthed elves."
The Cambro-Britian v. I.p. 348

In Prembrokeshire, the Fairies are called *Dynon Bach Teg* or the Small Fair People.

Another name applied to the Fairies is *Plant Annwfn* or *Plant Annwn*. This, however, is not an appellation in common use. The term is applied to the Fairies in the third paragraph of a Welsh prose poem called *Bard Cuag*, thus:

"*Y bwriodd y Tylwyth Teg fi…oni baif y nyfod; mawn pryd i'th achub o' gigweinau Plant Annwfn.*"

"Where the *Tylwyth Teg* threw me……If I had not come in time to rescue thee from the clutches of *Plant Annwfn*"

Annwn or *Annwfn* is defined in Canon Silvan Evans's Dictionary as an abyss, Hades etc. Plant Annwfn, therefore, means the children of the lower regions. It is a name derived from the supposed place of abode—the bowels of the earth—of the Fairies. *Guragedd Annwn*, the dames of Elfin land, is a name applied to Fairy ladies.

Ellis Wynne, the author of *Bard Cuag*, was born in 1671, and the probability that the words *Plant Annwfn* formed in his days part of the vocabulary of the people. He was born in Merionethshire.

Gwyll, according to Richards and Dr. Owen Pughe is a Fairy, a goblin etc. The plural of *Gwyll* would be *Gwylliaid* or *Gwyllion* but this latter word Dr. Pughe defines as ghosts, hobgoblins etc. Formerly there was, in Merionethshire, a red-haired family of robbers called *Y Gwylliaid Cochion* or the Red Fairies, of whom I shall speak hereafter.

Coblynau or Knockers have been described as a species of Fairies whose abode was within the rocks, and whose province it was to indicate to the miners by the process of knocking etc., the presence of rich lodes of lead and other metals in this or that direction of the mine.

That the words *Tylwyth Teg* and *Ellyll* are convertible terms appears from the following stanza, which is taken from the *Cumbrian Magazine* vol ii p. 58.

"*Pan dramwych ffrid yr Ywan,*
Lle mae Tylwyth Teg rhodien,
Dos yamlaen, a phaid a sefyll,
Gwillia'th droed—rhag dawnsva'r Ellyll"

"When the forest of the Yew,
Where Fairies haunt, thou passest through,
Tarry not, thy footsteps guard,
From the Goblin's dancing sward"

Although the poet mentions *Tylwyth Teg* and *Ellyll* as identical, he might have done so for rhythmical reasons. Undoubtedly, in the first instance, a distinction would be drawn between these two words, which originally were intended perhaps to describe two different kinds of beings but in the course of time the words became interchangeable, and thus there distinctive character is lost. In English, the words Fairies and elves are used without any distinction. It would appear from *Brand's Popular Antiquities* vol. II p. 478. that, according to Gervaise of Tilbury there were two types of Goblin in England, called *Portuni* and *Grant*. This division suggests a difference between the *Tylwyth Teg* and the *Ellyll*. The *Portuni*, we are told, were very small of stature and old in appearance, "*statura pusilli dimidium pollicis non habentes*" but then they were "*senili vultu facie corrugata*". The wrinkled face and aged appearance of the *Portuni* remind us of nursery Fairy tales in which the ancient female Fairy figures. The pranks of the *Portuni* are similar to those of Shakespeare's Puck. The species *Grant* is not described, and consequently it cannot be ascertained how far they resembled any of the many kinds of Welsh Fairies. Gervaise, speaking of one of these species says:—"If anything should be carried on in the house, or any kind of laborious work to be done, the join themselves to the work, and expedite it with more than human facility."

In Scotland, there are at least two species of elves, the *Brownies* and the *Fairies*. The Brownies are so called from their tawny walnut colour, and the Fairies from their fairness. The *Portuni* of Gervaise appear to have corresponded in character to the Brownies, who were said to have employed themselves in the night to the discharge of laborious undertakings, acceptable to the family to which they had devoted themselves. [*Editor's Note*: In this they appear to be a folkloric remnant of the ancient household gods of Rome who were in charge of the maintenance and well-being of house, home, and property.] The Fairies proper of Scotland strongly resembled the Fairies of Wales.

The term *Brownie*, or swarthy elve, suggests a connection between them and the *Gwylliaid Cochion* or Red Fairies of Wales.

Fairy Ladies Marrying Mortals

In the mythology of the Greeks, and other nations, gods and goddesses are spoken of as falling in love with human beings, and many an ancient genealogy began with a celestial ancestor. Much of the same thing is said of the Fairies. Tradition speaks of them as being enamoured of the inhabitants of this earth, and content for awhile to be wedded to mortals. And there are families in Wales who are said to have Fairy

69

blood coursing through their veins, but they are, or were, not so highly esteemed as were the offspring of the gods among the Greeks. The famous physicians of Myddfai, who owed their talent and supernatural knowledge to their Fairy origin are, however, an exception, for their renown, notwithstanding their parentage, was always great, and increased in greatness as the rolling years removed them from their traditionary parent, the Fairy lady of the Van Pool.

The Pellings are said to have sprung from a Fairy mother and the author of *Observations on the Snowdon Mountainside* states that the best blood in his veins is Fairy blood. There are, in some parts of Wales, reputed descendants on the female side of the *Gwilliaid Cochion* race; and there are other families among us who the aged of fifty years ago, with an ominous shake of the head, would say were of Fairy extraction. We are not, therefore, in Wales void of families of doubtful parentage or origin.

All the current tales of men marrying Fairy ladies belong to a class of stories called, technically, Taboo stories. In these tales the lady marries her lover conditionally, and when this condition is broken, she deserts her husband and children, and hies back to Fairy land.

This kind of tale is current among many people. Max Muller in *Chips from a German Workshop* vol. II pp. 104-6 records one of these ancient stories, which is found in the Brahamna of Yagur-Veda. Omitting a few particulars, the story is as follows:

"Urvasi, a kind of Fairy, fell in love with Pururavas, son of Ida and when she met him she said: 'Embrace me three times a day, but never against my will, and let me never see you without your royal garments for this is the manner of women'. In this manner she lived with him a long time, and she was with child. Then her former friends, the Gandharvas, said:

"This Urvasi has now dwelt a long time among mortals, let us see that she come back." Now, there was a ewe with two lambs, tied to the couch of Urvasi and Pururavas and the Gandharvas stole one of them. Urvasi said: "They take away my darling as if I had lived in a land where there is no hero and no man." They stole the second and she upbraided her husband again. Then Proves looked and said: 'How can that be a land without heroes and men where I am?' And naked he sprang up; he thought it too long to put on his dress. Then the Gandharvas sent a flash of lightning, and Urvasi saw her husband naked as by daylight. Then she vanished: 'I am come back' she said, and went.

Puruavas bewailed his love in bitter grief. But whilst walking along the border of a lake full of lotus flowers, the Fairies were playing there in the water, in the shape of birds and Urvasi discovered him and said:

'That is the man with whom I dwelt so long'. Then her friends said. 'Let us appear to him.' She agreed and they appeared before him. Then the king recognised her and said:

'Lo! my wife, stay, thou cruel in mind! Let us now exchange some words! Our secrets, if they are not told now, will not bring us back on any later day!'

She replied: 'What would I do with thy speech! I am gone like the first of the dawns. Puruavaras, go home again. I am hard to be caught, like the wind'.

The Fairy wife by and by relents, and her mortal lover became, by a certain sacrifice, one of the Gandharvas.

This ancient Hindu Fairy tale resembled in many particulars similar tales found in Celtic Folk-lore and possibly the original story in its main features, existed before the Ayrian family had separated. The very words, "I am hard to be caught" appear in one of the Welsh legends, which shall hereafter be given:

"*Nidd hawdd fy mala*"

"I am hard to be caught"

And the scene is similar: in both cases the Fairy ladies are discovered in a lake. The immortal weds the mortal, conditionally, and for awhile the union seems to be a happy one. But, unwittingly, when engaged in an undertaking suggested by, or in agreement with the wife's wishes, the prohibited thing is done and the lady vanished away.

Such are the chief features of these mythical marriages. I will now record like tales that have found a home in several parts of Wales.

Welsh Legends of Fairy Ladies Marrying Men

I. The Pentrevoleas Legend.

I am indebted to the Rev. Owen Jones, Vicar of Pentrevoelas, a mountain parish in West Denbighshire for the following tale, which was written in Welsh by a native of those parts and appeared in competition for a prize on the Folk-lore of that parish.

The son of Hafodgarrog was shepherding his father's flock on the hills and while thus engaged, he, one misty morning, came suddenly upon a lovely girl, seated on the sheltered side of the peat-stack. The maiden appeared to be in great distress and she was crying bitterly. The young man went up to her, and spoke kindly to her, and his attention and sympathy were not without effect on the comely stranger. So beautiful was the young woman, that from the expression of sympathy, the smitten youth proceeded to words of love, and his advances were not repelled. But while the lovers were holding sweet conversation, there appeared on the scene a venerable and aged man, who, addressing the female as her father, bade her follow him. She immediately obeyed, and both departed, leaving the young man alone. He lingered about the place until the evening, wishing and hoping that she might return, but she came not. Early the next day, he was at the spot, where he first felt what love was. All day long, he lingered about the place, hoping that the beautiful girl would pay another visit to the mountain, but he was doomed to disappointment and night again drove him homewards. Thus, daily, went he to the place where he had first met his beloved, but she was not there, and, lovesick and lonely, he returned to Hafodgarrog. Such devotion deserved its reward. It would seem that the young lady loved the young man quite as much as he loved her. And in the land of allurement and illusion (yen nhir hud a lledrith), she planned a visit to the earth, and met her lover, but she was soon missed by her father, and he suspecting her love for this young man came upon them, and found them conversing lovingly together. Much talk took place between the sire and his daughter, and the shepherd, waxing bold, begged and begged her father to give him his daughter in marriage. The sire, perceiving that the man was in earnest, turned to his daughter and asked her whether it were her wish to be married to a man of the earth? She said it was. Then the father told the shepherd he should have his daughter to wife, and that she should stay with him, until he should strike her with *iron*, and that as a marriage portion, he would give her a bag filled with bright money. The young couple were duly married and the promised dowry was received. For many years, they lived lovingly and happily together, and children were born to them. One day this man and his wife went to the hill to catch a couple of ponies, to carry them to the Festival of the Saint of Capel Garmon. The ponies were very wild and could not be caught. The man, irritated, pursued the nimble creatures. His wife was by his side and now he thought he had them in his power, but just at the moment he was about to grasp their manes, off they wildly galloped, and the man in anger, finding that they had again eluded him, threw the bridle after them, and, sad to say, the bit struck his wife and, as this was of *iron*, they both knew that their marriage contract was broken. Hardly had they time to realise the dire accident, ere the aged father of the bride appeared, accompanied by a host of Fairies, and there and then departed with his daughter to the land whence she came, and that too, without even allowing her to bid farewell to her children. The money though, and the children were left behind, and these were the only memorials of the lovely wife and the kindest of mothers, that remained to remind the shepherd of the treasure he had lost in the person of his Fairy spouse.

Such is the Pentrevoelas Legend. The writer had evidently not seen the version of this story in the *Cambro-Briton* nor had he read Williams's tale of a like occurrence, recorded in *Observations on the Snowdon Mountains*. The account, therefore, is all the more valuable as being an independent production.

A fragmentary variant of the preceding legend was given me by Mr. Lloyd, late schoolmaster of Llanfibangal-Glyn-Mylyr, a native of South Wales who heard the tale in the parish of Llanfibangel. Although but a fragment, it may not be altogether useless, and I will give it as I received it:

Shon Rolant, Haford y Dre, Pentrevoelas, when going home from Llanrwst market, fortunately caught a Fairy-maid whom he took home with him. She was a most handsome woman, but rather short and slight in person. She was admired by everybody on account of her great beauty. Shon Rolant fell desperately in love with her and would have married her but this she would not allow. He, however, continued pressing her to become his wife and by and by, she consented to do so, provided she could find out her name. As Shon was again going home from the market about a month later, he heard some one saying, near the place where he had seized the Fairy maid: "Where is little Penloi gone? Where is little Penloi gone?" Shon thought that some one was searching for the Fairy he had captured, and when he reached home, he addressed the Fairy by the name he had heard, and Penloi consented to become his wife. [*Editor's Note*: This portion of the tale seems

74

to be a variant of a very old legend that has come down to us in the form of the children's fairy tale Rumpelstiltskin. As with many other ancient peoples, the early Celts believed in both the importance and power of names—which was, after all, a person's identity, and speaking another's name would give one power over them.) She, however, expressed displeasure at marrying a dead man, as the Fairies call us. She informed her lover that she was not to be touched with *iron* or she would disappear at once. [*Editor's Note*: Fairies were supposed to have a particular aversion to iron. In certain parts of the Celtic world, iron horseshoes were placed close to a sleeping child until it could be baptised, to prevent it being stolen by the fairy-kind.] Shon took great care not to touch her with iron. However one day, when he was on horseback, talking to his beloved Penloi, who stood at the horse's head, the horse suddenly threw up its head and the curb, which was of iron, came in contact with Penloi, who immediately vanished out of sight.

The next legend is taken from Williams's *Observations on the Snowdon Mountains*. His work was published in 1802. He himself was born in Anglesey, in 1738, and migrated to Carnarvonshire about the year 1760. It was in this latter county that he became a learned antiquary, and a careful recorder of events that came under his notice. His "*Observations*" throw a considerable light upon the life, the customs and the traditions of the inhabitants of the hill parts and secluded glens of Carnarvonshire. I have thought fit to make these few remarks about the author I quote from, so as to enable the reader to give him the credence which he is entitled to. Williams entitles the following story "A Fairy Tale", but I will for the sake of reference, call it "The Ystrad Legend."

2. The Ystrad Legend

In a meadow belonging to Ystrad, bounded by the river which flows from Cwellyn Lake, they say the Fairies used to assemble, and dance on fair moon-light-nights. One evening a young man who was the heir and occupier of this farm, hid himself in a thicket close to the spot where they used to gambol; presently they appeared, and when in their merry mood, out he bounced from his covert and seized one of their females; the rest of the company dispersed themselves and disappeared in an instant. Disregarding her struggles and screams; he hauled her to his home, where he treated her so very kindly that she became content to live with him as his maid servant; but he could not prevail upon her to tell him her name. Some time after, happening to see the Fairies again upon the same spot, he heard one of them saying: "The last time we met here, our sister *Penelope* was snatched away from us by one of the mortals". Rejoiced at knowing the name of his *Incognita*, he returned home: and, as she was very beautiful and extremely active, he proposed to marry her, which she would not for a long time consent to; at last however she complied but on this condition: 'That if ever he should strike her with *iron*, she would leave him and never return to him again'. They lived happily for many years together, and he had by her a son and a daughter; and by her industry and prudent management as a house-wife, he became one of the richest men in the country. He farmed, besides his own household, his own freehold, all the lands on the north side of Nant-y-Bettws to the top of Snowdon and all of Cwmbrynog in Llanberis, an extent of about five thousand acres or upwards.

Unfortunately, one day Penelope followed her husband into the fields to catch a horse; and he being in rage at the animal as he ran away from him, threw the bridle that was in his hand, which unluckily fell on poor Penelope. She disappeared in an instant and he never saw her afterwards, but heard her voice in the window of his room, one night after, requesting him to take care of the children in these words:

"Rhag bod anwyd ar fy mab,
Yn rhodd rhowch arno gob ai dad,
Rhag bod anwyd ar liwr cann,
Rhoddwch arni bais ei mam".

That is:

"Oh! Lest my son should suffer cold,
Him in his father's coal infold.
Lest cold should seize my darling fair,
For her, her mother's robe prepare".

These children and their descendants, they say, were called *Pellings*; a word corrupted from their mother's name Penelope.

Williams proceeds thus with reference to the descendants of this union:

"The late Thomas Rowlands Esq., of Caeran in Anglesey, the father of the late Lady Bukeley, was a descendant of this lady if it be true that the name *Pellings* came from her; and there are still living several opulent and respectable people who are known to have sprung from the *Pellings*. The best blood in my own veins is this Fairy's."

This tale was chronicled in the last century but it is not known whether every particular incident connected therewith was recorded by Williams. *Glasynys*, the Rev. Owen Wynne Jones, a clergyman, relates a tale in the *Brython* which he regards as the same tale as that given by Williams, and he says that he heard it scores of times when he was a lad. [*Editor's Note*: Glasynys was the pen name used by another celebrated Welsh folklorist and antiquarian: Owen Wynne Jones, who contributed to the *Brython*, a Welsh journal of history, tradition and folklore, to which Elias Owen alludes.] Glasynys was born in the parish of Rhostryfan in Carnarvonshire in 1827, and as the place of his birth is not far distant from the scene of this legend, he may have heard a different version of Williams's tale and that too of equal value with Williams's Possibly, there are not more than from forty to fifty years between the time when that older writer heard the tale and the time when it was heard by the younger man. An octogenarian or even a younger person could have conversed with both Williams and Glasynys. *Glasynys* tale appears in Professor Rhys's *Welsh Fairy Tales, Cymmrodor*, vol iv, p. 188. It originally appeared in the *Brython* for 1863 p. 193. It is as follows:

"One fine sunny morning, as the young heir of Ystrad was busied with his sheep on the side of Moel Eilio, he met a very pretty girl, and when he got home he told the folks there of it. A few days afterwards, he met her again, and this happened several times, when he mentioned it to his father, who advised him to seize her when he next met her. The next time he met her he proceeded to do so, but before he could tale her away, a little fat old man came to them and begged them to give her back to him, to which the youth would not listen. The little man uttered terrible threats, but he would not yield, so an agreement was made between them that he was to have her to wife until he touched her skin with iron, and great was the joy both of the son and his parents in consequence. They lived together for many years, but once on a time, on the evening of Bettws Fair, the wife's horse got restive, and somehow as the husband was attending to the horse, the stirrups touched the skin of her bare leg, and that very night, she was taken away from him. She had three or four children and more than one of their descendants, as *Glasynys* maintains, were known to him at the time he wrote in 1863".

No Welsh Taboo story can be complete without the pretty tale of the Van Lake Legend or, as it is called "The Myddfai Legend". Because of its intrinsic beauty and worth and for sake of comparison with the preceding stories, I will relate this legend. There are various versions. [*Editor's Note*: For comparative purposes I have chosen a version to which Elias Owen alludes and recounts in his Notes and which appeared in a volume of the Cambro-Briton in 1821.]

3. The Myddvai Legend

"A man who lived in the farmhouse called Esgair-Ileathdy, in the parish of Myddvai in Carmarthenshire, having bought some lambs in a neighbouring fair, brought them to graze near *Llyn a Van Voch* on the Black Mountains. Whenever he visited the lambs, three most beautiful female figures presented themselves to him from the lake and often made excursions on the boundaries of it. For some time, he pursued and endeavoured to catch them, but always failed; for the enchanting nymphs, and, when they had reached the lake they tauntingly exclaimed:

> *Cras dy fara,*
> *Anhawdd ein dala.*

which, with a little circumlocution, means "For thee, who eatest baked bread, it is difficult to catch us".

One day some moist bread from the lake came to shore. The farmer devoured it with great avidity, and on the following day he was successful in his pursuit and caught the fair damsels. After a little conversation with them, he commanded courage sufficient to make a proposal of marriage to one of them. They consented to accept him on the condition that he would distinguish her from her two sisters on the following day. This was a new and very great difficulty to the young farmer, for the fair nymphs were so similar in form and features, that he could scarcely perceive any difference between them. He observed, however, a trifling singularity in the strapping of her sandal by which he recognised her the following day. Some indeed who relate this legend, say that this Lady of the Lake hinted in a private conversation with her swain that upon the day of the trial, she would place herself between her two sisters and that she would turn her right foot a little to the right and by this means, he distinguished her from her sisters. Whatever were the means, the end was secured, he selected her and she immediately left the lake and accompanied him to his farm. Before she quitted, she summoned to attend her from the lake, seven cows, two oxen, and one bull.

The lady engaged to live with him until such time as he would strike her three times without cause. For some years they lived together in comfort and she bore him three sons, who were the celebrated Meddygon Myddvai.

One day when preparing for a fair in the neighbourhood, he desired her to go to the field for his horse. She said she would, but being rather dilatory, he said to her humorously, "dos, dos. Dos—i.e. go, go, go" and he slightly touched her on the arm, three times with his glove.

As she now deemed the terms of her marriage broken, she immediately departed, and summoned with her her seven cows, her two oxen and the bull. The oxen were at that very time ploughing in the field but they immediately obeyed her call and took the plough with them. The furrow from the field in which they were ploughing, to the margin of the lake is to be seen in several parts of that country to the present day.

After her departure, she once met her two sons in a Cwm, now called *Cwm Meddygon* (Physicians Combe) and delivered to each of them a bag containing some articles which are unknown but which are supposed to have been some discoveries in medicine.

The Meddygon Myddvai were Rhiwallon and his sons, Cadwgan, Gruffydd, and Einion. They were the chief physicians of their age, and they wrote about A.D. 1230. A copy of their works is in the Welsh School Library, in Grey's Inn Lane.

Such are the Welsh Taboo tales. I will now make a few remarks upon them.

The age of these legends is worthy of consideration. The legend of *Meddygon Myddvai* dates from about the thirteenth century. Rhiwallon and his sons, we are told by the writer of the *Cambro-Briton* wrote about 1230 A.D. but the editor of that publication speaks of a manuscript written by these physicians about the year 1300. Modern experts think that their treatise on medicine in the *Red Book of Hengist* belongs to the end of the fourteenth century, about 1380 or 1400.

Dyfydd ab Gwilym, who is said to have flourished in the fourteenth century, says in one of his poems, as given in the *Cambro-Briton*, vol ii, p 313, alluding to these physicians:

"*Meddyg nis gwnai modd y gwaeth*
Myddfai, o chai ddyn maddfaeth"

"A Physician he would not make,
As Myddvai made, if he had a mead fostered man"

It would appear, therefore, that these celebrated physicians lived somewhere about the thirteenth century. They are describes as the Physicians of Rhys Gryg, a prince of South Wales, who lived in the early part of the thirteenth century. Their supposed supernatural origin dates therefore from the thirteenth or at the latest, the fourteenth century.

I have mentioned *Y Gwylliaid Cochion*, or as they are generally styled, *Gwylliaid Cochion Mawddwy*, the Red Fairies of Mawddwy as being of Fairy origin. The Llanfrothen Legend [*Editor's Note*: There is an ancient story from Llanfrothen in Merionethshire in which a shepherd marries a maiden who emerges from a hill. She lives with him for a number of years and they have several children. When touched with iron, she tells him that she must now depart and return to her former life. He asks what will become of the children without a mother, to which she replies, "Let them be red-headed and big-nosed."] seems to account for a race of men in Wales differing from their neighbours in certain features. The offspring of the Fairy

81

union were, according to the Fairy mother's prediction in that legend, to have red hair and prominent noses. That a race of men having these characteristics did exist in Wales is undoubted. They were a strong tribe, the men were tall and athletic, and lived by plunder. They had their head quarters at Dinas Mawddwy, Merionethshire and taxed their neighbours in open day, driving away sheep and cattle to their dens. So unbearable did their depredations become that John Wynn ap Meredydd of Gwydir and Lewis Owen, or as he is called Baron Owen, raised a body of stout men and overcame them on Christmas Eve, 1554, succeeded in capturing a large number of the offenders and, then and there, some hundred or so of the robbers were hung. Tradition says that a mother begged hard for the life of a young son, who was to be destroyed, but Baron Owen would not relent. On perceiving that her request was unheeded, baring her breast, she said:

"*Y bronan melynion hyn a fagasant y rhai a didialant waed fy mab, ac a olchant en dwylaw yu ugwaed calon Ilolrudd en brawd*"

"These yellow breasts have nursed those who will revenge my son's blood and will wash their hands in the heart's blood of this murderer of their brother"

According to Pennant this threat was carried out by the murder of Baron Owen in 1555 when he was passing through the thick woods of Mawddwy on his way to Montgomeryshire Assizes at a place called to this day *Llidiart y Barwn*, the Baron's Gate, from the deed. Tradition further tells us that the murderers had gone a distance off before they remembered their mother's threat and returning thrust their swords into the Baron's heart and washed their hands in his heart's blood. This act was followed by vigorous action, and the banditti were extirpated, the females only remaining, and the descendants of these women are occasionally still to be met with in Montgomeryshire and Merionethshire.

For the preceding information, the writer is indebted to *YrHynafion Cmyru rig* pp. 91-94, *Archaeologia Cambrensis* for 1854 pp. 119-20: *Pennant* vol ii, pp. 225-27. ed. Carnarvon , and the tradition that was told him by the Rev. D. James, Vicar of Garthbeibio, who likewise pointed out to him the very spot where the Baron was murdered.

But now, who were these *Gwylliaid*? According to the hint conveyed by their name, they were of Fairy parentage, an idea which the writer in the Archaeologia *Cambrensis,* vol v 1854 p.119, intended to throw out. But, according to *Brut y Tywysogion, Myf. Arch.,* p. 706 A.D. 1114, Denbigh edition, the *Gwylliaid Cochion Mawddwy* began in the time of Cadwgan ab Bleddyn ab Cynwyn.

From William's *Eminent Welshmen,* we gather that Prince Cadwgan died in 1110 A.D. and, according to the above-mentioned *Brut,* it was in his days that the Gwylliaid commenced their career if not their existence.

Unfortunately, for this beginning of the red-headed banditti of Mawddwy, Tacitus states in his *Life of Agricola* ch. xi that there were in Britain, men with red hair whom he surmises were of German extraction. We must, therefore, look for the commencement of a people of this description long before the twelfth century, and the Llanfrothen legend either dates from remote antiquity or it was some tale that found in its wanderings, a resting place in that locality in ages long past.

From a legend recorded by Geraldus Cambrensius which shall by and by be given, it would seem that a priest named Elidorus lived among the Fairies in their home in the bowels of the earth, and this would be in the early part of the twelfth century. [*Editor's Note*: In another part of his work, Owen refers to a legend from Cambrensius's "Itinerary through Wales," which the Archdeacon had learned in 1188 during a visit to St.David's. The legend, already ancient at the time, relates how a boy, Elidorus, being trained for the priesthood and anxious to escape his rigorous masters, fled into an underground world inhabited by a smaller race of men and women who spoke a language similar to Greek. He lived amongst them for a time, returning occasionally to his own sphere and at last was prevailed upon by friends and family to return permanently and to resume his priestly studies. Cambrensius cites the source of this tale as being David II, former Bishop of St. David's who died in 1176 and who allegedly had spoken to Elidorius when the priest was in his old age and who also had learned some of the language of the underground world.] The question arises, is the priest's tale credible, or did he merely relate a story of himself which had been ascribed to some one else in the traditions of the people? If his tale is true, then, there lived even in that late period a remnant of the aborigines of the country, who had their homes in caves. The Myddvai Legend in part corroborates this supposition for the story apparently belongs to the thirteenth century

It is difficult to fix the date of the other legends here given, for they are dressed in modern garb with, however, trappings of remote times. Probably all these tales have reached, through oral tradition, historic times but in reality they belong to that far-off distant period when the prehistoric inhabitants of this island dwelt in Lake-habitations, or in caves. And the marriage of Fairy ladies, with men of a different race, intimate that the more ancient people were not extirpated but were amalgamated with their conquerors.

The Tale of Connal

As Christianity began to spread across the Celtic world, the ancient tales began to adapt in order to include elements of the new faith. Many of these old stories concerned the deeds of mighty heroes of times long past and of their battles against monsters and giants. Some of them would later form the basis of well-known fairy tales such as 'Jack the Giant Killer,' which is the adaptation of an old tale from Cornwall where giants and monstrous men were believed to be plentiful.

Scotland, too, has several legends of these monstrous ogres, usually living in the Western Highlands and who were defeated by ancient Scottish kings and heroes. According to extremely ancient travelers' tales, a race of huge and mighty men lived along the coasts of Argyll and Kintyre and in the North Antrim area of Ireland who preyed on passing ships, luring them to their doom on the rocks with fires and torches, which the sailors mistook for signals. According to these same stories, these giants were cannibals who quickly

85

devoured those who survived the shipwrecks. For example, it was said that three great cannibal sisters dwelt in the coastal Ballypatrick Forest, near the present-day town of Ballycastle in North Antrim, devouring those who were washed up on the beaches below or who passed by their huge stone house beside a trail that led through the forest to the clifftops beyond. They were slain by a Highland hero (different names are given for him, and in some cases more than one hero is mentioned) who came from the Mull of Kintyre to accomplish the deed. In some variants of the tale, they were slain by a bishop, emphasising the power of the Church over the pagan past and bringing Christian elements into the story.

The following story comes from the Western Highlands. It is part of a series of folktales collected there by J. F. Campbell from a number of old people whom he interviewed. Two sources are given for it. Campbell notes a Hector Urquart, whom he spoke to on June 27, 1859, but the actual story was recited by Kenneth MacLennan, aged 70, from Turnaig, Pool Ewe in Ross-shire, who was able to repeat the story, which he'd heard when only a young boy. It is probably a remnant of a number of ancient hero stories from the Highland Celtic tradition that have been given some passing and superficial Christian elements. According to the notes, the tale was originally recited in Scots Gaelic and the translation is Campbell's own.

Story by J.F. Campbell

There was a king over Eirinn once, who was named King Cruachan, and he had a son who was called Connal MacRigh Cruachan. The mother of Connal died, and the father married another woman. She was for finishing Connal, so that his kingdom might belong to her own posterity. He had a foster mother, and it was in the house of his foster-mother that he made his home. He and his eldest brother were right-hand of each other [*Editor's Note*: They were close.]; and the mother was vexed because Connal was so fond of her big son. There was a bishop in the place, and he died; and he desired that his gold and silver should be placed beside him in the grave. Connal was at the bishop's burying, and he saw a great bag of gold being placed at the bishop's head and a bag of silver at his feet, in the grave. Connal said to his five foster-brothers that they would go in search of the bishop's gold and when they reached the grave, Connal asked them which they would rather; go down into the grave, or hold up the flagstone. They said that they would hold up the flag. Connal went down and whatever the squealing was that they heard, they let go the flag and took to their soles home. Here he was, in the grave, on top of the bishop. When the five of the foster brothers reached the house, their mother was somewhat more sorrowful for Connal than she would have been for the five. At the end of seven mornings, there went a company of young lads to take the gold out of the bishops grave, and when they reached the grave, they threw the flag to the side of the further wall; Connal stirred below, and when he stirred they went, and they left each arm and dress that they had. Connal arose and he took with him the gold, and arms and dress, and he reached his foster mother with them. They were all merry and lighthearted as long as the gold and silver lasted.

There was a great giant near the place, who had a great deal of gold and silver in the front of a rock; and he was promising a bag of gold to any being that would go down in a creel. Many were lost in this way, when the giant would let them down, and they would fill the creel, the giant would not let down the creel more till they died in the hole.

On a day of days, Connal met with the giant and he promised him a bag of gold, for that he should go down the hole to fill a creel with gold. Connal went down, and the giant was letting him down with a rope, Connal filled the giant's creel

A hero displays the head of the last of the giants.

with gold but the giant did not let down the creel to fetch Connal and Connal was in the cave among the dead men and the gold.

When it beat the giant to get another man who would go down into the hole, he sent his own son down into the hole, and the sword of light in his lap, so that he might see before him.

When the young giant reached the ground of the cave, and when Connal saw him, he caught the sword of light, and he took off the head of the young giant.

Then Connal put the gold in the bottom of the creel, and he put the gold over him; and then he hid in the midst of the creel and he gave a pull on the rope. The giant drew the creel, and when he did not see his son, he threw the creel over the top of his head. Connal leaped out of the creel, and the black back of the giant's head (being) towards him, he laid a swift hand on the sword of light, and he took the head off the giant. Then he betook himself to his foster-mother's home with the creel of gold and the giant's sword of light.

After this, he went to hunt one day on Sliamh na lierge. He was going forwards, till he went into a great cave. He saw in the upper part of the cave, a fine fair woman, who was thrusting the flesh-stake into a big lump of a baby, and every thrust she would give the spit, the baby would give a laugh and she would begin to weep. Connal spoke, and he said: "Woman, what ails thee at the child without reason?"

"Oh", said she, "since thou art an able man thyself, kill the baby and set it on this stake till I roast it for the giant". He caught hold of the baby and he put a plaid that he had on about the babe, and he had the baby at the side of the cave.

There were a great many dead bodies at the side of the cave and he set one of them on the stake and the woman was roasting it.

Then he heard under ground trembling and thunder coming, and he would rather he was out. Here he sprang in place of the corpse that was in the fire, in the very middle of the bodies. The giant came and he asked, "Was the roast ready?" He began to eat and he said:

"Fiu fau hoagrich, it's no wonder that thy own flesh is tough, it is tough on thy brat".

When the giant had eaten that one, he went to count the bodies and they way he had of counting them was, to catch hold of them by the two smalls of the leg and toss them past the top of his head; and he counted them back and forwards thus, three or four times; and he found Connal somewhat heavier and that he was soft and fat, he took that slice out of him from the back of his head to his groin. He roasted this at the fire, and he ate it, and then he fell asleep. Connal winked at the woman to set the flesh-stake in the fire. She did this, and when the spit grew white after it was red, he thrust the spit through the giant's heart, and the giant was dead.

Then Connal went, and he set the woman on her path homewards, and then he went home himself. His stepmother sent him and her own son to steal the whitefaced horse from the King of Italy, "Eadilt" [*Editor's Note*: This was the name of the people who had charge of the horse, which was supposed to be a magnificent animal and one of the swiftest in the world.] and they went together to steal the whitefaced horse, and every time they would lay a hand on him, the whitefaced horse would let out an ialt [neigh?]. A "company" me out and they were caught. The binding of the three smalls was laid on them painfully. [*Editor's Note*: This was a form of torture allegedly used in Italy and other Mediterranean countries. It was said to involve tightening knots in a rope against various sensitive parts of the body.]

"Thou big red man", said the king, "wert thou ever in such hard a case as that?"

"A little tightening for me and a little loosening for my comrade and I will tell thee that" said Connal.

The Queen of the Eadailt was beholding Connal.
Then Connal said:

"Seven morns so sadly mine,
As I dwelt on the bishop's top,
That visit was longest for me,
Though I was the strongest myself.
At the end of the seventh morn,
An opening grave was seen,
And I would be up before,
The one that was soonest down.
They thought I was a dead man,
As I rose from the mould of the earth;
At the first of the harsh bursting,
They left their arms and their dresses;
I gave the leap of the nimble one,
As I was naked and bare,
'Twas for me, a vagabond,
To enjoy the bishop's gold."

"Tighten well, and right well," said the king, "it was not in the one good place that he ever was; great is the ill that he has done" [*Editor's Note*: By desecrating a bishop's grave and by spending his gold, he enraged the Italian Christian king.] Then he was tightened somewhat tighter, and somewhat tighter; and somewhat tighter; and the king said:

"Thou great red man, was thou ever in a harder case than that?"

"Tighten myself and let a little slack with this one beside me, and I will tell thee that."

They did that. "I was," said he:

"Nine morns in the cave of gold;
My meat was the body of bones,

91

Sinews of feet and hands,
At the end of the numb morn,
A descending creel was seen;
Then I caught hold on the creel,
And laid gold above and below;
I made my hiding within the creel:
I took with me the glave of light,
The luckiest turn that I did."

They gave him the next tightening, and the king asked him. "Wast thou ever in case, or extremity, as hard as that?"

"A little tightening for myself and a slack for my comrade and I will tell thee that". They did this.

"On a day on Slaibh na leirge,
As I went into a cave,
I saw a smooth, fair, mother-eyed wife,
Thrusting the stake for the flesh,
At a young unreasoning child. 'Then,' said I,
'What causes thy grief, oh wife,
At that unreasoning child?'
'Though he's tender and comely' said she,
'Set this baby at the fire'
Then I caught hold on the boy.
And wrapped my maundal' (plaid) a round;
Then I brought up the great big corpse,
That was up in front of the heap,
Then I heard Turstar, Turstar and Turnaich,
The very earth mingling together,
But when it was his to be fallen,
Into the soundest of sleep,
There fell by myself the forest fiend,

92

I drew back the stake of the roast,
And thrust it into his maw".

There was the Queen and she was listening to each thing that Connal suffered and said, and when she heard this, she sprang and cut each binding that was on Connal and on his comrade: and she said "I am the woman that was there", and to the king, "thou are that son that was yonder".

Connal married the king's daughter, and together they rode the whitefaced horse home, and there I left them.

[*Editor's Note*: In his notes on the tale Campbell mentions other fragmentary variants of it, collected in other parts of the Western Highlands. For example, he draws attention to similar stories in a collection gathered together by a Mr. Thomas Cameron, a schoolmaster, at the request of Mr. Osgood H. McKenzie Esq. in July 1859. These were collected in a form of Gaelic prevalent around Gearrloch, also in Ross-shire, and contains elements of the tale, which it attributes to various local legendary heroes. He further mentions a collection taken from old men around Inverasdale by Alexander MacDonnell that attributes the deeds of Connal to another localized hero, Uisdean Mor MacIlle Phadraig—a gentleman famous for killing "Fuathan" (bogles, or the half-dead). The basic similarities of many of the versions serve to show the undoubted antiquity of the tale itself.]

Fireside

Tales

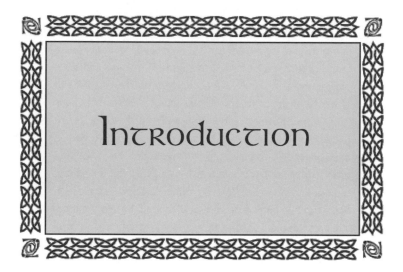

Introduction

The passing of the great Gaelic lordships and the increasing modernization of the Celtic world did not mean that the storytelling tradition died out. Indeed, it had become far too imbedded in the Celtic psyche to do so. It now largely became the preserve of those who had always owned it: the common people.

Across the centuries, folktales and legends had formed a central and important part of Celtic society. As the great Mythological Tales of old, they recorded events and characters within the communities, but they also served as an explanation for occurrences within a locality. Thus the tales of heroes and kings, of gods and monsters were added tales of ghosts and fairies. These stories were not mere *recitations* of monarchs and warriors (as under the Bards) but now reflected the perspectives and beliefs of the Celtic people and their descendants. At night, the noises that emerged out of the dark were the sounds of *sheehogues*, or supernatural creatures that traversed the gloom. Milk that had somehow soured overnight was the result of the intervention of the *marbh bheo* (the nightwalking dead) or the fairies, whose touch could accomplish this. The fact that cows did not give milk or hens did not lay was put down to the evil of witches in the community. Odd shapes, glimpsed at twilight in the middle of some ancient earthworks were unquestionably the *Sidhe* (the ancient and secretive people of the mounds). That these may have been ordinary objects distorted by the poor light that the milk curdled for natural reasons that the sounds from the darkness were no more than night creatures going about their nocturnal business did not suffice to explain them away, and so a body of lore and belief began to build up. Certain places in the area were *sheehoguey* (frequented by supernatural entities); certain precautions had to be taken to avoid unearthly visitations; certain actions had to be carried out in order to placate Otherworldly beings—all these became a part and parcel of later Celtic life. And these beliefs and perceptions were carried across the generations in the tales that were told.

As were the mythological warrior tales before, such stories were mainly oral in their transmission. They were told around the firesides in country cottages and in places where people gathered. And they had a community element as well, for they bound neighbors together in a common consciousness and identity. As with the great Bardic gatherings centuries before, people came together to hear these stories and take them away as part both of themselves and of their culture. The Bards themselves were replaced by traditional local storytellers (in Ireland, these people were known as *seanachie,* or men—and women—of lore) who could spin a fine yarn concerning histories, events, and places in the local community. Such people were accorded the status that had once been given to the Bards. The tales that they told not only served as entertainment and explanation, they actually shaped and honed who their listeners were and how those people saw themselves. Not only this, but the stories gave shape and meaning to the countryside around them and their relationship to it. The haunted fort at the foot of the field might be haunted or the abode of fairies, but it was haunted for a *purpose*. There might have once been a mighty battle fought within its earthen walls, or there might have been an awful murder committed there. The resonances of these events and actions percolated down across the centuries and immersed themselves in rural folklore.

As with the warrior tales before them, the tales that were often told around the fireside were oral ones, simply conveyed by word of mouth between relatives or from one neighbor to another. Sadly, unlike the mythological tales, in the majority of cases, no attempt was made to record them. Although a number of anthologies of Celtic folktales have been recorded, many of them vanished into oblivion as the years passed.

This loss has accelerated as the modern era has taken hold. New and 'scientific' and 'reasoned' explanations have been found for events and phenomena in the Celtic countryside, and our notions of what constitutes 'culture' have changed. Much of our cultural entertainment nowadays comes from a box in the corner of our living rooms, much of it is imported, and this has almost dissolved the indigenous ancient cultures of the Celtic past. And yet, there is still a hankering for the perspectives of yesterday; we all still love a good story, well told. Perhaps not all of our Celtic heritage has completely vanished.

A Selection of Cornish Healing Charms and Spells

Throughout the rural Celtic world, charms, spells, and protections were important; so important that many of them survived until comparatively recent times—until at least the early 20th century in some cases. In an uncertain world, and perhaps in the absence of formal medical and social services, it was vital that people had some form of protection against whatever life threw at them. Charms and talismans were often the stock-in-trade of local 'wise women' or 'fairy doctors' who could trace their ancestry back to Celtic shamans, more than a thousand years before. Such people were often integral members of their communities, serving as midwives, soothsayers, healers, and cursers, and were usually treated with awe and respect by those around them. In some cases, such as that of the wise woman Tamsin Blight (Tammy Blee) in Cornwall, such persons were even according the distinction of being able to drive out demons and spirits (a privilege normally reserved for the clergy) that were believed to bring sickness and danger to those whom they attacked. Most charms, however, were designed to alleviate or protect against common ailments—colds, toothache, a heavy flow of blood—and were largely concerned with people's health and welfare.

Although many of the charms and spells undoubtedly had pagan origins, a distinctly Christian note soon began to creep in. As with pagan wells and shrines, the Christian Church in the Celtic West wasn't slow to take them over. Throughout the years, significant elements of the Christian faith were to be found alongside pagan beliefs in most charms.

The following is a selection of charms and protections dealing with common ailments that were collected by celebrated Cornish folklorist William Bottrell (1816-1881) in the rural West of Cornwall, beyond the town of Hayle, where old pagan Celtic beliefs had once been prevalent but where Christianity had made great inroads. They were widely in use in Western Cornwall around mid-19th century and show a melding of ancient and Christian traditions in the Celtic mind. The selection comes from Bottrell's own *Traditions of West Cornwall* (published in 1873).

Selections From
Traditions of West Cornwall

by William Bottrell

Charm for a scald, wild-fire, burn, or any other inflammatory disease

The person to be charmed gathers nine bramble leaves which are put into a vessel of spring water; then each leaf is passed over and from the diseased part whilst repeating three times to each leaf as follows:

A noble is given a grim warning.

"Three ladies come from the east,
One with fire and two with frost;
Out with thee fire and in with thee frost,
In the name of the Father, Son and Holy Ghost".

A stick of fire is then taken from the hearth and passed over and around the diseased part whilst the above is repeated nine times.

[*Editor's Note*: The charm/spell is probably a Christian variant of a much older Celtic ritual, drawing on the natural elements of fire—which was a potent healing symbol throughout the Celtic world—and of frost, a coolant. The reference to "the three ladies" may be a variation of ancient goddesses, making use of the significant number three: the nine brambles suggest a multiplication of three times three, adding to the potency of the magical number.]

Charm for a pick of a thorn, boils, kennels etc.

"Christ was crowned with thorns,
The thorns did bleed but did not rot
No more shall thy finger (or whatever part it may be),
In the name of the Father, Son and Holy Ghost".

[*Editor's Note*: Although this is obviously a Christian charm, its roots are probably pagan Celtic. Older variations speak of pagan or classical gods—Osiris, for example—who have expelled foreign elements from their bodies. The name of Christ and the biblical reference to the crown of thorns have been substituted. The recitation of the charm was accompanied by the touch to the infected area of the wonder-worker or charmer—something that probably had its origins in the Celtic shaman tradition.]

Charm for staunching blood

"Christ was born in Bethlehem,
Baptised in the River Jordan.
There he digg'd a well
And turned the water against the hill,
So shall they blood stand still
In the name of Father, son and Holy Ghost".

[*Editor's Note*: This is another almost completely Christian charm that most probably has pagan Celtic origins. Although the charm contains references to Christ, there is also an oblique hint at magical wells and the notion of water running uphill, which was a magical notion in Celtic lore. Water collected from such sources was deemed to have curative properties, as at St. Patrick's Tub at Belcoo, County Fermanagh in the North of Ireland, where an optical illusion makes a feeder stream appear to run uphill. Water from this course is considered to be especially remedial.]

Charm for toothache

"Christ pass'd by his brother's door,
Saw his brother lying on the floor.
'What aileth thee brother?
Pain in thy teeth?
Thy teeth shall pain thee no more'
In the name of the Father, Son and Holy Ghost".

[*Editor's Note*: As with all the other charms and spells mentioned here, apart from the first, the charmer must touch the infected part with his or her finger. This is perhaps harking back to the ancient Celtic shamans who could reputedly heal with a touch. The later Celtic Church, with its emphasis on miracles and healing, encouraged its clergy to do the same.]

105

A Holy Well in Cornwall

The transition from the pagan to Christian traditions in Celtic lands was not an easy one. Ancient traditions had become so embedded in the Celtic way of life that they were practically impossible to erase. These traditions included charms and spells that had been used for centuries by local shamans and had been passed down from one generation to the next. Dotted throughout the landscape too were sacred streams and wells in which spirits and ancient gods were said to dwell, and over the years many of these sites had become associated with healing and protection. Consequently, they had attracted pilgrims who came in the hope of receiving cures or some form of good fortune from the spirit that lived there. The druids—the near-shamanistic religious leaders of the Celtic world—were the guardians of such places and received offerings for the spirits in these places. When the Church asserted itself and the druids began to fade away, the wells still retained their former reputations as magical places, and indeed some were places of pilgrimage for a nominally Christian but still largely pagan people. The Church moved quickly to take these places over, replacing their old pagan names with those of Christian saints, many of whom had nothing at all to do with the sites involved. The miraculous powers of the waters, formerly attributed to the pagan spirits, were now attributed to these holy men and women. Even the power to foresee the future in the well's depths (often a pagan attribute) was now ascribed to holy intervention.

Cornish folklorist William Bottrell visited and cataloged a number of these wells all dedicated to saints but which had pagan associations. The most famous of his accounts of such places concerns a site widely known as St. Madron's Well. Who St. Madron was is unknown, and, indeed, the saint may not even have existed at all. The name may actually be a corruption of the name of some ancient pagan deity associated with the well itself. The account is taken from Bottrell's pamphlet "West Country Superstitions" (1874-75).

Excerpt from
"West Country Superstitions"

by William Bottrell

"On passing over a stile and entering the moor in which the well is situated, cross the moor at right angle to the hedge and a minute's walk will bring one to the noted spring which is not seen until very near, as it has no wall above the surface, nor any mark by which it can be distinguished at a distance.

Much has been written of the remarkable cures affected by its holy waters and the intercession of St. Madron or Motran, when it was so famous that the maimed, halt and lame made pilgrimages from the distant parts to the heathy moor.

It is still resorted to on the first three Wednesdays in May, by some few women of the neighbourhood, who bring children to be cured of skin diseases by being bathed in it. Its old reputation as a divining fount has not yet quite died out, though many young people visit it now to drop pebbles or pins into the well, more for fun and the pleasure of each other's company than through any belief that the falling together or the separation of pins or pebbles will tell how the course of love will run between the two parties indicated by the objects dropped into the spring; or that the number of bubbles which rise in the water or stamping near the well, mark the years in answer to any question of time; but there was not such want of faith, however, half a century ago.

A short time since, I visited an elderly dame of Madron who was a highly reputed charmer for the cure of various skin ailments; I had known her from my childhood; and my object was to glean what I could about the rites practised within her remembrance at Madron Well, the Crick-stone and elsewhere.

She gave the following account of the usages at Madron Well about fifty years ago. At that time when she lived in Lanyon, scores of women from Morvah, Zennor, Towednack and other places brought their children to be cured of the shingles, wild-fires, tetters and other diseases as well as to fortify against witchcraft or being blighted with an evil eye.

An old dame called An' Katty, who mostly lived in the Bossullows, or some place near, and who did little but knitting-work picked up a good living in May by attending at the well, to direct the high country folks how they were to proceed in using the waters.

First, she had the child stripped as naked as it were born; then it was plunged three times against the sun; next the creature was passed quickly nine times around the spring, going from east to west, or with the sun; the child was then dressed, rolled up in something warm and laid to sleep near the water; if it slept and plenty of bubbles in the well; it was a good sign. I asked if a prayer, charm or anything was spoken during the operations. 'Why no, to be sure' my old friend replied 'don't 'e know any better, there musn't be a word spoken all the time they are near the water, it would spoil the spell; and a piece rented not cut, from the child's clothes or from that of anybody using the well must be left near it for luck; ever so small a bit will do.' This was mostly placed out of sight between the stones bordering the brooklet or hung on a thorn that grew on the chapel wall.

Whilst one party went through their rites at the spring, all the others remained over the stile in the higher enclosure or by the hedge because "if a word were spoken by anybody near the well during the dipping, they had to come again". The old woman An' Katty was never paid in money but balls of yarn and other things she might want were dropped on the road outside the well moors for her; she also had good pickings by instructing young girls how to "try for sweethearts" at the well. "Scores of maidens"—the dame's words—"used, in the summer evenings, to come down to the well from ever so far, to drop into it pins, gravels, or any small thing they could sink". The names of the persons were not always spoken whom the objects which represented them were dropped into the water; it sufficed to think of them and as the pins or pebbles remained together or separated, such would be the couples' fate. It was only when the spring was working (rising strongly) that it was of any use to try the spells: and it was unlucky to speak when near the well at such times.

The old woman that I visited said she had never heard that any saint had anything to do with the water, except from a person who told her that there was something about it in a book; nor had she or anybody also heard the water called St. Madron's Well except by the new gentry who go about now naming places and think they know more about them than the people who have lived there ever since the world was created. She never heard of any ceremony being performed at the old Chapel, except that some persons hung a bit of their clothing on a thorn tree that grew near it. High Country folks, who mostly resort to the spring, pay no regard to any saint, or to anyone else, except some old women who may come down with them to show them how everything used to be done.

There is a spring, not far from Bosporthenes in Zennor which was said to be as good as Madron Well; and children were often taken thither and treated in the same way.

Such is the substance of what the dame related; and she regarded the due observance of ancient customs as a very solemn matter.

In answer to the questions of 'What was the reason for going round the well nine times? Leaving bits of clothing? Following the sun etc.?' It was always the same reply. 'Such were the old customs and everybody know it was unlucky to do any such work and many things beside against the sun's course; no woman who know anything, would place pans of milk in a dairy, so as to have to unream (skim) them, in turn, against the sun, nor stir cream in that direction to make butter'.

Mrs. Sheridan: Encounters With the Fairies

The fairies are often central in Irish folklore, existing alongside humankind as an independent and separate race. Indeed, it has often been argued that the name "fairy" comes from an early Celtic description, "fah-ri" (the spirit race); but, because they objected to that name, they were frequently referred to as "the Good People" or "the Other Crowd" to avoid angering them. The only day on which anyone was allowed to talk about them was Tuesday, and any remark regarding them had to be prefaced with "may their heels be turned toward us," hoping that they were looking the other way!

Despite these prohibitions, it was believed that humans and fairies lived cheek by jowl across the Celtic landscape. However, there was only limited contact between the two for the fairies were a secretive species and greatly mistrustful of Men.

For the most part, the fairy kind remained invisible to the human eye, going about their business, unseen by their mortal neighbors. Occasionally, of course, there was contact between the two races—sometimes accidental, sometimes deliberate on the part of the fairies. Some mortals had the fortune (or sometimes misfortune) to either see the Good People or to visit them where they lived. Occasionally, too, certain mortals might be taken away for a time to be the with fairies, perhaps to return later with their wits all but gone and little recollection as to where they'd been. Some had been away a long time, as an hour in the fairy world was said to be more than a hundred years in its human counterpart; some had been away no time at all.

One of those who had been 'away' with the fairy kind was a lady from County Sligo who was interviewed at the end of the 19th century by Lady Augusta Gregory (1859-1931), a fairy abductee whom she refers to as 'Mrs. Sheridan.' This lady had benefited from her time amongst the fairy kind in several ways. First, though poorly sighted, she was nevertheless able to see the fairy kind around her; and second, on her return from the fairy country, she had become a great healer. A contemporary of the famous County Clare wise woman, Biddy Early, Mrs. Sheridan may even have at one time challenged that famous wise women as the most famous in Ireland. Describing this 'fairy woman,' Lady Gregory writes:

'Mrs Sheridan, as I call her was wrinkled and half blind and had gone barefoot through her lifetime. She was old for she had once met Raftery, the Gaelic poet at a dance and he died well before the famine of '47. She must have been comely then for he said to her 'Well planed you are; the carpenter that planed you knew his trade' and she was ready of reply and answered him back 'Better than you know yours' for his fiddle had two or three broken strings". It was to Lady Gregory that Mrs. Sheridan recounted some of her experiences with the fairies. Her stories contain a number of interesting elements, including the strong association in the Irish west

between the fairies and the dead. This account is taken from
Lady Gregory's "Visions and Beliefs in the West of Ireland"
(published 1920).

Excerpt From "Visions and Beliefs in the West of Ireland"

by Lady Augusta Gregory

"Come here close and I'll tell you what I saw at the old
castle there below (Ballinamantane). I was passing there in the
evening and I saw a great house and a grand one with screens
(clumps of trees) at the ends of it and the windows open—
Coole house is nothing like what it was for size or grandeur.
And there were people inside and ladies walking about and a
bridge across the river. For they can build up such things all in
a minute. And two coaches driving up and across the bridge to
the castle, and in one of them I saw two gentlemen and I knew
them well and both of them had died long before. As to the
coaches and the horses I didn't take much notice of them for I
was too much taken up with looking at the two gentlemen.
And a man came and called out and asked me would I come
across the bridge, and I said I would not. And he said "It
would be better for you if you did, you'd go back heavier than
you came". I suppose they would have given me some good
thing. And then two men took up the bridge and laid it against
the wall. Twice I've seen that some thing, the house and the
coaches and the bridge and I know well that I'll see it a third
time before I die."

"One time when I was living at Ballymacduff there were
two little boys drowned in the river there, one was eight years
old and the other eleven years. And I was out in the fields, and
the people looking in the river for their bodies and I saw a man
coming away from it, and the two boys with him, he holding
a hand of each and leading them away. And he saw me stop

115

and look at them and he said "Take care, would you bring them from me, for you have only one in your own house and if you take these from me she'll never come home to you again". And one of the little chaps broke from his hand and ran to me and the other cried out to him, "Oh Pat, would you leave me!" So he went back and the man led them away. And then I saw another man, very tall he was, and crooked and watching me like this with his head down and he was leading two dogs the other way and I knew well where he was going and what he was going to do with them.

And when I heard the bodies were laid out, I went to the house to have a look at them and those were never the two boys that were lying there but the two dogs that were in their places. I knew this by a sort of stripes on the bodies such as you'd see in the covering of a mattress; and I knew that the boys couldn't be in it, after me seeing them being led away.

And it was at that time I lost my eye, something came on it, and I never got the sight again. All my life, I've seen *them* and enough of them. One time I saw one of the fields below full of them, some were picking up stones and some were ploughing it up. But the next time I went by, there was no sign of it being ploughed at all. They can do nothing without some live person is looking at them, that's why they were always so much after me. Even when I was a child I could see them, and once they took my walk from me and gave me a bad foot, and my father cured me, and if he did, in five days after he died.

But there's no harm in them, not much harm.

There was a woman who lived near me at Ballymacduff and she used to go about to attend women [*Editor's Note*: She was a "handy woman"—a local midwife.]: Sarah Redington was her name. And she was brought away one time by a man that came for her into a hill, through a door, but she didn't know where the hill was. And there were people in it and cradles and a woman in labour and she helped her and the baby was born and the woman told her it was only that night she was brought away. And the man led her out again and put her on the road near her home and he gave her something rolled in a bag and he bid her not to look at it till she'd get home and to throw the first handful of it away from her. But she couldn't wait to get home to look at it and she took it off her back and opened it, and there was nothing in it but cowdung. And the man came to her and said; "You have us near destroyed looking in that, and we'll never bring you in again among us".

There was a man I know well was away with them often and often, and he was passing one day by the big tree and they came about him and he had a new pair of breeches on, and one of them came and made a slit in them, and another tore a little bit out, and they all came running and tearing little bits till he hadn't a rag left. Just to be humbugging him they did that. And they gave him good help, for he had but an acre of land and he had as much on it as another would have on a big farm. But his wife didn't like him to be going and some one told her of a cure for him, and she said she'd try it and if she did, within two hours after she was dead, killed her they had before she'd try it. He used to say that where he was brought was into a round, very big house and Cairns that went with him told me the same.

Three times when I went for water to the well, the water spilled over me and I told Bridget after that they must bring the water themselves, I'd go for it no more. And the third time it was done there was a boy, one of the Heniffs, was near and when he heard what had happened me he said, "It must have been the woman that was at the well along with you that did that". And I said there was no woman at the well along with me. "There was" says he; "I saw her there beside you, and the two little tins in her hand".

One day after I came to live at Coole, a strange woman came into the house and I asked what was her name and she said: "I was in it before ever you were ever in it" and she went into the room inside and I saw her no more.

But Bridget and Peter saw her coming in and they asked me who she was for they never saw her before. And in the night when I was sleeping at the foot of the bed, she came and threw me out on the floor, that the joint of my arm has a mark on it yet. And every night she came and she'd spite me or annoy me in some way. And at last we got Father Nolan to come and to drive her out. As soon as he began to read, there went out of the house a great blast, and there was a sound as loud as thunder. And Father Nolan said, "It's well for you that she didn't have you killed before she went".

I know that I used to be away among them myself, but how they brought me I don't know, but when I'd come back I'd be cross with the husband and with all. I believe that when I was with them, I was cross that they wouldn't let me go, and that's why they didn't keep me altogether, they don't like cross people to be with them. The husband would ask me where I was, and why I stopped so long away but I think he knew I was *taken* and it fretted him, but he never spoke much about it. But my mother knew it well, but she tried to hide it. The neighbours would come in and ask where was I and she'd say I was sick in the bed—for whatever was put in the place of me would have the head in under the bed-clothes. And when a neighbour would bring me in a drink of milk, my mother would just put it by and say 'Leave her now, maybe she'll drink it tomorrow". And maybe in a day or two, I'd meet someone and he'd say 'Why wouldn't you speak to me when I went into the house to see you?" And I was a young, fresh woman at the time.

Himself died but it was *they* took him from me. It was in the night and he lying beside me and I woke and heard him move, and I thought I heard someone with him. And I put out my hand and what I touched was an iron hand, like knitting needles it felt. And I heard the bones of his neck crack, and he gave a sort of a choked laugh and I got out of bed and struck a light and I saw nothing but I thought I saw someone go through the door. And I called to Bridget and she didn't come, and I called again and she came and she said she struck a light when she heard a noise and was coming and someone came and struck the light from her hand. And when we looked in the bed, himself was lying dead and not a mark on him".

[*Editor's Note*: Lady Gregory concludes her account of the conversations with Mrs. Sheridan in the following manner:]

"She died some year ago and I am told:

There is a ghost in Mrs. Sheridan's house. They got a priest to say Mass there, but with all that there's not one in it has leave to lay a head on the pillow till such time as the cock crows".

About the Fairies

For the Celtic people and their descendants, fairies and their nature presented something of a problem. There was no doubt in the popular mind that such beings existed, but what exactly were they? Were they, for example, spirits? A separate race of men? Ancient gods? Were they well intentioned towards Mankind or were they hostile? Were they agents of the Devil seeking to lead God's children astray? Or were they something else? Views on them were ambivalent. In later years, the Christian Church taught that fairies were inherently evil and should be avoided, and local wisdom suggested that they should be feared. And yet the debates continued.

Arguably, nowhere in the Celtic world was the imminence of the fairy kind so closely felt than in Ireland. Within every bush and beyond every stone throughout the countryside, the fairy kind were said to dwell. And it was here that many of the debates about the exact nature of the Good Folk were conducted. Local sages turned their minds to explaining fairy nature and fairy ways and to placing them within the rural context around them. The debate even seems to have made its way across the Atlantic Ocean to America, with folklorists there examining the tales of Irish fairies and even comparing them with Native American stories. As did the Irish, the Native Americans had their 'little people,' and certain comparisons between the two are to be found.

The following extract comes from Dr. David Rice McAnally's book *Irish Wonders* (published in 1888). Dr. McAnally (1810–1895) was an Irish-American folklorist who had amassed a fair amount of orally based material from the Irish countryside. Rather than adopting a scientific or philological approach to the tales, as many folklorists do, he preferred to concentrate on their literary, poetic, and narrative aspects. His was an attempt to present them as they would initially have been delivered by the storytellers themselves, and his work is nonetheless scholarly for that. What we find in this collection, therefore, is the authentic voice and belief of the Irish country people. The following is a discourse rooted in this tradition, concerning the origins and nature of the fairies, and it gives us insight as to how these enigmatic beings were viewed by rural Irish people during the 19th and early 20th centuries.

Excerpt From *Irish Wonders*

by Dr. David Rice McAnally

The Oriental luxuriance of the Irish mythology is nowhere more conspicuously displayed than when dealing with the history, habits, characteristics and pranks of the "good people". According to the most reliable of the rural "fairy men", a race now nearly extinct, the fairies were once angels, so numerous as to have formed a large part of the population of heaven.

When Satan sinned and drew throngs of the heavenly host with him into open rebellion, a large number of the less war-like spirits stood aloof from the contest that followed, fearing the consequences and not caring to take sides till the issue of the conflict was determined. Upon the defeat and expulsion of the rebellious angels, those who had remained neutral were punished by banishment from heaven, but their offence being only one of omission, they were not consigned to the pit with Satan and his followers, but were sent to earth where they still remain, without hope that on the last day they may be pardoned and readmitted to Paradise. They are thus on their good behaviour, but having power to do infinite harm, they are much feared, and spoken of either in whisper or aloud, as the "good people."

Unlike Leprechawns, who are not considered fit associates for reputable fairies, the good people are not solitary; but quite sociable, and always live in large societies, the members of which pursue the co-operative plan of labor and enjoyment, owning all their property, the kind and amount of which are somewhat indefinite, in common, and uniting their efforts to accomplish any desired object, whether of work or play. They travel in large bands, and although their parties are never seen in the daytime, there is little difficulty in ascertaining the line of their march, for, "sure they the terriblest little cloud o' dust iver raised, an' not a bit o' wind in it at all", so that a fairy migration is sometimes the talk of the country. "Though be nacher (by nature), they're not the length av yer finger, they can make themselves the bigness av a tower when it plazes them an' av that ugliness that ye'd faint wid the looks o' thim, as knowin' they can shtrike ye dead on the shpot or change ye into a dog, a pig, or a unicorn or anny other dirthy baste they plaze".

As a matter of fact, however, the fairies are by no means so numerous at present as they were formerly, a recent historian remarking that the National Schools and societies of Father

Matthew are rapidly driving the fairies out of the country, for "they hate larnin' an' wisdom an' are lovers av nacher entirely".

In a few remote districts where schools are not yet well established, the good people are still found and their doings are narrated with a childlike faith in the power of the first inhabitants of Ireland, for it seems to be agreed that they were in the country long before the coming either of the Irishman or of his Sassenagh oppressor.

The bodies of the fairies are not composed of flesh and bone but of an ethereal substance, the nature of which is not determined. "Ye can see themselves as plain as the nose on yer face an' can see through thim like it was a mist". They have the power of vanishing from human sight, when they please, and the fact that the air is sometimes full of them. Inspires the respect entertained for them, by the peasantry. Sometimes they are heard without being seen and when they travel through the air, as they often do, are known by a humming noise similar to that made by a swarm of bees. Whether or not they have wings is uncertain. Barney Murphy of Kerry thought they had; for several seen by him a number of years ago seemed to have long, semi-transparent pinions, "like thim that grows on a dhraggin-fly". Barney's neighbors, however, contradicted him by stoutly denying the good people the attribute of wings and intimated that at the time Barney saw the fairies he was too drunk to distinguish a pair of wings from a pair of legs, so this branch of the subject must remain in doubt.

With regard to their dress, the testimony is undisputed. Young lady fairies wear pure white robes and usually allow their hair to flow loosely over their shoulders; while fairy matrons bind up their tresses in a coil on the top or back of their head, also surrounding the temples with a golden band. Young gentleman elves wear green jackets, with white breeches and stockings; and when a fairy of either sex has need of a cap or head covering, the flower of the fox-glove is brought into requisition.

124

Male fairies are perfect in all military exercises for, like the other inhabitants of Ireland, fairies are divided into factions, the objects of contention not, in most cases, being definitely known. In Kerry a number of years ago, there was a great battle among the fairies, one party inhabiting a rath or sepulchral mound and the other an unused and lonely graveyard. Paddy O'Donohue was the sole witness of this encounter, the narrative being in his own words:

"I was lyin' be the road, bein' on my way home an' tired wid the walkin'. A bright moon was out that night, an' I heard a noise like a million av sogers (soldiers) thrampin' on the road, so I riz (rose) an' looked, an' the way was full av little men, the length o' me hand, wid green coats on, an' all in rows like wan o' the ridgmints; aitch wid a pike on his showldher an' a shield on his arrum. Wan was in front, beway he was the ginral, walkin' wid his chin up, proud as a paycock. Jagers, but I was skairt an' prayed fasther than iver I did in me life, for it was too clost to me entirely they wor for comfort or convaynience aither. But they all went by, sorra the wan o' thim turnin' his head to raygard me at all, Glory be to God for that same; so they left me. Afther they were clane gone by, I had curiosity to see phat they were after, so I folly'd thim, a good bit aff, an' ready to jump an' run like a hare at the laste noise, for I was afeerd if they caught me at it, they'd make a pig o' me at wanst or change me into a baste completely. They marched into the field bechuxt the graveyard an' the rath an' there was another army there wid red coats, from the graveyard an' the two armies had the biggest fight ye iver seen, the granes agin the reds. Afther lookin' on a bit, I got axcited, for the granes were batin' the reds like blazes, an' I up an' gave a whilloo an' called out 'At 'em agin. Don't lave one o' the blaggards'. An' wid that word, the sight left me eyes an' I remember no more till mornin', an' there was I, layin' on the road where I'd seen thim, as stiff as a crutch."

125

Leaving all behind him, the hero sets off into the mystic realm.

The homes of the fairies are commonly in raths, tumuli of the pagan days of Ireland and. On this account, raths are much dreaded and after sundown are avoided by the peasantry. Attempts have been made to move some of these raths but the unwillingness of some of the peasants to engage in the work, no matter what inducements may be offered in compensation, has generally resulted in the abandonment of the undertaking. On one of the islands in the Upper Lake of Killarney there is a rath, the proprietor finding it occupied too much ground, resolved to have it levelled to increase the arable surface of the field. The work was begun, but one morning, in the early dawn, as the laborers were crossing the lake on their way to the island, they saw a procession of about two hundred persons, habited like monks, leave the island and proceed to the mainland, followed, as the workmen thought, by a long line of small, shining figures. The phenomenon was perhaps genuine, for the mirage is by no means an uncommon appearance in some parts of Ireland, but work on the rath was at once indefinitely postponed. Besides raths, old castles, deserted graveyards, ruined churches, secluded glens in the mountains, springs, lakes and caves, all are the homes and resorts of fairies, as is very well known on the west coast.

The better class of fairies are fond of human society and often act as guardians to those they love. In parts of Donegal and Galway they are believed to receive the souls of the dying and escort them to the gates of heaven, not, however being allowed to enter with them. On this account, fairies love graves and graveyards, having often been seen walking to and fro among the grassy mounds. There are indeed, some accounts of faction fights among the fairy bands at or shortly after a funeral, the question in dispute being whether the soul of the departed belonged to one or the other faction.

The amusements of the fairies consist of music, dancing and ball-playing. In music their skill exceeds that of men, while their dancing is perfect, the only drawback being the fact that it blights the grass, "fairy rings" of dead grass, apparently caused by a peculiar fungous growth, being common in Ireland. Although their musical instruments are few, the fairies use those few with wonderful skill. Near Colooney, in Sligo, there is a "knowledgeable woman", whose grandmother's aunt once witnessed a fairy ball, the music for which was furnished by an orchestra which the management had no doubt been at great pains and expense to secure and instruct.

"It was the cutest sight alive. There was a place fro thim to shtand on an' a wonderful big fiddle av the size ye could slape [*Editor's Note*: sleep] in it, that was played by a monshtrous frog an' two little fiddles, that two kittens fiddled on, an' two big drums baten be cats an' two trumpets played be fat pigs. All around the fairies were dancing like angels, the fireflies givin' thim light to see by an' the moonbames shinin' on the lake, for it was be the shore it was, an' if ye don't believe it, the glen's still there, that they call the fairy glen to this blessed day."

The fairies do much singing, seldom, however, save in chorus, and their songs were formerly more frequently heard than at present. Even now as belated peasant, who has been at a wake, or is coming home from a fair, in passing a rath will sometimes hear the soft strain of their voices in the distance and will hurry away lest they discover his presence and be angry at the intrusion on their privacy. When in unusually good spirits, they will sometimes admit a mortal to their revels, but if he speaks, the scene at once vanishes, he becomes insensible and usually finds himself by the roadside the next morning, "wid that degray av pains in his arums an' legs an' back, that if sixteen thousand devils were afther him he cudn't stir a toe to save the sowl av him, that's phat the fairies do be pinchin' an' punchin' him for comin' on them an' shpakin' out loud".

Kindly disposed fairies often take great pleasure in assisting those who treat them with proper respect, and as their favors always take a practical form, there is sometimes a business value in the show of reverence for them. There was Barney Noonan from County Leitrim, for instance: "An' sorra a better boy was in the country than Barney. He'd work as reg'lar as a pump an' liked a bit av divarshun as well as anybody when he'd the time for it, that was n't often to be sure, but small blame to him, for he was n't rich be no manner o' manes. He'd a power av ragard av the good people an' when he wint be the rath beyant his field, he'd pull off his caubeen an' take the dudheen out av his mouth, as p'lite as a dancin' masther, an' say 'God save ye ladies an' gintlemen' that the good people always heard though they never showed themselves to him. He'd a bit o' a bog that the hay was on, an' afther cuttin' it, he left it for to dhry, an' the sun came out beautiful an' in a day or so the hay was as dhry as powdher an' ready to put away.

So Barney was goin' to put it up, but it bein' the day av the fair, he thought he'd take the calf an' sell it, an' so he did, comin' up wid the boys, he stayed over his time, bein' hindhered wid dhrinkin' an' dancin' an' palaverin' at the gurls so it was afther dark when he got home an' the night as black as a crow, the clouds gatherin' on the tops av the mountains like avil sper'ts an' crapin' down into the glens like disthroyin' angels an' the wind howlin' like tin thousand Banshees, but Barney did n't mind it all wan copper, bein' glorified wid the dhrink he'd had. So the hay niver enthered the head av him, but he wint an' tumbled in bed an' was shnorin' like a horse in two minnits for he was a bach'ler, God bless him, an' had no wife to gosther him an' ax him where he'd been an' phat he'd been at, an' make him tell a hundred lies about not getting' home afore. So it came on to thunder an' lightnin' like as all the avil daymons in the univarse were fightin' wid cannons in the shky, an' by an' by there was a clap loud enough to shplit yer skull an' Barney woke up.

'Tattheration to me' says he to himself 'it's goin' for to rain an' me hay on the ground. Phat'll I do?' says he.

So he rowled over on the bed, an' looked out av a crack for to see if it was ralely rainin'. An' there was the biggest crowd he iver seen av little men and wimmen. They'd built a row o' fires from the cow-house to the bog an' were comin' in a shtring like cows goin' home, aitch wan wid his two arums full o' hay. Some were in the cow-house, recayvin' the hay, some were in the field, rakin' the hay together, an' some were shtandin' wid their hands in their pockets, beways they were the bosses, tellin' the rest for to make haste. An' so they did, for every wan run like he was afther goin' for the docther, an' brought a load an' hurried back for more.

Barney looked through the crack at thim a crossin' himself ivery minnit wid admiration for the spheed they had. 'God be good to me', says he to himself, "t is not ivery gossoon in Leitrim that's got haymakers like thim' only he never spake a word out loud, for he knewn very well the good people 'ud n't like it. So they brought in all the hay an' put it in the house an' thin let the fires go out an' made another big fire in front o' the dure, an' begun to dance round it wid the sweetest music Barney iver heard.

Now be this time he'd got up an' feelin' aisey in his mind about the hay, began to be very merry. He looked on through the dure at thim dancin' an' by an' by, they brought out a jug wid little tumblers an' began to drink summat that they poured out o' the jug. If Barney had the sense av a herrin', he'd a kept shtill an' let thim drink their fill without opening the big mouth av him, bein' that he was full as a goose himself an' naded no more; but when he seen the jug an' the fairies drinkin' away wid all their mights, he got mad and bellered out like a bull 'Arrah-a-a-h now, ye little attomies, is it drinkin' ye are an' never givin' a sip to a thirsty mortial that always thrates ye as well as he knows how' an' immejitly the fairies an' the fire an' the jug all wint out av his sight an' he to bed again in a timper. While he was layin' there he thought he heard talkin' an' a cugger-mugger goin' on but when he peeped out agin, sorra a thing did he see but the black night an' the rain comin' down an' aitch dhrop the full av a wather-noggin. So he wint to slape (sleep), continted that the hay was in, but not plazed that the good people 'ud be pigs entirely, to be afther dhrinkin' under his eyes an' not offer him a taste, no not so much as a shmell at the jug.

In the mornin' up he gets an' out for to look at the hay an' see if the fairies put it in right, for he says, 'It's a job they're not used to'. So, he looked in the cow-house an' thought the eyes 'ud lave him when there was n't a shtraw in the house at all. 'Holy Moses', says he, 'phat have they done wid it?', an he could n't consave phat had gone wid the hay. So he looked in the field an' it was all there; bad luck to the bit av it had the fairies left in the house at all, but when he shouted at thim, they got tarin' mad an' took all the hay back agin to the bog, puttin' every shtraw where Barney laid it an' it was as wet as a drownded cat. But it was a lesson to him that he niver forgot, an' I go bail that the next time the fairies help him in wid his hay, he'll kape shtill an' let thim dhrink thimselves to death if they plaze without sayin' a word."

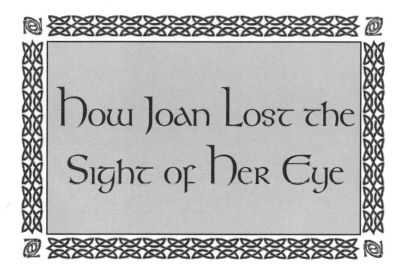

How Joan Lost the Sight of Her Eye

Although humans and fairies lived alongside each other, it was usually impossible for mortals to actually see their fairy neighbors. For the most part, rural Celtic peoples went about their daily lives oblivious to the thriving but unseen fairy world that existed all around them. It was, nevertheless, possible to see into this world, albeit briefly, but only with the permission of the fairies themselves. Sometimes they granted individuals direct sight of their world simply through personal contact and 'bringing them away' with them; they allowed a human to find a four-leafed clover, which allowed the fairy world to be seen; and at other times they granted the sight by means of a magical ointment that could be applied to mortal eyes. This latter method was merely a temporary one, for the ointment's effects soon wore off and normal sight returned, but with another application, sight of the fairy world was often restored. Wise women and conjurers were always supposed to have this ointment to aid them in their dealings with the fairy folk, and so stories about these potent salves are legion throughout Irish, Scottish, Welsh,

133

and Cornish folklore. It is thought that such ointments had a detrimental long-term effect on human eyes (because humans were not really supposed to see the fairy world at all). This is perhaps not surprising, because some conjurers were trying to actually make the salve from noxious ingredients and applying it to their own eyes! Any loss of sight was attributed to fairy annoyance. The following interesting and rather unique story, which comes from St. Leven in Cornwall, is taken from Robert Hunt's "The Drolls, Traditions, and Superstitions of Old Cornwall" (published in 1881).

Excerpt From "The Drolls, Traditions, and Superstitions of Cornwall"

by Robert Hunt

Joan was housekeeper to Squire Lovell and was celebrated for her beautiful knitting. One Saturday afternoon, Joan wished to go to Penzance to buy a pair of shoes for herself and some things for the Squire. So the weather being particularly fine, away she trudged.

Joan dearly loved a bit of gossip and always sought for company. She knew Betty Trenance was always ready for a jaunt: to be sure everybody said that Betty was a witch; but says Joan "Witch or no witch, she shall go: bad company is better than none."

Away went Joan to Lemorna, where Betty lived. Arrived at Betty's cottage, she peeped through the latch-hole (the finger-hole) and saw Betty rubbing some green ointment on the children's eyes. She watched till Betty Trenance had finished and noticed that she put the salve on the inner end of the chimney stool and covered it over with a rag.

Joan went in and Betty was delighted sure enough to see her and sent the children out of the way. But Betty wouldn't walk to Penzance, she was suffering with pain and she had been taking milk and suet and brandy and rum and she must have some more. So away went Betty to the other room for the bottle.

Joan seized the moment and taking a very small bit of the ointment on her finger, she touched her right eye with it. Betty came with the bottle and Joan had a drink; when she looked round she was surprised to see the house swarming with small people. They were playing all sorts of pranks on the key-beams and rafters. Some were swinging on cobwebs, some were riding the mice, and others were chasing them in and out of the holes in the thatch. Joan was surprised at the sight and thought that she must have a four-leafed clover about her.

However, without stopping to take much drink, she started alone for Penzance. She had wasted, as it was that it was nearly dark when she reached the market.

After having made her purchases and as she was about to leave the market, who should she spy but Betty's husband, Tom Trenance. There he was, stealing about in the shadows, picking from the standings, shoes and stockings from one, hanks of yarn from another, pewter spoons from a third and so on. He stuffed these things into his capacious pockets and yet no-one seemed to notice Tom.

Joan went forth to him.

"Aren't ye ashamed to be here in the dark carrying such a game?"

"Is that you Dame Joan?" says Tom; "which eye can you see me upon?"

After winking, Joan said she could see Tom plain enough with her right eye. She had no sooner said the word than Tom Trenance pointed his finger to her eye and she lost the sight of it from that hour.

"The work of the world" had Joan to find her way out of Penzance. She couldn't keep the road, she was always tumbling into the ditch on her blind side. When near the Fawgan, poor Joan who was so weary that she could scarcely drag one leg after the other, prayed that she might find a quiet old horse on which she might ride home.

Her desire was instantly granted. There by the roadside, stood an old bony white horse, spanned with its halter.

Joan untied the halter from the legs and placed it on the head of the horse; she got on the hedge and seated herself on the horse's back.

There she was mounted, "Gee wup; gee wup; k'up; k'up; k'up." The horse would not budge. Busy were Joan's heels rattling against the ribs of the poor horse and thwack, thwack went a thorn stick over his tail, and by and by the old blind brute began to walk. Joan beat and kicked and k'uped and coaxed, the horse went but little faster until it got to the top of the hill.

Then away, away like the wind it went through Toldava Lanes, and it swelled out until the horse became as high as the tower. Over hedges and ditches, across all the corners that came into the road, on went the horse. Joan held on by the mane with both hands and shouted: "Woa! Woa! Woey!" until she could shout no longer.

At length they came to Toldava Moor: the "ugly brute" took right away down towards the fowling-pool when Joan fearing he might plunge in and drown her, let go her hold.

The wind was blowing so strong, and the pair were going so fast against it, that Joan was lifted off over the hindquarters of the horse and by luck she fell soft on the rushes at the very edge of the fowling-pool.

When she looked up, Joan saw whatever she had been riding going down to the "bottom" in a blaze of fire, and the devil riding after with lots of men, horses and hounds, all without heads. All the marketing was lost; and in getting through the bogs, Joan had her shoes dragged from her feet. At last she got to Trove Bottoms and seeing the Bouge (sheep house), she clambered over the hedge as best she could, got into it and, laying herself down amongst the sheep, she soon fell fast asleep, thoroughly wearied out.

She would have slept for a week, I believe, if she had not been disturbed. But, according to custom on Sunday morning, the Squire and his boys came out to the Downs to span the sheep and there, greatly to their surprise, they found her.

They got the miserable woman home between them. The Squire charged her with having got drunk and said her eye had been scratched out by a furze-bush; but Joan never wandered from her story, and to the day of her death she said it to all young women, warning them never to meddle with "Fairy salve."

[*Editor's Note*: The folklore motif of the mad dash through the countryside appears in many Celtic legend, comprising the Wild Hunt in England and Brittany and a number of tales concerning the Pooka—the fairy horse—in Ireland, but this is one of the few known stories in which it is directly linked to the fairy ointment.]

The Priest's Supper

All across the Celtic world, the fairies were regarded
as another race. In Ireland they are referred to as "the Good
folk," "the Other Kind," "the Other Crowd"; in Scotland they
were known as "the Host" or "the Sluagh" (giving us our
word *slogan*; sluagh gairn "the cry of the Host"). For the
pagan peoples, the fairies were all powerful, and they were
everywhere. As Christianity began to move slowly across
the West however, debates arose as to what manner of beings
the fairies were, particularly in Ireland where the fairy faith
was strong. Did they have immortal souls, for example? Did
they acknowledge God as Lord of the World? Or, as many
suspected, were they instruments of the Devil? Actual Church
teaching tended towards the latter view: that fairies were
the servants of the Enemy of All Mankind and their ultimate
aim was to lead God's people astray and into wickedness.
Trafficking with them was forbidden. And yet, speculation
about their true nature persisted. Were they bound for Heaven,
people asked? Several old tales attempt to answer that
question. There were stories, for instance, of the fairies at

139

certain times of the year escorting the souls of the dead to the very Gates of Heaven, which they themselves were not allowed to enter. There are stories of fairy mothers attempting to get their supernatural offspring baptized by a Christian priest in order to gain them some hope of Salvation. Some people asserted that they were actually fallen angels, cast out of Heaven during the rebellion of Lucifer—not good enough to remain, but not evil enough to be condemned to Hell, and therefore unable to return to the place of their origin. This ancient tale, which queries the suitability of the fairies for Heaven, is particularly well known all over Ireland. There are several variations of the story; arguably the most famous one being given by Kate Ahern, the celebrated Limerick storyteller. This version together with commentary, however, comes from Thomas Crofton Croker's (1798–1854) 'Fairy Legends and Traditions of the South of Ireland' (first published in 1825) and closely parallels Kate Ahern's story.

Excerpt From "Fairy Legends and Traditions of the South of Ireland"

by Thomas Crofton Croker

It is said by those who ought to understand such things, that the good people, or the fairies, are some of the angels who were turned out of heaven, and who landed on their feet in this world, while the rest of their companions who had more sin to sink them went down further to a worse place. Be this as it may, there was a marry troop of fairies, dancing and playing all manner of wild tricks on a bright moonlit evening towards the end of September. The scene of their merriment was not far distant from Inchegeela, in the west of County Cork—a poor village although it had a barrack for soldiers; but great mountains and barren rocks, like those round about it, enough

Two warriors shade a terrifying tale of great valous.

to strike poverty into any place: however fairies can have anything they want for wishing; poverty does not trouble them much and all their care is to seek out unfrequented rocks and places where it is not likely that any one will come to spoil their sport.

On a nice green sod by the river's side were the little fellows dancing in a ring as gaily as may be, with their red caps wagging about at every bound in the moonshine; and so light were these bounds that the lobes of dew, although they trembled under their feet were not disturbed by their capering. Thus did they carry on their gambols, spinning round and round and twirling and bobbing and diving and going through all manner of figures, until one of them chirped out:

"Cease, cease with your drumming,
Here's an end to all your mumming,
By my smell,
I can tell,
A priest this way is coming!"

And every one of the fairies scampered off as hard as they could, concealing themselves under the green leaves of the lusmore, where if their little red caps should happen to peep out, they would only look like its crimson bells; and more hid themselves at the shady side of stones, and brambles and others under the bank of the river, and in holes and crannies of one kind or another.

The fairy speaker was not mistaken, for along the road, within view of the river, came Father Harrigan on his pony, thinking to himself that it was so late he would make an end of his journey at the first cabin he came to and, according to this determination, he stopped at the dwelling of Dermod Leary, lifted the latch and entered with "My blessing on all here."

I need not say that Father Harrigan was a welcome guest wherever he went, for there was no man more pious or better beloved in the country. Now it was a great trouble to Dermod that he had nothing to offer his reverence for his supper as a relish to the potatoes which "the old woman", for so Dermod called his wife though she was not much past twenty, had down boiling in the pot over the fire: he thought of the net which he had in the river, but as it had been there only a short time, the chances were against his finding a fish in it. "No matter", thought Dermod "there can be no harm in stepping down to try and may be as I want the fish for the priest's supper that it will be there before me."

Down to the river side went Dermod, and he found in the net as fine a salmon as ever jumped out of the bright waters of "the spreading Lee"; but as he was going to take it out, the net was pulled from him, he could not tell how or by whom, and away got the salmon and went swimming along with the current as gaily as if nothing had happened.

Dermod looked sorrowfully at the wake which the fish had left upon the water, shining like a line of silver in the moonlight, and then with an angry motion of his right hand, and a stamp of his foot, gave vent to his feelings by muttering: "May bitter bad luck attend you day and night for a blackguard schemer of a salmon, wherever you go! You ought to be ashamed of yourself, if there's any shame in you, to give me the slip after this fashion! And I'm clear in my own mind you'll come to no good for some sort of evil thing or other helped you—did I not feel it pull the net against me as strong as the devil himself".

"That's not true for you", said one of the little fairies, who had scampered off at the approach of the priest, coming up to Dermod Leary, with a whole throng of companions at his heels, "there was only a dozen and a half of us pulling against you."

Dermod gazed on the tiny speaker with wonder, who continued: "Make yourself no way uneasy about the priest's supper, for if you will go back and ask him one question from us, there will be as fine a supper as ever was put on a table spread out before him in less than no time".

"I'll have nothing at all to do with you," replied Dermod, in a tone of determination: and after a pause, he added, "I'm much obliged to you for your offer, sir, but I know better than to sell myself to you or the like of you for a supper, and more than that, I know Father Harrigan has more regard for my soul than to wish me to pledge it for ever, out of regard of any thing you could put before him—and there's an end to the matter".

The little speaker, with a pertinacity not to be repulsed by Dermods manner, continued. "Will you ask the priest one civil question for us?"

Dermod considered for some time and he was right in doing so, but he thought that no one would come to harm out of asking a civil question. "I see no objection to do that same gentlemen," said Dermod; "but I will have nothing in life to do with your supper,—mind that".

"Then," said the little speaking fairy, whilst the rest came crowding after him from all parts, "go and ask Father Harrigan to tell us whether our souls will be saved on the last day, like the souls of good Christians; and if you wish us well, bring back word what he says without delay."

Away went Dermod to his cabin, where he found the potatoes thrown out on the table and his good woman handing the biggest of them all, a beautiful laughing red apple, smoking like a hard ridden horse on a frosty night, over to Father Harrigan.

"Please your reverence", said Dermod after some hesitation, "may I make bold as to ask your honour one question?"

"What may that be?" asked Father Harrigan.

"Why then, begging your reverences's pardon for my freedom it is, if the souls of the good people are to be saved at the last day?"

144

"Who bid you ask me that question Leary?" said the priest, fixing his eyes upon him very sternly, which Dermod could not stand before at all.

"I'll tell no lies about the matter, and nothing in live but the truth", said Dermod. "It was the good people themselves who sent me to ask the question, and they are in thousands down on the bank of the river waiting for me to go back with the answer".

"Go back by all means", said the priest, "and tell them if they want to know, to come here to me by themselves and I'll answer that or any other question they are pleased to ask, with the greatest pleasure in life".

Dermod accordingly returned to the fairies who came swarming around him to hear what the priest had said in reply; and Dermod spoke out among them like a bold man as he was; but when they heard that they must go to the priest, away they fled, some here and more there; some this way and more that, whisking by poor Dermod so fast and in such numbers, as he was quite bewildered.

When he came to himself, which was not for a long time, back he went to his cabin and ate his dry potatoes along with Father Harrigan, who made quite light of the thing; but Dermod could not help thinking it a mighty hard case that his reverence, whose words had the power to banish the fairies at such a rate; should have some sort of relish to his supper, and that the fine salmon he had in the net should have got away from him in such a manner.

It is curious to observe the similarity of legends, and of ideas concerning imaginary beings, among nations that for ages have had scarcely any communication. In the 4th vol of the *Danske Folkesagan* or Danish Popular Legends lately collected by Mr. Thiele, the following story occurs which has a great resemblance to the adventure of Dermod Leary: "A priest was going in a carriage one night from Kjeslunde to Roeskilde, in the island of Zealand and on his way passed by a hill, in which there was music and dancing and other merry-making going on. Some dwarfs suddenly jumped out of the hill, stopped the carriage and asked, "Where are you going?" "To the chapter-house" said the priest. They then asked him whether he thought they could be saved; to which he replied, that at present he could not tell: on which they begged him to meet with them with an answer that day twelvemonth. Notwithstanding, the next time the coachman drove that way, an accident befell him, for he was thrown on the level ground and severely hurt. When the priest returned at the end of the year, they asked him the same question to which he answered "No you are all damned!" and scarcely had he spoken the word, when the whole hill was enveloped in a bright flame."

[*Editor's Note*: Not only are there variants of the tale in Denmark, but the story also has various permutations all over Ireland. In the County Down, for example, a fairy approaches a serving man to inquire from a priest if there is any hope of salvation for the fairy kind. The servant conveys a reply from the cleric, which states that Christ died for all of Adam's children and if there is but one drop of Adam's blood in fairy veins, then they shall be saved and shall see Heaven. This reply sends the fairy away in great distress. It was generally accepted that the fairies were not covered by Christ's sacrifice and were so condemned to Hell on the great Day of Judgement.]

The Night Dancers

As did many other ancient peoples, the Celts viewed borders and thresholds with suspicion and fear. Thresholds and crossings were places where dark powers—many inimical to Mankind—tended to gather. Even the transition of one time-period into another, such as at midnight or noonday, was fraught with danger. Celtic lore is filled with stories of strange happenings that occur as one day merges into another, or morning moves into afternoon. The thresholds of houses were also sinister places. In some areas of rural Ireland, for example, open scissors or naked iron blades were left under doormats to ward away witches, fairies, or the returning dead who were supposed to congregate there.

If thresholds and crossings were supernaturally troublesome places, crossroads were twice as dangerous. At crossroads, ghosts and fairies thronged, and travelers had to be wary (or adequately protected by holy charms) before approaching them.

Nowhere was the lore of crossroads more prevalent than in Brittany. Here, at the crossing of trails and paths, such spectral terrors as ghouls, Midnight Washerwomen (who washed the shrouds of those who were about to die), and Night Dancers (fairies who often danced to tunes unheard by mortal ears) waited to waylay passersby. To those who ignored them, they could mete out awful punishment, but to those who showed proper respect they could dispense largesse.

Variants of the following Breton story, which comes from the rural Breton folktales collected by F. M. Luzel during the mid-19th century, can be found all over the Celtic world. Even in Brittany itself another variation, "The Two Hunchbacks and the Dwarves," can still be found, and in Ireland it is known as "The Legend of Knockgrafton." It also contains many elements of a traditional fairy-tale.

Listen if you wish
Here's a pretty little tale,
In which there's never a lie,
Except perhaps a word or two.

Excerpt From a Breton Folktale

collected by F.M. Luzel

Once there was a rich widow who married a rich widower.

The man had a pretty well behaved daughter by his previous wife called Levenes. The widow also had a daughter by her first husband, called Margot, who was bad and ugly.

The husband's daughter, as so often happens in such cases, was detested by her stepmother. They lived in a fine manor house at Guernaour, near Coathuel. At the crossroads at Croazann-neud, which is on the road going from Guernaour

148

to the village of Plouaret, the night dancers were often seen in those days, or so they say, and whoever passed them as they danced in circles in the moonlight and did not wish to dance with them, became a victim of their bad humour.

The Lady of Guernaour knew this well and one Sunday evening, after supper, she said to Levenes:

"Go and fetch my book of hours, which I've left in church beneath my pew."

"Yes mother" replied the young girl.

And she went alone, although night had already fallen

It was a clear moonlit night. When she reached the cross-roads, she saw a crowd of little men who were dancing in a circle holding hands. She was afraid, poor child, and thought of going back, but her stepmother would grumble and perhaps beat her so she resolved to pass them. One of the dancers ran after her and said:

"Would you like to dance with us pretty girl?"

"Willingly" she replied, trembling.

And she joined in the circle and danced.

Then one of the dancers said to the others.

"What present should we give this charming girl for dancing with us?"

"She's quite pretty, but she should become even prettier," said one of the dancers.

"And with each word she speaks, a pearl should fall from her mouth" said a second.

"And everything she touches with her hand should change to gold if she wishes it to" said a third.

"Yes, yes," cried all the others together.

"Many thanks sirs, I'm much obliged," she said with a curtsy.

Then she went on her way.

When she reached the village, she went to the sacristan's for the church was locked, and told him why she had come.

The sacristan went with her and unlocked the door. She touched the door with her hand and it became gold and with every word she spoke, a pearl fell from her mouth. The sacristan could not believe his eyes and was dumbfounded. He picked up the pearls and put them in his pocket. Levenes went inside, took her stepmother's book from her pew, and went straight back home.

The night dancers were no longer at the crossroads when she passed by.

"Here's your book of hours mother", she said giving her a golden book.

"What", she asked her, surprised to see her unharmed. "you didn't see the night dancers?"

"Yes I did" she replied, "I saw them at the crossroads."

"And they didn't hurt you?"

"No, quite the opposite; they're very pleasant, these little men, they invited me to dance with them".

"And did you?"

"Yes I did".

"That's good, go to bed".

The stepmother had noticed her stepdaughter's extraordinary beauty and also the pearls that fell from her mouth each time she spoke, and the way her book of hours had changed to gold, but she pretended not to notice but inside herself she thought:

"Good! I know what to do. Tomorrow night I'll send my own daughter to the night dancers. These little men have inexhaustible treasures of gold and pearls hidden underground and amongst the rocks".

Next day, at the same time, she said to her daughter Margot.

150

"Margot, you must go and fetch me another book of hours from my pew in the church".

"No, I won't go," replied Margot

"I want you to and you're going", replied the mother, "and when you pass by the crossroads if you see the night dancers and they invite you to dance with them, and have no fear; they'll do you no harm, but quite the contrary, they'll give you a fine present."

Margot answered rudely and her mother had to threaten her with a stick to make her go.

When she reached the crossroads, the night dancers were dancing in circles in the moonlight. One of them ran up to Margot and politely invited her to dance with them.

"Shit," she replied.

"What present should we give this girl for the way she has welcomed our proposition?" said the dwarf to his companions.

"She's quite ugly, but she could become uglier yet," replied one of them.

"She should have only one eye in the middle of her head," said another.

"A toad shall fall out of her mouth with every word she speaks, and everything she touches should turn dirty", said a third.

"That's what should happen," cried all the others in a chorus.

Then Margot went to church, took her mother's book from her pew and went back home.

"Here's your book," she said, throwing it at her, all dirty and smelly.

And at the same time three toads fell from her mouth.

"What's happened to you my poor child?" cried the mother, upset. "What a mess you've come back in!...... Who did this to you? Did you see the night dancers, and did you dance with them?"

151

"Me?....Dance with such ugly creatures! Shit on them!"

And again she spat as many toads as the words.

"Go to bed daughter," said her mother, furious at what she saw, and promising herself revenge on Levenes.

But fortunately, the stepdaughter was married shortly afterwards, to a young gentleman of the land who took her to his castle, and the stepmother and her daughter almost died of spite and jealousy.

The Blood-Drawing Ghost

To the ancient Celts, death meant something far different than it does today. Nowadays we consider it to be the end of our involvement in the affairs of the world, but for them it was no more than a transition from one sphere of existence to another. From a place known as the Otherworld, a sort of halfway house between this world and some half-imagined Eternity, the dead watched the lives of their descendants with a mixture of concern and pride. And they had the power to come back into the world to carry out certain tasks on their descendants' behalf or to complete business that they'd left unfinished when alive. These, of course, were not the wispy, ethereal phantoms of Victorian ghost-lore. These were the substantial, corporeal entities that could eat, drink, and work as they had done when alive. For the most part, many of the dead returned for altruistic motives to warn, advise, or reward their descendants, but occasionally some came back from the grave with a more malign purpose. They could, for example, punish their descendants for some slight against them. Indeed, this was

153

what the Church itself taught. If congregations were remiss in remembering their loved ones in Masses for the dead a regular source of income for local priests, then their ancestors, condemned to another time in Purgatory, would return to take vengeance on their neglect. Thus the seeds for an idea of the hostile dead were sewn. The following story from Ireland, taken from Jeremiah Curtin's (1835–1906) *Tales of the Fairies and of the Ghost World from Oral Tradition in South-West Munster* (1895), reflects this popular belief and presents a cadaver so terrible that it might have come from a modern horror story.

Excerpt From *Tales of the Fairies and of the Ghost World from Oral Tradition in South-West Munster*

by Jeremiah Curtin

There was a young man in the parish of Drimalegue, county Cork, who was courting three girls at one time and he didn't know which one of them would he take, they had equal fortunes and any of them was a pleasing to him as any other. One day, when he was coming home from the fair with his two sisters, the sisters began:

"Well John" said one of them "why don't you get married? Why don't you take either Mary, or Peggy, or Kate?"

"I can't tell you that" said John, "'till I find which of them has the best wish for me."

"How will you know?" asked the other.

"I will tell you that as soon as any person will die in the parish."

In three weeks time from that day an old man died. John went to the wake and then to the funeral. While they were burying the corpse in the graveyard John went and stood near a tomb which was next to the grave and when all were going away after burying the old man, he remained standing a while by himself, as if thinking of something, then he put his blackthorn stick on top of the tomb, stood a while longer, and on going from the graveyard left the stick behind him. He went home and ate his supper. After supper, John went to a neighbour's house where young people used to meet of an evening, and the three girls happened to be there that time. John was very quiet so that every one noticed him.

"What is troubling you this evening John?" asked one of the girls.

"Oh I am sorry for my beautiful blackthorn," said he.

"Did you lose it?"

"I did not," said John "but I left it on the top of the tomb next to the grave of the man who was buried today and whichever of you three will go for it is the woman I'll marry. Well Mary, will you go for my stick?" he asked.

"Faith then, I will not," said Mary.

"Well Peggy, will you go?"

"If I were without a man for ever" said Peggy "I wouldn't go"

"Well Kate" said he to the third, "Will you go for my stick? If you go I'll marry you"

"Stand to your word" said Kate "and I'll bring the stick"

"Believe me, that I will" said John

Kate left the company behind her and went for the stick. The graveyard was three miles away and the walk was a long one. Kate came to the place at last and made out the tomb by the fresh grave. When she had her hand on the blackthorn, a voice called from the tomb:

"Leave the stick where it is and open the tomb for me"

Kate began to tremble and was greatly in dread but something was forcing her to open the tomb—she couldn't help herself.

"Take the lid off now," said the dead man when Kate had the door open and was inside the tomb "and take me out of this—take me on your back"

Afraid to refuse, she took the lid from the coffin and raised the dead man on her back and walked on in the way he directed. She walked about the distance of a mile. The load, being very heavy, was near breaking her back and killing her. She walked half a mile further and came to a village; the houses were at the side of the road.

"Take me to the first house" said the dead man.

She took him.

"Oh we cannot go in here," said he when they came near. "The people have clean water inside, and they have holy water too. Take me to the next house."

She went to the next house.

"We cannot go in there," said he, when they stopped in front of the door. "They have clean water, and there is holy water as well."

She went to the third house.

"Go in there" said the dead man. "There is neither clean water nor holy water in this place; we can stop in it"

They went in.

"Bring a chair now and put me sitting at the side of the fire. Then find me something to eat and to drink"

She placed him in a chair by the hearth, searched the house and found a dish of oatmeal and brought it. "I have nothing to give you to drink but dirty water" said she.

"Bring me a dish and a razor"

She brought the dish and the razor.

"Come now" said he "to the room above."

They went up to the room, where three young men, sons of the man of the house, were sleeping in bed, and Kate had to hold the dish while the dead man was drawing their blood.

156

"Let the father and mother have that" said he "in return for the dirty water", meaning that if there was clean water in the house, he wouldn't have taken the blood of the young men. He closed their wounds in the way that there was no sign of a cut on them. "Mix this now with the meal, get a dish of it for yourself and another for me"

She got two plates and put the oatmeal in it after mixing it, and brought two spoons. Kate wore a handkerchief on her head, she put this under her neck and tied it, she was now pretending to eat but she was putting the food to hide in the handkerchief till her plate was empty.

"Have you your share eaten?" asked the dead man.

"I have" answered Kate.

"I'll have mine finished this minute," said he, and soon after he gave her the empty dish. She put the dishes back in the dresser, and didn't mind washing them. "Come now" said he, "and take me back to the place where you found me"

"Oh how can I take you back, you are too great a load; 'twas killing me you were when I brought you". She was in dread of going from the house again.

"You are stronger after that food than what you were in coming, take me back to my grave"

She went against her will. She rolled up the food inside the handkerchief. There was a deep hole in the wall of the kitchen by the door, where the bar had slipped in when they barred the door; into this hole she put the handkerchief. In going back she shortened the road by going through a big field at the command of the dead man. When they were at the top of the field she asked, was there any cure for those young men whose blood was drawn?

"There is no cure", said he, "except one. If any of that food had been spared, three bits of it in each young man's mouth would bring them back to life again, and they'd never know of their death"

"Then" said Kate in her own mind, "that cure is to be had"

"Do you see this field?" asked the dead man

"I do"

"Well there is so much gold buried in it as would make rich people of all who belong to you. Do you see those three leachtans (piles of small stones)? Underneath each of them is a pot of gold" "The dead man looked around for a while, then Kate went on without stopping till she came to the wall of the graveyard, and just then they heard the cock crow.

"The cock is crowing" said Kate, "it's time for me to be going home"

"It is not time yet", said the dead man, "that is a bastard cock"

A moment after that another cock crowed. "There the cocks are crowing a second time," said she. "No" said the dead man, "that is a bastard cock again, that's no right bird". They came to the mouth of the tomb and a cock crowed the third time.

"Well," said the girl, "that must be the right cock"

"Ah, my girl, that cock has saved your life. But for him I would have had you in the grave with me for evermore, and if I knew this cock would crow before I was in the grave, you wouldn't have the knowledge you have now of the field and the gold. Put me in the coffin where you found me. Take your time and settle me well. I cannot meddle with you now and 'tis sorry I am to part with you."

"Will you tell me who you are?" asked Kate.

"Have you heard your father or mother mention a man called Edward Derrihy or his son Michael?"

"It's often I've heard tell of them" said the girl.

"Well, Edward Derrihy was my father, I am Michael. That blackthorn stick that you came for to night, to this graveyard was the lucky stick for you, but if you had any thought of the danger that was before you, you wouldn't be here. Settle me carefully and close the door of the tomb well behind you."

She closed him in the coffin carefully, closed the door behind her, took the blackthorn stick, and away home with Kate. The night was far spent when she came. She was tired and it's good reason the girl had. She thrust the stick into the thatch above the door of the house and rapped. Her sister rose up and opened the door.

"Where did you spend the night?" asked the sister. "Mother will kill you in the morning for spending the whole night from home"

"Go to bed" said Kate, "and never mind me"

They went to bed and Kate fell asleep the minute she touched the bed, she was that tired after the night.

When the father and mother of the three young men rose the next morning and there was no sign of their sons, the mother went to the room to call them, and there she found the three dead. She began to screech and wring her hands. She ran to the road, screaming and wailing. All the neighbours crowded round to see what trouble was on her. She told them her three sons were lying dead in their beds after the night. Very soon the report spread in every direction. When Kate's father and mother heard it they hurried off to the house of the dead men. When they came home Kate was still in bed, the mother took a stick and began to beat the girl for being out all the night and in bed all the day.

"Get up now, you lazy stump of a girl," said she, "and go to the wake house, your neighbour's three sons are dead"

Kate took no notice of this. "I am very tired and sick," said she. "You'd better spare me and give me a drink"

The mother gave her a drink of milk and a bite to eat, and in the middle of the day she rose up.

"'Tis a shame for you not to be at the wake house yet", said the mother, "hurry over now"

When Kate reached the house, there was a great crowd of people before her and great wailing. She did not cry but was looking on. The father was as if wild, going up and down the house, wringing his hands.

"Be quiet", said Kate. "Control yourself"

"How can I do that, my dear girl, and my three fine sons lying dead in the house?"

"What would you give" asked Kate "to the person who would bring them back to life again?"

"Don't be vexing me" said the father.

"It's neither vexing you I am or trifling," said Kate. "I can put life in them again"

"If it was true that you could do that, I would give you all that I have inside the house and outside as well"

"All that I want" said Kate "is the eldest son to marry and Gort na Leachtan [*Editor's Note*: the field of the stone heaps] as fortune"

"My dear you will have that from me with the greatest blessing"

"Give me in writing from yourself, whether the son will marry me or not"

He gave her the field in his handwriting. She told all who were inside in the wake house to go outside the door, every man and woman of them. Some were laughing at her and some were crying, thinking it was mad she was. She bolted the door inside, and went to the place where she left the handker-chief, found it and put three bites of the oatmeal and the blood in the mouth of each young man, and as soon as she did that the three got their natural colour and they looked like men sleeping. She opened the door, then called on all to come inside, and told the father to go and wake his sons.

He called each one by name, and as they woke they seemed very tired after their night's rest; they put on their clothes,

160

and were greatly surprised to see all the people around. "How is this?" asked the eldest brother

"Don't you know of anything that came over you in the night?" asked the father.

"We do not," said the sons. "We remember nothing at all since we fell asleep last evening"

The father then told them everything but they could not believe it. Kate went away home and told her father and mother of her night's journey to and from the graveyard, and said that she would soon tell them more.

That day she met John.

"Did you bring the stick?" asked he

"Find your own stick," said she, "and never speak to me again in your life"

In a week's time, she went to the house of the three young men and said to the father, "I have come for what you promised me."

"You'll get that with my blessing" said the father. He called the eldest son aside and asked would he marry Kate, their neighbours' daughter. "I will," said the son. Three days after that, the two were married and had a fine wedding. For three weeks they enjoyed a pleasant life without toil or trouble, then Kate said, "This will not do for us; we must be working. Come with me tomorrow and I'll give yourself and your brothers plenty to do, and my own father and brothers as well."

She took them next day to one of the stone heaps in Gort na Leachtan. "Throw these stones to one side," said she.

They thought that she was losing her senses, but she told them that they'd soon see for themselves what she was doing. They went to work and kept at it until they had six feet deep of a hole dug, and then they met with a flat stone three feet square and an iron hook in the middle of it.

"Sure there must be something underneath this" said the men. They lifted the flag and under it was a pot of gold. All were happy then. "There is more gold yet in the place", said Kate "Come now, to the other heap". They moved that heap, dug down and found another pot of gold. They moved the third pile and found a third pot of gold. On the side of the third pot was an inscription and they could not make out what it was. After emptying it they placed the pot by the side of the door.

About a month later, a poor scholar walked the way, and as he was going in at the door, he saw the old pot and the letters on the side of it. He began to study the letters.

"You must be a good scholar if you can read what's on that pot," said the young man.

"I can," said the poor scholar, "and here it is for you. 'There is a deal more at the south side of each pot'"

The young man said nothing, but putting his hand in his pocket, he gave the poor scholar a good day's hire. When he was gone they went to work and found a deal more gold at the south side of each stone heap. They were very happy then and very rich, and bought several farms and built fine houses, and it was supposed by all of them in the latter end that it was Derrihy's money that was buried under the leachtans, but they could give no correct account of that, and sure why would they care? When they died they left property to make their children rich to the seventh generation.

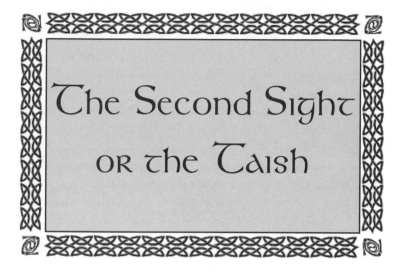

The Second Sight or the Taish

Amongst the Celts, the idea of prognostication—the foretelling of the future—was highly important. Warriors wished to know whether or not they would return from battle; young men and young women wanted to know whom they would marry; others simply wished to know what the future might hold in store for them. The gift of foretelling the future resided with the druids (the pagan Celtic priests) who could determine what lay in store by the movements of birds or clouds, from the way in which certain engraved sticks might fall after being thrown in the air, from the entrails of certain animals. There were those too who were deemed to possess a certain power—to actually 'see' the future. This was said to have been given as a gift either from the gods themselves or from other supernatural beings such as the Good Folk (fairies). The tradition of 'seeing' another future world or deriving interpretations from visions that no one else could see continued long after the druids were gone. In certain communities, there were individuals who were deemed to have the gift of what became known as 'the second sight'

163

(the ability to 'see' things that were either to come or that lay beyond the sight of ordinary mortals). Many people who possessed this ability actually considered it to be a curse, as the visions were often involuntary and liable to come upon them without warning. In many instances they were the harbingers of doom, placing a dreadful knowledge and responsibility upon the seer.

Nowhere was this ability more prevalent than in the Highlands and Western Islands of Scotland. The Highland Seers men and women with the gift of the 'second sight'—were famous the length and breadth of the Celtic world. These ranged from the celebrated Brahan Seer (Kenneth MacKenzie) of Ross-shire to the local 'spae-wives' of the Hebrides. The Irish referred to the 'gift' as the *taish* and declared it to be infallible. They paid homage to their Scottish cousins in whom 'the greatest gift' resided.

The following account concerning the second sight is taken from Martin Martin's almost indispensable book *A Description of the Western Isles of Scotland* (first published about 1695).

Excerpt From *A Description of the Western Isles of Scotland*

by Martin Martin

The second-sight is a singular faculty of seeing an otherwise invisible object, without any previous means used by the person who sees it for that end: the vision makes a lively impression upon the seers that they neither see nor think of anything else except the vision as long as it continues—and then they appear pensive or jovial, according to the object which was represented to them.

At the sight of a vision, the eye-lids of the person are erected; the eyes continue staring until the object vanishes. This is obvious to others who are by, when the person happens to see a vision, and occurred more than once to my own observation, and to others that were with me.

There is one in Skye, of whom his acquaintance observed, that when he sees a vision, the inner part of his eye-lids turn so far upwards, that after the object disappears, he must draw them down with his fingers, and sometimes employs others to draw them down, which he finds to be much the easier way.

The faculty of the second sight does not lineally descend in a family, as some imagine, for I know several parents who are endowed with it and their children are not, and vice versa. Neither is it acquired by any previous compact. And, after a strict enquiry, I could never learn from any among them, that this faculty was communicable in any way whatsoever.

The seer knows neither the object, time nor the place of a vision before it appears: and the same object is often seen by different persons, living at a considerable distance from one another. The true way of judging as to the time and circumstance of an object is by observation; for several persons of judgement, without this faculty, are more capable to judge of the design of a vision, than the novice that is a seer. If an object appear in the day or night, it will come to pass sooner or later accordingly.

If an object is seen early in the morning (which is not frequent) it will be accomplished in a few hours afterwards. If at noon it will commonly be accomplished that very day. If in the evening, perhaps that night; if after the candles be lighted, it will be accomplished that night: the latter always in accomplishment by weeks, months and sometimes years, according to the time of night the vision is seen.

When a shroud is perceived about one, it is a sure prognostic of death. The time is judged according to the height of it about the person; for if it is not seen above the middle, death is not to be expected for the space of a year, and perhaps some months longer; and as it is frequently seen to ascend higher towards the head, death is concluded to be at hand within a few days, if not hours, as daily experience confirms. Examples of this kind were shown me; when persons of whom the observations then made enjoyed perfect health.

One instance was lately foretold by a seer that was a novice, concerning the death of one of my acquaintance; this was communicated to a few only and with great confidence; I being one of the number, did not in the least regard it, until the death of the person about the time foretold, did confirm me of the certainty of the prediction. The novice mentioned above is now a skilful seer, as appears from many late instances; he lives in the parish of St. Mary's, the most northern in Skye.

If a woman is seen standing at a man's left hand, it is a presage that she will be his wife, whether they be married to others, or unmarried at the time of the apparition.

If two or three women are seen at once standing near a man's left hand, she that is next to him will undoubtedly be his wife first, and so on, whether all three or the man be single or married at the time of the vision; of which there are several late instances among those of my acquaintance. It is an ordinary thing for them to see a man that is to come to the house shortly after; and if he is not of the seer's acquaintance, yet he gives such a lively description of his stature, complexion, habit etc. that upon arrival he answers the character given him in all respects.

If the person so appearing be one of the seer's acquaintance, he will tell his name as well as other particulars; and he can tell by his countenance whether he comes in good or bad humour.

I have been seen thus myself by seers of both sexes at some hundred miles distance; some that saw me in this manner had never seen me personally, and it happened according to their visions, without any previous design of mine to go to these places, any coming there being purely accidental.

It is ordinary with them to see houses, gardens and trees, in places void of all three; and this in process of time used to be accomplished; as at Mogstot in the Isle of Skye, where there are but a few sorry cow-houses thatched with straw, yet in a few years after, the vision which appeared often was accomplished, by the building of several good houses on the very spot represented to the seers, and by the planting of orchards there.

To see a spark of fire fall upon ones arm or breast is a forerunner of a dead child to be seen in the arms of those persons; of which there are several fresh instances.

To see a seat empty at the time of ones sitting in it, is a presage of that person's death quickly after.

When a novice, or one that has lately obtained the second-sight, sees a vision in the night-time without doors, and comes near a fire, he presently falls into a swoon.

Some find themselves as it were in a crowd of people, having a corpse, which they carry along with them; and after such visions, the seers come in sweating and describe the people that appeared: if there be any of their acquaintance among them, they give an account of their names, as also of the bearers, but they know nothing concerning the corpse.

All those who have the second-sight do not always see these visions at once, though they be together at the time. But if one who has this faculty designedly touch his fellow-seer at the instant of a vision's appearing, then the second sees it as well as the first; and this is sometimes discerned by those that are near them on such occasions.

There is a way of foretelling death by a cry that they call taisk, which some call a wraith in the Lowlands.

They hear a loud cry without doors, exactly resembling the voice of some particular person, whose death is foretold by it. Last instance was given to me of this kind was in the village Rigg, in the isle of Skye.

Five women were sitting together in the same room, and all of them heard a loud cry passing by the window; they thought it plainly to be the voice of a maid who was one of the

Dark forces seek to lure away a child.

number; she blushed at the time, though not sensible of her so doing, contracted a fever next day, and died that week.

Things also are foretold by smelling, sometimes as follows. Fish or flesh is frequently smelled in a fire, when at the same time neither of the two are in the house, or in all probability likely to be hand in it for some weeks or months; for they seldom eat flesh and though the sea be near them, yet they catch fish but seldom in the winter and spring. This smell several persons have, who are not endued with the second-sight, and it is always accomplished soon after.

Children, horses and cows see the second-sight, as well as men and women advanced in years.

That children see it is plain from their crying aloud at the very instant that a corpse or any other vision appears to an ordinary seer. I was present in a house where a child cried out of a sudden and being asked the reason of it, he answered that he had seen a great white thing lying on the board which was in the corner: but he was not believed, until a seer present told them that the child was in right; for said he, I saw a corpse and the shroud about it, and the board will be used as part of a coffin or some way employed about a corpse; and accordingly it was made into a coffin for one who was in perfect health at the time of the vision.

That horses see it is likewise plain from their violent and sudden starting when the rider or seer in company with him sees a vision of any kind, night or day. It is observable of the horse that he will not go forward that way, until he be led about at some distance from the common road, and then he is in a sweat.

A horse fastened by the common road on the side of Loch Skeriness in Skye, did break his rope at noon-day and run up and down without the least visible cause. But two of the neighbourhood that happened to be at a little distance and in view of the horse, did at the same time see a considerable number of men about a corpse directing their course to the church of Snizort; and this was accomplished within a few days after by the death of a gentlewoman who lived thirteen miles from that church and came from another parish from whence very few came to Snizort to be buried.

That cows see the second-sight appears from this; that when a woman is milking a cow and then happens to see the second-sight the cow runs away in great fright at the same time and will not be pacified for some time after.

Before I mention more particulars discovered by the second-sight, it may not be amiss to answer the objections that have lately been made against the reality of it.

Object 1. These seers are visionary and melancholy people and fancy they see things that do not appear to them or anybody else.

Answer. The people of these isles, and particularly the seers are very temperate, and their diet is simple and moderate in quantity and quality, so that their brains are not in all probability disordered by undigested fumes of meat or drink. Both sexes are free from hysteric fits, convulsions, and several other distempers of that sort; there's no madmen among them, nor any instance of self-murder. It is observed among them that a man drunk never sees the second-sight; and that he is a visionary, would discover himself in other things as well as in that; and such as see it are not judged to be visionaries by any of their friends or acquaintance.

Object 2. There is none among the learned able to oblige the world with a satisfying account of these visions, therefore it is not to be believed.

Answer. If everything for which the learned are not able to give a satisfying account be condemned as impossible we may find many other things generally believed that must be rejected by this rule. For instance, yawning and its influence and that the lodestone attracts iron; and yet these are true as well as harmless, though we can give no satisfying account of their causes, how much less can we pretend to things that are supernatural?

Object 3. Seers are impostors, and the people who believe them are credulous, and easily imposed upon.

Answer. The seers are generally illiterate and well meaning people, and altogether void of design, nor could I ever learn that any of them made the least gain by it, neither is it reputable among them to have that faculty; besides the people of isles are not so credulous as to believe the thing implicitly before the thing foretold is accomplished; but when it actually comes to pass afterwards it is not in their power to deny it without offering violence to their senses and reason. Besides, if the seers were deceivers, can it be reasonable to imagine that all the islanders who have not the second-sight should combine together and offer violence to their understandings and senses, to force themselves to believe a lie from age to age. There are several persons among them whose birth and education raise them above the suspicion of concurring with an imposture merely to gratify an illiterate and contemptible sort of persons; nor can a reasonable man believe that children, horses or cows could be pre-engaged in a combination to persuade the world of the reality of the second-sight.

Such as deny these visions give their assent to several strange passages in history upon the authority of historians that lived several centuries before our time and yet they deny the people of this generation the liberty to believe their intimate friends and acquaintance, men of probity and unquestionable reputation, and of whose veracity than we have of any ancient historian.

Every vision that is seen comes exactly to pass according to the true rules of observation, though novices and heedless persons do not always judge by those rules. I remember the seers returned me this answer to my objections and gave me several instances in that purpose whereof the following is one.

A boy of my acquaintance was often surprised by the sight of a coffin close by his shoulder, which put him into a fright and made him to believe it was a forerunner of his own death, and this his neighbours judged to be the meaning of that vision; but a seer who lived in the village of Knockow, where the boy was then a servant, told them that they were under a great mistake, and desired the boy to take hold of the first opportunity that offered; and when he went to a burial to remember to act as a bearer for some moments; and this he did accordingly within a few days after when one of his acquaintance died; and from that time forward he was never troubled with seeing a coffin at his shoulder, though he has seen many at a distance, that concerned others. He is now reckoned one of the exactest seers in the parish of St. Mary's in Skye where he lives.

There is another instance of a woman in Skye, who frequently saw a vision representing a woman having a shroud about her up to the middle, but always appeared with her back towards her, and the habit in which it appeared to be dressed resembled her own: this was a mystery for some time, until the woman tried an experiment to satisfy her curiosity, which was to dress herself contrary to the usual way; that is, she put that part of her clothes behind, which was always before, fancying the vision at the next appearing would be easier distinguished: and it fell out accordingly, for the vision soon after presented itself with its face and dress looking towards the woman, and it proved to resemble herself in all points, and she died in a little time after.

There are visions seen by several persons, in whose days they were not accomplished; and this is one of the reasons why some things have been seen that are said to never come to pass, and there are also several visions seen which are not understood until they are accomplished.

The second-sight is not a late discovery seen by one or two in a corner, or a remote isle, but it is seen by many persons of both sexes, in several isles, separated above forty or fifty leagues from one another: the inhabitants of many of these isles never had the least converse by word or writing; and this faculty of seeing visions, having continued, as we are informed by tradition, ever since the plantation of these isles, without being disproved by the nicest sceptic, after the strictest inquiry, seems to be a clear proof of its reality.

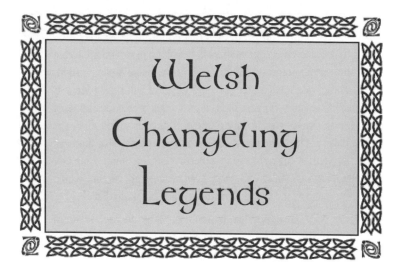

Welsh Changeling Legends

If fairies were indeed another race, separate from Mankind, then there was a widespread belief throughout the Celtic world that their population remained reasonably static. Fairy women, it was said, had great difficulty in giving birth. There are many stories from Ireland, Scotland, Wales, and Brittany of human midwives being called to assist at exhausting fairy deliveries, none of which seem to have been successful, whilst the more elderly of the species lingered on for centuries through a cantankerous old age. In order to alleviate this situation and to bring new blood into the fairy line, it was believed that the fairies often carried away human children—particularly small girls or one of a set of twins—to live amongst them and add to their population. In return, they left one of their own—an old, wizened, whining creature which magically they "disguised" as the child that they had abducted. However, they couldn't really disguise the fact that this being was thin and wasted or that it had a disagreeable nature.

173

In times and areas where infantile diseases such as tuberculosis were common, such beliefs often served to explain how a normal-sized, healthy baby turned into a thin, wasted, and crying invalid almost overnight. And if the child were to die (as many of them did), then the idea provided at least some form of solace for the grieving parents. After all, it was not *their* child who had died— he or she was still alive amongst the fairies—but rather some withered ancient thing. If the tiny bodies were later exhumed, it was declared, all that would be found in the coffin was an old and blackened stick.

Of course, parents did not want their children taken at all, so a series of measures and protections was devised to rid the house of these potential 'changelings' (a fairy changed for a human being). If a child were suspected of being a changeling, then there were ways of finding out. The most common way was to trick the changeling into revealing its true age, which would be far older than that of a human infant. There were of course more drastic measures in Ireland, they might be given a mixture of milk and powdered lusmore (foxglove) to drink. Because foxglove is a poison, this only hastened the demise of the unfortunate infant, though it was supposed to burn the entrails out of a fairy creature. Even more drastic was to place the infant on an iron shovel and hold it over an open fire. It was far better, then, to protect the child from being taken in the first place.

Baptism by the Church was the surest way of preventing a child from being 'taken,' but in many remote country areas it was maybe a few days before the cleric could attend to perform the ceremony. The child therefore had to be protected during the crucial days directly after birth. Crucifixes and religious ornaments were often placed around the crib to deter the Other People from coming too close; an open pair of scissors might be left at the crib-foot to turn evil powers back; and there were numerous other deterrents. Open iron tongs from the hearth, for instance, might be left crosswise on the bedding, or an iron nail from a horseshoe could be hidden amongst the bedclothes. (Iron was considered to be anathema to the fairy kind.) As someone who has never been baptized myself, I vaguely remember my grandmother laying an item of my father's clothes across my bed in order to remind "the fairies and the dead" that I was a human child and my father's property. This, I think, continued until I was well into my fifth year. Despite these protections, human children might still be "taken away" and a changeling left in their place.

The following selection of changeling stories comes from rural Wales and is found in Reverend Elias Owen's *Welsh Folk-lore* (published 1896).

Selections From *Welsh Folk-lore*

by Reverend Elias Owen

Corwrion Changeling Legend

Once on a time in the fourteenth century, the wife of a man at Corwrion had twins and she complained one day to the witch who lived close by at Tyddyn y Barcut, that the children were not getting on, but that they were always crying, day and night. "Are you sure that they are your children?" asked the witch, adding that it did not seem to her that they were like hers.

"I have my doubts also," answered the mother.

"I wonder has somebody changed children with you," said the witch.

"I don't know," said the mother

"But why do you not seek to know?" asked the other.

175

"But how am I to go about it?" said the mother. The witch replied,

"Go and do something rather strange before their eyes and watch what they will say to one another."

"Well I do not do what I should do," said the mother.

"Oh," said the other "take an egg-shell and proceed to brew beer in it in a chamber aside and come here to tell me what the children will say about it". She went home and did as the witch had directed her, when the two children lifted their heads out of the cradle to see what she was doing, to watch and to listen. Then one observed to the other—

"I remember seeing an oak having an acorn" to which the other replied: "And I remember seeing a hen having an egg" and one of the two added "But I do not remember before seeing anybody brew beer in the shell of a hen's egg"

The mother then went to the witch and told her what the twins had said and she directed her to go to a small wooden bridge, not far off, with one of the strange children under each arm and there to drop them from the bridge into the river beneath. The mother then went back home again and did as she had been directed. When she reached home this time to her astonishment she found that her own children had been brought back.

[*Editor's Note*: This tale is an extremely popular one with many variations all across the Celtic world. In Ireland, it is known as "The Brewery of Eggshells," where a changeling is driven out by fire from the grate after being tricked into revealing its true age: more than a thousand years old.]

Another version of this tale was related to me by my young friend, the Rev. D.H. Griffiths of Clocaenog Rectory near Ruthlin. The tale was told to him by Evan Roberts, Ffriddagored, Llanfwrog. Mr. Roberts is an aged farmer.

Llanfwrog Changeling Legend

A mother took her child to the gleaning field and left it sleeping under the sheaves of wheat whilst she was busily engaged gleaning. The Fairies came in the field and carried off her pretty baby, leaving in its place one of their own infants. At the time, the mother did not notice any difference between her own child and the one that took its place, but after awhile she observed with grief that the baby she was nursing did not thrive, nor did it grow, nor would it try to walk. She mentioned these facts to her neighbours and was told to do something strange and then listen to its conversation. She took an eggshell and pretended to brew beer in it and she was surprised to hear the child who had observed her actions intently, say:

Mi welais fesan gan dderwen,
Mi welais wy gan iar
Ond ni welais I eriod ddarllaw
Mewn cinyn wy iar.

I have seen an oak having an acorn,
I have seen a hen having an egg
But I never saw before brewing
In the shell of a hen's egg.

This conversation proved the origin of the precocious child who lay in the cradle. The stanza seems to have been taken down from Roberts' lips. But he would not say what was done to the fairy changeling.

In Ireland, a plan for reclaiming the child carried away by the Fairies was to take the Fairy's changeling and place it on the top of a dunghill, and then to chant certain innovatory lines beseeching the Fairies to return the stolen child.

There was, it would seem, in Wales, a certain form of incantation resorted to reclaim children from the Fairies, which is as follows—The mother who had lost her child was to carry the changeling to a river but she was to be accompanied by a conjuror, who was to take a prominent part in the ceremony. When at the river's brink the conjuror was to cry out:

Crap ar y wrach—

A grip on the bag

And the mother was to respond—

Rhy hwyr gyfraglach

Too late decrepit one

And having uttered these words, she was to throw the child into the stream and to depart and it was believed that on reaching her home she would find her own child, safe and sound.

I will now relate a tale somewhat resembling those already given but in this latter case, the supposed changeling became the mainstay of the family. I am indebted for the *Gors Goch* legend to an essay written by Mr. D Williams, Llanfachreth, Merionethshire which took the prize at the Liverpool Eisteddfod 1870 and which appears in a publication called *Y Gordofigion* published by Mr. I Foulkes, Liverpool.

The Gors Goch Changeling Legend

This tale, rendered into English is as follows—There was once a happy family living in a place called Gors Goch. One night, as usual, they went to bed but they could not sleep a single wink, because of the noise outside the house. At last, the master of the house got up and trembling enquired: What was there and what was wanted. A clear sweet voice answered him this:

"We want a warm place where we can tidy the children." The door was opened when there entered half-full the house of the *Tylwyth Teg* (Welsh fairies) and they began forthwith washing their children. And when they had finished, the commenced singing and the singing was entrancing. The dancing and singing were both excellent. On going away, they left behind them money, not a little for the use of the house. And afterward they came pretty often to the house and received a hearty welcome in consequence of the large presents which they left behind them on the hob. But at last a sad affair took place which was no less than the exchange of children. The Gors Goch baby was a dumpy child, a sweet, pretty, affectionate little dear, but the child which was left in its stead was a sickly, thin, shapeless, ugly being which did nothing but cry and eat, though it ate ravenously like a mastiff, it did not grow. At last the wife of Gors Goch died of a broken heart and so did all her children but the father lived a long life and became a rich man, because his new heirs family had brought him abundance of gold and silver

Garth Uchaf, Llanuwchllyn Changeling Legend

The wife of Garth Uchaf, Llanuwchllyn, went out one day to make hay and left her baby in the cradle. *Unfortunately she did not place the tongs crossways on the cradle,* and consequently the Fairies changed her baby and by the time she came home there was nothing in the cradle but some old decrepit changeling which looked as if it was half famished but, nevertheless, it was nursed.

The reason why the Fairies exchanged babies with human beings was their desire to obtain healthy well-formed children in the place of their own puny, ill-shaped offspring but this is hardly a satisfactory explanation of such conduct. A mother's love is ever depicted as being so intense that deformity on the part of her child rather increases then diminishes her affection for her unfortunate babe. There was once thought that the Fairies were obliged every seventh year to pay the great enemy of mankind an offering of one of their own children or a human child instead and as a mother is ever a mother whether she be elve's flesh or Eve's flesh, she always endeavoured to

179

substitute some one else's child for her own, and hence the reason for exchanging children.

The Rev. Peter Roberts's theory was that the smaller race kidnapped the children of the stronger race who occupied the country concurrently with themselves for the purpose of adding to their own strength as a people.

Gay, in lines quoted in *Brand's Popular Antiquities*, laughs at the idea of changelings. A Fairy's tongue ridicules the superstition:

> *Whence sprung the vain conceited lye,*
> *That we the world with fools supply,*
> *What! Give our sprightly race away*
> *For the dull, hapless sons of clay.*
> *Besides, by partial fondness shows*
> *Like you we dote upon our own.*
> *Where ever yet was found a mother*
> *Who'd give her booby for another?*
> *And should we change with human breed*
> *Well might we pass for fools indeed.*

With the above fine satire I bring my remarks on Fairy Changelings to a close.

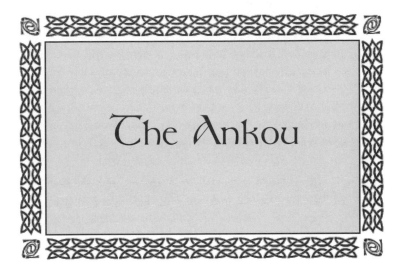

The Ankou

For the ancient Celts, death was a transition from one form of existence into another: from the material world that we know and experience every day to a mystical Otherworld that lay just outside our realm of consciousness. This transition from one reality to another was accomplished in a number of ways. The dying person could be carried off by beautiful maidens, as in the death of the Celtic King Arthur, or he or she could be carried off by dark horsemen, who appear in several Irish and Manx tales.

The most common method for carrying off the souls of the dead in Ireland, Scotland, and Brittany, however, was the "death coach," a fearsome vehicle that traveled about the night-bound roads, collecting the spirits of those who had died to take them to the Otherworld (and during the Christian period to Paradise or Hell). In Ireland, it was known as the "coshta-bodhr" (coach-a-bower) or "deaf coach," as it's passing made no sound—although this wasn't always the case. Sometimes, the thing rumbled along so fast along the Irish roads that it set the very bushes along the roadsides on fire. It was a conveyance that inspired awe and terror.

181

In Brittany, this horrible vehicle was no more than a creaking cart, loaded with the souls of the dead and driven by a creature known as the Ankou. Explanations as to what this being actually was vary from place to place. In some areas of Brittany, he is the Lord of the Dead, responsible for the safekeeping of the dead until they receive their Ultimate Reward; in order regions, he is a ghost or specter. He is always the embodiment of Death or Father Time.

The following account of the Ankolu—possibly the best that there is—is taken from Breton writer and folklorist Anatole Le Braz's (1859-1926) seminal work on Breton death and the supernatural, *La Legende de la mort en Basse-Britagne, croyances et usages des Bretons armoricaines* (published in Paris in 1893).

Excerpt From *La Legende de la mort en Basse-Britagne, croyances et usages des Bretons armoricaines*

by Anatole Le Braz

In many places, the last one to die in each year becomes the Ankou; in a few places it is the first one to die.

When there have been more deaths than usual in a year, they say the Ankou is a wicked one.

Sometimes they depict the Ankou as a tall, thin man with long white hair and a face shaded by a large felt hat; sometimes in the form of a skeleton draped in a shroud, and whose head turns continuously, just like a weather cock, so that he can see all the region he has to cover at a single glance.

In one case or the other he holds a scythe. It differs from ordinary scythes in having its blade turned the other way round, so that when he uses it, instead of bringing it towards him, he pushes it forward.

The Ankou's coach is like the ones they used in the old days for transporting the dead.

It is usually pulled by two horses harnessed in line. The one in front is thin, emaciated and scarcely able to stand on its feet. The one behind is fat, with a shiny coat, and without a collar.

The Ankou stands in the coach.

He is escorted by two companions, both of whom walk. One of them leads the first horse by the bridle. The other has the job of opening the field gates and the doors of the houses. He is also the one who piles the dead up in the coach; the dead whom the Ankou has harvested.

When the Ankou sets out on his tour, they say his coach is filled with pebbles that it will go more heavily, making more noise.

When he reaches the house where there is someone that he must harvest, he abruptly discharges his load, to make room for his new 'ballast.'

That is the cause of the sound of pebbles which is heard so often in home where they are watching over a dying person, just at the time of that person's last breath.

The coach of the dead

"It was a night in June, at a time when they leave the horses out all night.

A young man had taken his horses to the fields. He was whistling on his way back, for the night was clear and the moon was shining. He heard a coach coming towards him, a coach whose badly greased axle went 'squeak-squeak.'

But he was sure it was the coach of death.

'At least I'll be able to see that coach with my own eyes' he thought.

And he crossed the ditch and hid himself in a clump of hazels so that he could see without being seen.

The coach came into view.

It was drawn by three white horses harnessed one behind the other. Two men accompanied it, each dressed in black and wearing

183

wide-brimmed felt hats. One of them led the first horse by the bridle; the other was standing up in the front of the coach.

As the coach came opposite the hazel clump where the young man was hiding, the axle went 'crack.'

'Stop' said the man on the coach to the one who was leading the horses.

The man cried 'woa' and the team came to a halt.

'The axle pin's just broken', said the Ankou. 'Go and cut what you need to make a new one from that hazel clump over there.'

'I'm lost' thought the young man, who right then regretted his indiscreet curiosity very much.

However, he was not punished there and then. The coachman cut off a branch, shaped it, inserted it into the axle and then the horses went on their way.

The young man was able to return home safe and sound, but towards morning, he was taken with an unknown fever and they buried him the next day."

[*Editor's Note*: Told by Francoise, daughter of Jean Le Gac, 1890]

Gab Lucas

"Gab Lucas worked at Rune-Riou. He went back every night to Kerdrenkenn where he lived with his wife Madelaine and five children in the most wretched thatched cottage of the poor village. For Gab Lucas had only the ten pennies that he earned by very hard work each day. This did not prevent him from having a happy nature and being a good worker. The owners of Rune-Riou valued him. At the end of the week, they often invited him to spend Saturday evening with them, drinking flip (rum and cider) and eating roast chestnuts. At the stroke of ten the farmer would give Gab his weekly wage and his wife would always add some present for the household at Kerdrenkenn.

One Saturday night she said to him

'Gab, I've put a sack of potatoes aside for you. Give them to Madelaine on my behalf'.

Gab Lucas thanked her, threw the sack on his back and set off home, after having wished everyone good night.

It is a good three quarters of a league from Rune-Riou to Kerdrenkenn. Gab walked sprightly at first. The moon was shining and the good flip he had drunk warmed his stomach. He whistled a Breton air to keep himself company, happy that Madelaine would be pleased when she saw him return with a good sack of potatoes. They would cook a large potful for the next day; they would add a slice of pork belly to it, and they would all enjoy themselves.

All went well for a quarter of a league.

But then the virtue of the flip wore off in the coolness of the night. Gab felt all the tiredness of the day's work come back to him. The sack of potatoes began to weigh heavy on his shoulders. Soon he no longer felt like whistling.

'If only a wagon would come by' he thought.... 'But I'll have no such luck.'

But just then he reached the cross where the track from the farm at Nizilzi joins the road.

'Well,' said Gab 'I can always sit on the steps of the cross for a moment whilst I catch my breath.'

He set his load down, sat beside it, and lit his pipe.

The countryside was silent all around.

Suddenly the dogs at Nizilzi began to howl pitifully.

'Why on earth are they making such a din?' wondered Gab.

Then he heard the sound of a cart coming from Nizilzi. Its badly greased axle went squeak, squeak.

'It looks as though my wish is about to come true; they must be going for a load of sand, they'll take my sack right to my door,' said Gab to himself.

He saw the horses come into view, and then the cart. They were terribly thin and emaciated those horses. They were certainly not from Nizilzi, because their horses always looked so fat and shiny. As for the cart, its base was made of a few loosely fitted planks, two rude hurdles served as sides. A great gawk of a man, who was just as scraggy as his beasts, led this pitiful team. A large felt hat shaded his face. Gab could not recognise him. He greeted him all the same.

'Comrade would you have room for this sack in your cart? My back's aching. I'm only going as far as Kerdrenkenn.'

The carter did not reply.

'He must not have heard me,' said Gab to himself. 'That awful cart makes such a noise.'

The opportunity was too good to be missed. Gab hurriedly put his pipe out, stuffed it into his jacket pocket, grabbed the sack of potatoes, and ran after the cart, which was going fast enough. He ended by catching up with it and dropped his sack inside, letting out a sigh of relief.

But how do you explain this? The sack went through the old planks and landed on the ground.

'What sort of a cart is this?' said Gab to himself.

He picked up the sack and once more put it in the cart, but this time further forward.

But the base of the cart had no solidity, for the sack and Gab went through it. Both of them rolled on the ground.

The strange team wound on its way. Its mysterious leader had not even turned his head.

Gab let them move away from him. When they had disappeared, he took his own turn to go up to Kerdrenkenn, where he arrived half-dead from fright.

'What's wrong' asked Madeaine, seeing him so upset.

Gab told her of his adventure.

'It's quite simple.' said his wife to him, 'You've met the coach of the dead.'

Gab almost had a fit. The next day, they heard the church bell ringing. The Master of Nizilzi had died on the previous night, towards half-past ten."

[*Editor's Note*: Told by Marie-Yvonne, Port Blanc]

Canwyll Corph:
Corpse Candle

Throughout the Celtic world, prognostication, particularly the foretelling of death, was widespread. In their earliest times, the Celts were a war-like people, and it was advantageous to local leaders to know in advance what the outcome of a particular battle might be or if they would return alive from it. For this reason, both soothsayers and supernatural warnings were of the utmost importance. One of the best-known Celtic death warnings is, of course, the Irish banshee. The 'woman of the fairy' is usually portrayed as a wailing specter whose unearthly keen heralds the death of the hearer or of some close relative. She was said to appear only to those with ancient Irish blood in their veins or who had some family connection to them. Although now considered to be a ghost, it is thought that the banshee was originally a living person, a woman who served as a soothsayer to the ancient royal houses of Ireland, warning kings and chieftains of death or approaching danger. There are, in fact, references in certain stories to a living banshee named Aoibheall who is described as the Banshee of the

187

Royal House of Munster and who is said to have foretold the death of Brian Boru, High King of Ireland, at the battle of Clontarf in 1014. The banshee has become *the* most celebrated death-warning worldwide.

However, she is not the only such portent. Other Celtic countries have their own harbingers of death and doom. At one time, the Welsh canwyll corph, or corpse candle, was as central to the Celtic mind as the banshee—even in Ireland. Everywhere across the Gaelic world, there are tales of flickering lights, signaling a demise or even guiding people to their final resting places. This exposition concerning this particular supernatural phenomenon comes from the Reverend Edmund Jones's (1702–1793) 'A Relation of Ghosts and Apparitions' (published in 1840), with a commentary added in 1896 by Welsh folklorist Reverend Elias Owen.

Excerpt From "A Relation of Ghosts and Appartitions"

by Reverend Edmund Jones

"The corpse candle or *canwyll corph* was a light like that of a candle which was said to issue from the house where a death was about to occur and to take the course of the funeral procession to the burial place. This was the usual way of proceeding but this mysterious light was also thought to wend its way to the abode of a person about to die. Instances could be given of both kinds of apparitions.

I have met with persons in various parts of Wales who told me that they had seen a corpse candle. They described it as a pale bluish light moving slowly along a short distance above the ground. Strange tales are told of the course the light has taken. Once it was seen to go over hedges and to make straight for the churchyard wall. This was not then understood, but when the funeral actually took place the ground was covered with snow, and the drift caused the procession to proceed along the fields and over the hedges and churchyard wall as indicated by the corpse candle.

It was ill jesting with the corpse candle. The Rev. J. Jenkins, Vicar of Hirnant told me that a drunken sailor at Borth said he went up to a corpse candle and attempted to light his pipe at it but he was whisked away and when he came to himself he discovered that he was well off the road in the bog.

Some have seen the resemblance of a skull carrying the candle, others the shape of the person that is to die carrying the candle between his fore-fingers, holding the light before his face. Some said that they saw the shape of those who were to be at the burying.

Those who have followed the light state that it proceeded to the church, lit up the building, emerged therefrom, and then hovered awhile over a certain spot in the churchyard, and then sank into the earth at the place where the deceased was to be buried.

There is a tradition that St. David, by prayer, obtained the corpse candle as a sign to the living of the reality of another world and that originally it was confined to his diocese. This tradition finds no place in the *Life of the Saint*, as given in the *Cambro-British Saints*, and there are many wonderful things recorded of that saint.

It was thought possible for a man to meet his own Candle. There is a tale of a person who met a candle and struck it with his walking-stick, when it became sparks which, however, reunited. The man was greatly frightened, became sick and died. At the spot where he had struck the Candle, the bier broke and the coffin fell to the ground, thus corroborating the man's tale."

I will now record one tale, not of the usual kind, which was told me by a person who is alive:

Tale of a Corpse Candle

My informant told me that one John Roberts, Felin-y-Wig, was in the habit of sitting up a short time, after his family had retired to rest to smoke a quiet pipe, and the last thing he usually did before retiring for the night was to take a peep into the night. One evening, whilst peering around, he saw in the distance a light, where he knew there was no house and on further notice he observed that it was slowly going along the road from Bettws-Gwerfil-Goch to Felin-y-Wig. Where the road dipped, the light disappeared only, however, to appear again in such parts of the road as were visible from John Roberts' house. At first Roberts thought that the light proceeded from a lantern but this was so unusual an occurrence in those parts that he gave up this idea and intently followed the motions of the light. It approached Roberts house and evidently this was its destination. He endeavoured to ascertain whether the light was carried by a man or woman, but he could see nothing save the light. When therefore, it turned into the lane approaching Roberts's house, in considerable fear he entered the house and closed the door awaiting with fear the approach of the light. To his horror, he perceived the light passing through the shut door and it played in a quivering way underneath the roof, and thus vanished. That very night, the servant man died and his bed was right above the spot where the light had disappeared.

Spectral Funerals or Drychiolaeth

This was a kind of shadowy funeral which foretold the real one. In South Wales it goes by the name *toilu, toila* or *teulu* (the family) *anghladd* (unburied); in Montogomeryshire it is called *Drychiolaeth* (spectre)

I cannot do better than quote from Mr. Hamer's *Parochial Account of Llanidloes* (*Montgomeryshire Collections* vol x., p.256) a description of one of these phantom funerals. He writes:

"It is only a few years ago that some excitement was caused amongst the superstitious portion of the inhabitants by the statement of a certain miner, who at the time was working in Brynpostig mine. On his way to the mine one dark night, he said that he was thoroughly frightened in China Street in seeing a spectral funeral leaving the house of one Hoskiss who was then very ill in bed. In his fright the miner turned his back on the house with the intention of going home, but almost fainting he could scarcely moved out of the way of the advancing procession, which gradually approached and at last surrounded him and then passed down Longbridge Street in the direction of the church. The frightened man managed with difficulty to drag himself home, but he was so ill that he was unable to go to work for several days."

The following weird tale I received from the Rev. Philip Edwards. I may state that I have heard variants of the story from other sources.

"While the Manchester and Milford Railway was in course of construction there was a large influx of navvies into Wales and many a frugal farmer added to his incomings by lodging and boarding workmen engaged on the line. Several of the men were lodged at a farm called Penderlwyngoch occupied by a man called Hughes.

One evening when the men were seated round the fire, which burned brightly, they heard the farm dogs bark as they always did at the approach of strangers. By and by they heard the tamp of feet mingled with the howling of the frightened dogs, and then the dogs ceased barking, just as if they had slunk away in terror. Before many minutes had elapsed, the inmates heard the back door opened, and a number of people entered the house, carrying a heavy load resembling a dead man, which they deposited in the parlour, and all at once the noise ceased. The men in great dread struck a light and proceeded to the parlour to ascertain what had taken place. But they could discover nothing there, neither were there any marks

191

of feet in the room, nor could they find any footprints outside the house, but they saw the cowering dogs in the yard looking the picture of fright. After this fruitless investigation of the cause of this dread sound, the Welsh people present only too well knew the cause of this visit. On the very next day one of the men who sat by the fire was killed, and his body was carried by his fellow-workmen to the farm house, in fact everything occurred as rehearsed the previous night. Most of the people who witnessed the vision are, my informant says, still alive."

The Fairy Commonwealth

Throughout the Celtic world, the imminence of the fairy realm was very keenly felt. It lay, said conventional wisdom, all around, just beyond the sight of ordinary mortals. The ancient fairy people came and went everywhere unseen by those living beside them. Occasionally, however, they would allow favored mortals fleeting glimpses through the veil that lay between the worlds and might even allow them to cross from one realm into another.

What sort of place was the realm of the Sidhe? How was it organized? How did its inhabitants live, and, more importantly, what did they look like? These questions and others could only be answered by someone who had seen into the Otherworld.

The Reverend Robert Kirk (c. 1630-1692), Scottish minister of Balquhidder in Callandar (the burial place of the famous Scottish figure, Rob Roy) and later of Aberfoyle in the Trossachs, was one of those who stole a glimpse into that other realm and who was able to write about what he saw and learned. Kirk, the seventh son of a seventh son, was believed to have the "gift" of seeing the world of the ancient Sidhe and had the knowledge and skills to record what he knew. His book, *The Secret Commonwealth,* is considered to be one of the most detailed studies of the fairy world. His account lay in manuscript form until around 1815; certainly no prior edition of it has ever been traced.

Little is known about Kirk himself except that he was married twice and that he completed a translation of part of the Bible (the Book of Psalms) into Gaelic before he died. Given his almost-mystical pedigree, he was also considered as something of an expert in the supernatural. He was said to frequently go to meet and converse with the fairy kind on Doon Hill (a dun-shi, or fairy hill) near his manse, which was said to be a gateway into the Otherworld. With their blessing, it would seem, he wrote a highly absorbing account of the unseen world that, although it may have simply started out as personal notes or a memoir, gradually metamorphosized into *The Secret Commonwealth.*

Kirk died on May 14, 1692, while out on a regular walk to Doon Hill. His body was found by the side of the road and carried back to the manse. Legend states that, after the funeral, Kirk appeared to one of his cousins to announce that he was not dead at all but was, in fact, living in the fairy realm.

Robert Kirk, of course, reflected the beliefs and perspectives of his own community. As R.E. Cunningham-Graham remarked: "No doubt the congregation that the ingenuous minister served were most of them, devout believers in fairy lore...for they sucked it with their mother's milk and held it, not by conviction for they never had reasoned on it, but quite naturally, as part and parcel of themselves; and in such surroundings it was not strange that the writer of the book also believed in them". *The Secret Commonwealth* therefore represents a core of popular Scottish lore, which had, in Kirk's time, been passed down across the centuries more or less intact. This brief excerpt is taken from the original work, written around 1691. There has been some Anglicisation of the Scots dialect that Kirk used, in order to give a better understanding of the discourse.

Excerpt From
The Secret Commonwealth

by Reverend Robert Kirk

The Siths, or Fairies, they call *Sleagh Maith* (or Good people, it would seem to prevent the dint of their ill attempts) are said to be of a middle nature betwixt man and angel, as were demons thought to be of old, of intelligent studious spirits and light, changeable bodies (like those called astral), somewhat of the nature of a condensed cloud and best seen in twilight. These bodies be so pliable through the subtlety of the spirits that agitate them, that they can make them appear or disappear at pleasure. Some have bodies or vehicles so spongeous, thin and pure that they are fed by only sucking into some fine spirituous liquors, that pierce like pure air and oil; others feed more gross on the abundance or substance of corn and liquors, or corn itself that grows on the surface of the earth, which these fairies steal away, partly invisible and partly preying on the grain as do crows or mice; wherefore in this same age they are sometimes heard to break bread, strike hammers and to do such like services within the little hillocks they most do haunt; some whereof of old before the Gospel dispelled Paganism, and in some barbarous places as yet, enter houses after all are at rest, and set the kitchen in order, cleaning all vessels. Such dregs (spirits, supernatural beings) go under the name of Brownies. We have plenty, they have scarcity at their homes and, on the contrary (for they are not empowered

195

to catch as much prey everywhere as they please), their robberies, notwithstanding, oft-times occasion great ricks (stacks) of corn not to bleed so well (as they call it) or prove so copious by very far as was expected by their owner.

Their bodies of congealed air are sometime carried aloft, other whiles grovel in different shapes, and enter into any cranny or cleft of the earth where air enters, to their ordinary dwellings; the earth being full of dark cavities and cells, and there being no place, no creature, but is supposed to have other animals (greater or lesser) living in or upon it as inhabitants; and no such thing as a pure wilderness in the whole universe.

We then (the more terrestrial kind have now so numerously planted all countries) do labour for that abstruse people as well as for ourselves. Albeit when several countries are inhabited by us, these had their easy tillage above ground as we do now. The print of those furrows do yet remain to be seen on the shoulders of very high hills, which was done when the campaign ground was wood and forest.

They remove to other lodgings at the beginning of each quarter of the year, so traversing till doomsday, being impotent of staying in one place, and finding some ease by journeying and changing habitations. Their chameleon-like bodies swim in the air near the earth with bag and baggage; and at such revolution of time, seers or men of the second sight, (females being seldom so qualified) have very terrifying encounters with them, even on highways; who awfully shun to travel abroad at these four seasons of the year, and therefore have made it a custom to this day among the Scottish-Irish to keep church duly every first Sunday of the quarter to seun or hallow themselves, their corn and cattle, from the shots and stealth of these wandering tribes; and many of these superstitious people will not be seen in church again until the next quarter begins, as if no duty were to be learnt or done by them; but all the use of worship and sermons were to save them from the arrows that fly in the dark.

They are distributed in tribes and orders and have children, nurses, marriages, deaths and burials in appearance, even as we (unless they do so for a mock-show, or to prognosticate some such things among us).

They are clearly seen by these men of the second sight to eat at funerals and banquets. Hence many of the Scottish-Irish will not taste meat at these meetings, lest they have communion with, or be poisoned by, them. So are they seen to carry the bier or coffin, with the corpse among the middle-earth men to the grave? Some men of that exalted sight (whether by art or nature) have told me they have seen theses meetings as a double man, or the shape of a man in two places, that is a super-terranean and subterranean inhabitant, perfectly resembling one another in all points, when he, notwithstanding could easily distinguish one from another by some secret tokens and operations, and go and speak to the man, his neighbour and familiar, passing by the apparition or resemblance of him. They avouch that every element and different state of being has animals resembling those of another element; as there are fishes sometimes at sea, resembling monks of late order in all their hoods and dresses; so as the Roman invention of good and bad demons and guardian angels particularly assigned [*Editor's Note*: Kirk is here referring to the Roman Catholic Church, which was, in this time, considered to be highly superstitious and gullible.] is called by them an ignorant mistake, sprung only from this original. They call this reflex man, a co-walker, every way like the man, as a twin brother and companion, haunting him as his shadow, as is oft seen and known among men (resembling the original), both before and after the original is dead; and was often seen of old to enter a house by which the people knew that the person of that likeness was to visit them within a few days. This copy, echo, or living picture, goes at last to his won herd. It accompanied that person so long and frequently for ends best known to itself, whether to guard him from the secret assaults of some of its own folk, or only as a sportful ape to counterfeit all his actions. However, the stories of old witches prove beyond contradiction that all sorts of people, spirits which assume airy bodies, or crazed bodies concocted by foreign spirits, seem to have some pleasure (at least to assuage some pain or melancholy) by frisking and capering like satyrs, or whistling and screeching (like unlucky birds) in their unhallowed synagogues and Sabbaths. If invited and earnestly required, these companions make themselves known and familiar to men; otherwise being in a different state and element, they neither can nor will easily converse with them. They avouch that a heluo, or great eater has a voracious elve to be his attender, called a joint-eater or just-halver, feeding on the pith and quintessence of what the man eats; and that, therefore, he continues lean like hawk or heron; notwithstanding his devouring appetite, yet it would seem they convey his substance elsewhere, for these subterraneans eat but little in their dwellings, their food being exactly clean, and are served by pleasant children, like enchanted puppets.

Their houses are called large and fair and (unless at some odd occasions) unperceivable by vulgar eyes, like Rachland and other enchanted islands [*Editor's Note*: Rachland was believed to be a fairy island lying off the Northwest Coast of Scotland. It was allegedly inhabited either by fairies of by the descendants of Vikings and only appeared to mortal eyes once every seven years, but it could be seen by the pure-hearted almost at any time.] having fir lights, continual lamps and fires, often seen without fuel to sustain them. Women are yet alive who tell they were taken away when in child-bed to nurse fairy children, a lingering, voracious image of them being left in their place (like a reflection in a mirror) which (as if it were some insatiable spirit in an assumed body) made first

The hero confronts a dreadful monster.

semblance to devour the meats that it cunningly carried by, and then left the carcass as if it expired and departed thence by a natural and common death. The child and fire, with food and all other necessities, are set before the nurse how soon she enters, but she never perceives any passage out, nor sees what those people do in any other rooms of the lodging. When the child is weaned, the nurse dies, or is conveyed back, or gets it to her choice to stay there. But if any superterraneans be so subtle as to practice sleights for procuring the privacy to any of their mysteries (such as making use of their ointments, which, as Gyges' ring, make them invisible or nimble, or cast them in a trance, or alter their shape, or make things appear at a vast distance, etc.), they smite them without pain, as with a puff of wind, and bereave them of both the natural and acquired sights in the twinkling of an eye (both these sights, when once they come, being in the same organ and inseparable), or they strike them to death. [*Editor's Note*: The reference to the Ring of Gyges evokes a tale mentioned in Plato's *Republic* in which the Lydian shepherd Gyges enters a cave that had been revealed after an earthquake. Finding a ring upon the hand of an enthroned corpse there, he stole it and found that it had the power to make him invisible. Using the magical artifact, he murdered the ruler of Lydia to ascend the throne himself. King Croesus, the famous king with the golden touch, was reputedly descended from Gyges. Various and contradictory versions of this legend circulated throughout the ancient world—a vastly different story is told by Heroditas, for example.] The tramontanes to this day, place bread, the Bible, or a piece of iron, so save their women at such time from being stolen, and they commonly report that all uncouth, unknown weights (supernatural creatures) are terrified of nothing earthly as much as cold iron. [*Editor's Note*: The use of the word *tramontanes*, thought to be of French derivation, is interesting here. It has been used to describe Catalans but is here probably used in a religious sense to describe indigenous Gaelic Scots—predominantly

Catholic—who were deemed to be incredibly superstitious.] They deliver the reason to be that hell, lying between the chill tempests and firebrands of scalding metals, and iron of the north (hence the lodestone causes a tendency to that point) by antiquity thereto, these odious, far-scenting creatures shrug and fright at all that comes thence relating to an abhorred place, whence their torment is either begun, or feared to come hereafter.

Their apparel and speech is like that of the people and country under which they live; so are they seen to wear plaids and variegated garments in the Highlands of Scotland, and *suanachs* (plaids) therefore in Ireland. They speak but little, and by way of whistling clear, not rough. The very devils conjured in any country do answer in the language of that place; yet sometimes the subterraneans speak more distinctly than at other times. Their women are said to spin very fine, to dye, to tossue, and embroider, but whether it be as manual operation of industrial refined stuffs, with apt and solid instruments, or only curious cobwebs, unpalpable rainbows and a phantastic imitation of the actions of the more terrestrial mortals, since it transcended all the senses of the seer to discern whether, I leave to conjecture as I found it.

Their men travel much abroad, either presaging or aping the dismal and tragical actions of some amongst us; and have also many disastrous doings of their own, as convocations, fighting, gashes, wounds and burials, both in the earth and air. They live much longer than we, yet die, at last; or at least vanish from that state. 'Tis one of these tenets that nothing perisheth, but (as the sun and year) everything goes in a circle, lesser or greater, and is renewed and refreshed in its revolutions, as 'tis another, that every body in creation moves (which is a sort of life) and that nothing moves but has another animal moving on it; and so on until the utmost minutest corpuscle that's capable of being a receptacle of life.

201

They are said to have aristocratical rulers and laws, but no discernable religion, love, or devotion towards God, the blessed Maker of all; they disappear whenever they hear His name invoked, or the name of Jesus (at which all do bow willingly, or by constraint, that dwell above or beneath, within the earth) (Philip ii.10); nor can they act ought at that time after the hearing of the sacred name. The Taiblsdear or seer, that corresponds with this kind of familiars, can bring them with a spell to appear to himself or others when he pleases, as readily as the Endor Witch did those of her own kind. He tells that they are ever readiest to go on hurtful errands but seldom will be the messengers of great good to men. He is not terrified with their sight when he calls them, but seeing them in a surprise (as often as he does) frights him extremely, and glad would he be to be quit of such, for the hideous spectacles seen among them, as the torturing of some wight (spirit or goblin), earnest, ghostly, staring looks, skirmishes and the like. They do not all the harm which, appearingly, they have the power to do; nor are they perceived to be in great pain, save that they are usually silent and sullen. They are said to have many pleasant, toyish books; but the operation of these pieces only appears in some paroxysms of antic, corybantic jollity, as if ravished and prompted by a new spirit entering into them at that instant, lighter and merrier than their own. Other books they have of involved, abstruse sense, much like the Rosicurucian style. They have nothing of the Bible, save collected parcels for charms and counter-charms: not to defend themselves withal, but to operate on other animals, for they are a people invulnerable to weapons, and albeit werewolves and witches true bodies are (by the union of spirit and nature that runs through all, echoing and doubling the blow towards another) wounded at home, when the astral or assumed bodies are stricken elsewhere—as the strings of a second harp, tuned to a unison sound, though only one be struck—yet these people have not a second, or so gross a body at all, to be so pierced, but as the air which when divided, unites again; or if they feel pain by a blow, they are better physicians than we, and quickly cure. They are not subject to sore sicknesses, but dwindle and decay at a certain period, all about an age. Some say that their continual sadness is because of their pendulous state (like those men: Luke xiii. 2-6), as uncertain what at the last revolution will become of them; when they are locked up into an unchangeable condition; and if they have any frolic fits of mirth, 'tis as the constrained grinning of a mort's-head (death's-head) or rather as acted on a stage and moved by another, than by cordially coming of themselves. But other men of the second sight, being illiterate, and unwary in their observations, differ from those, one averring those subterranean people to be departed souls, attending a while in this inferior state, and clothed with bodies procured through their alms-deeds in this life, fluid, active, eternal vehicles to hold them that they may not scatter nor wander and be lost in the totum or their first nothing; but if any were so impious as to have given no alms, they say, when the souls of such do depart, they sleep in an inactive state till they resume the terrestrial bodies again; others that what the low-country Scotch call a wraith, and the Irish taibhse, or death's messenger (appearing sometimes as a little rough dog and if crossed and conjured in time will be pacified by the death of any other creature instead of the sick man) is only exuvious fumes of the man approaching death, exhaled and congealed into a various likeness (as ships and armies are sometimes shaped in the air) and called astral bodies, agitated as wildfire with the wind, and are neither souls nor counterfeiting spirits, yet not a few avouch (as is said) that surely these are a numerous people by themselves, having their own politics, which diversities of judgement may occasion several inconsistencies in this rehearsal after the narrowest scrutiny made about it.

Fictional

Tales

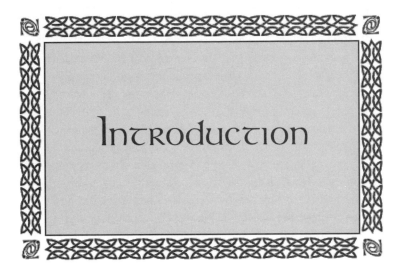

Introduction

It was not only local storytellers—those men and women who sat by the hearthside of a Winter's night and entertained their neighbors with stories of great deeds in times long past and tales of the imminent supernatural—who looked towards the ancient corpus of belief and tradition. The successors of the oral transmitters, writers and artists, also drew on the lore of former times for their stories and pictures. Some of the writers simply recorded the tales that they heard, but others used the themes and suggestions that they'd heard in the Celtic countryside as a basis around which to build tales of their own. In a sense, they were following a tradition that dated all the way back to the Celtic Bards who changed and embellished some of the ordinary events that they recited into something marvelous and strange.

Many of these writers had either Celtic backgrounds or were interested in Celtic matters. Relatively recent writers such as American H.P. Lovecraft, with his lurking terrors in the hills of rural Rhode Island, or British writers such as

Arthur Machen, with his stories of strange little people hiding in the hollows of rural Wales, owe much to the stories and storytellers of earlier times. They look toward talespinners such as Joseph Sheridan Le Fanu, who wrote about wizard Earls emerging out of lakes or young girls marrying mouldering corpses (a common theme in some of the more gruesome Irish and Scottish legends); or to the collectors of rural folklore such as Jeremiah Curtin, Elias Owen, or Lady Gregory, with their fearful stories of small children being carried away by shadowy creatures that dwelt amongst (or sometimes under) the gloomy hills. Such stories have provided a basis for much of the fantastic and spine-tingling literature that we have enjoyed over the years.

Even the greatest bogeyman of them all, the dark and cape-clad Count Dracula, may well have his origins in Celtic folktale. Although he is portrayed as a Transylvanian (East European) nobleman, it is possible to argue that the Count may have had his origins in the mists of Celtic folklore. Remember that Dracula's author, Bram Stoker, was Irish and had been brought up in Dublin, where his family had been attended by serving-maids from County Kerry. Undoubtedly, he would have heard old folktales of the blood-drinking fairies dwelling in the Magillycuddy Reeks Mountains. Later, as a man visiting his old friends Sir William and Lady Wilde, both collectors of folktales, he could have heard old stories of cannibalistic Irish chieftains from North Derry and all of these elements may well have influenced his portrayal of the vampiric Transylvanian nobleman. And similar tales may have also influenced his predecessor, Le Fanu, to pen one of the earliest vampire tales: the celebrated 'Carmilla.' Thus novels and even modern-day film may very well have been influenced by the tales told around the Celtic fires of long ago.

Other writers, too, have drawn on Celtic roots for their tales. Stories of unsettled spirits and ancient charms and *shehoguey* places have been featured in many tales right up to today. Even television series such as the *X-Files* and more recently *Buffy the Vampire Slayer* have, from time to time, drawn on Celtic themes and have reawakened interest in these ancient tales. And each year, novels and anthologies appear that reflect, either consciously or unconsciously, many of the motifs and perspectives of an earlier Celtic folklore.

The folktale has come a long way, from the whispered stories in the dark of the night as ancient warriors bedded down for the night; through the yarns and mysteries told and hinted at by local storytellers around the rural hearths as evening drew in; to the books, films, and television series of our fast, "sophisticated," modern world. Perhaps, in some ways at least, the ancient tales have adapted and have become, almost imperceptibly, a strand of our own culture, serving to show just what a clever animal the folktale is. It will be with us for years to come, for it is a fundamental part of our heritage and culture, and more: it is a fundamental part of *us*, whether we be Celt or not.

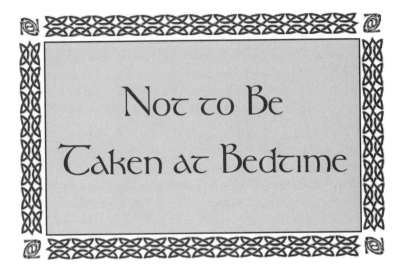

Not to Be Taken at Bedtime

Ever since earliest times, peoples all across the world have sought to influence or change the natural course of events through the use of charms and spells. The Celts were no different. In all probability, their shamans had used incantations and allegedly sorcerous materials to affect the outcomes of battles, of kingship, of day-to-day living. This was, of course, part of a continuing Celtic belief that continued down into relatively modern times. Even as late as the early 20th century, the use of certain magical 'rhymes' and of special herbs was still in evidence in many parts of the Celtic countryside.

Nowhere, arguably, was the use of charms, incantations and invocations more widespread than in the attempt to instill love into the heart of a desired one. The Celts used a variety of natural materials—herbs, parts of animals, pieces of sacred objects—that they ground into powders and potions as an aid to their charms. They also used waters from certain wells or extracts squeezed from special plants. Some of the ingredients were more repellent. The more noxious the charm, it seemed, the greater its chances of success. The most grisly of all lovecharms was the burragh-boos or burragh-bos, which had been reputedly handed down from pagan times and which smacked to the later Christian peoples of darkest sorcery.

In her eerie story "Not to Be Taken at Bedtime" (published in *All The Year Round* in 1865), Belfast-born Gothic writer Rosa Mulholland (1841–1921) draws upon the lore and traditions of this ghastly charm. This is a story of terrible love and madness that contains echoes of both J.S. Le Fanu and William Carleton. It is the story of the dark Coll Dhu and of the Devil's Inn.

"Not to Be Taken at Bedtime"

by Rosa Mulholland

This is the legend of a house called the Devil's Inn, standing in the heather on the top of the Connemara Mountains in a shallow valley between five peaks. Tourists sometimes come in sight of it on September evenings, a crazy and weather-stained apparition, with the sun glaring on it angrily between the hills and striking its shattered window-panes. Guides are known to shun it however.

The house was built by a stranger, who came no one knew whence, and whom the people named Coll Dhu (Black Coll) because of his sullen bearing and solitary habits. His dwelling they called the Devil's Inn because no tired traveller had ever been asked to rest under its roof or friend known to cross its threshold. No-one bore him company in his retreat but a wizen-faced old man, who shunned the good-morrow of the trudging peasant when he took occasional excursions to the nearest village for provisions for himself and master, and who was as secret as a stone concerning all the antecedents of both.

212

For the first year of their existence in the country, there had long been much speculation as to who they were and what they did with themselves up among the clouds and eagles. Some said that Coll Dhu was a scion of the old family from whose hands the surrounding lands had passed; and that, embittered by poverty and pride, he had come to bury himself in solitude, and brood over his misfortunes. Others hinted of crime, and flight from another country; others again whispered of those who were cursed from birth, and could never smile, nor yet make friends with a fellow-creature till the day of their death. But when two years had passed, the wonder had somewhat died out, and Coll Dhu was little thought of, except when a herd looking for sheep crossed the track of the big dark man walking the mountains gun in hand to whom he did not dare say 'Lord save you' or when a housewife rocking her cradle of a winter's night, crossed herself as a gust of storm thundered over her cabin-roof, with the exclamation "Oh then, it's Coll Dhu that has enough o' that fresh air about his head up there this night, the creature!"

Coll Dhu had lived thus in his solitude for some years, when it became known that Colonel Blake, the new lord of the soil, was coming to visit the country. By climbing one of the peaks encircling his eyrie, Coll could look sheer down a mountain-side and see in miniature beneath him a grey old dwelling with ivied chimneys and weather-slated walls, standing amongst straggling trees and grim, warlike rocks, that gave it the look of a fortress, gazing out onto the Atlantic for ever with the eager eyes of its windows, as if demanding perpetually 'What tidings from the New World?'

He could see now masons and carpenters crawling about below, like ants in the sun, over-running the old house from base to chimney, daubing here and knocking there, tumbling down walls that looked to Coll, up among the clouds, like a handful of jack-stones and building up others that looked like toy fences to a child's farm. Throughout several months he

213

must have watched the busy ants at their task of breaking and mending again, disfiguring and beautifying; but when all was done he had not the curiosity to stride down and admire the handsome panelling of the new billiard-room, nor yet the fine view which h the enlarged bay-window in the drawing room commanded of the water highway to Newfoundland.

Deep summer was melting into autumn and the amber streaks of decay were beginning to creep out and trail over the ripe purple of the moor and mountains when Colonel Blake, his only daughter and a party of friends arrived in the country. The grey house below was alive with gaiety but Coll Dhu no longer found an interest in observing it from his eyrie. When he watched the sun rise or set, he chose to ascend some crag that looked on no human habitation. When he sallied forth on his excursions, gun in hand, to set his face towards the most isolated wastes, dipping into the loneliest valleys, and scaling the nakedest ridges. When he came by chance within call of other excursionists, gun in hand he plunged into the shade of some hollow, and avoided an encounter. Yet it was fated for all that, that he and Colonel Blake should meet.

Towards the evening of one bright September day, the wind changed and in half an hour the mountains were wrapped in a thick, blinding mist. Coll Dhu was far from his den, but so well had he searched these mountains, and inured himself to their climate, that neither storm, rain, nor fog, had power to disturb him. But while he stalked on his way, a faint and agonised cry from a human voice reached him through the smothering mist. He quickly tracked the sound and gained the side of a man who was stumbling g along in danger of death at every step.

"Follow me!" said Coll Dhu to this man and in an hour's time, brought him safely to the lowlands and up to the walls of the eager-eyed mansion.

214

"I am Colonel Blake", said the frank soldier, who, having left the fog behind him, they stood in the starlight under the lighted windows. "Pray tell me quickly to whom I owe my life."

As he spoke, he glanced up at his benefactor, a large man with a sombre, sun-burned face.

"Colonel Blake" said Coll Dhu after a strange pause "your father suggested to my father to stake his estates at the gaming table. They were staked, and the tempter won. Both are dead; but you and I live, and I have sworn to injure you."

The colonel laughed good humouredly at the uneasy face above him.

"And you began to keep your oath tonight by saving my life?" said he. "Come! I am a soldier, and know how to meet an enemy; but I had far rather meet a friend. I shall not be happy till you have eaten my salt. We have merrymaking tonight in honour of my daughter's birthday. Come in and join us?"

Coll Dhu looked at the earth doggedly.

"I have told you" he said, "who and what I am, and I will not cross your threshold."

But at this moment (so runs my story) a French window opened among the flower-beds by which they were standing and a vision approached which stayed the words on Coll's tongue. A stately girl, clad in white satin, stood framed in the ivied window, with the warm light from within streaming about her richly-moulded figure into the night. Her face was as pale as her gown, her eyes were swimming in tears, but a firm smile sat on her lips as she held out both hands to her father. The light behind her touched the glistening folds of her dress—the lustrous pearls around her throat—the coronet of blood-red roses which encircled the knotted braids at the back of her head. Satin, pearls and roses—had Coll Dhu, of the Devil's Inn, never set eyes upon such things before?

Evleen Blake was no tearful miss. A few quick words—
"Thank God! You're safe; the rest have been home an hour"—
and a slight pressure on her father's fingers between her own
jewelled hands, were all that betrayed the uneasiness she had
suffered.

"Faith my love I owe my life to this brave gentleman" said
the blithe colonel. "Press him to come in and be our guest
Evleen. He wants to retreat in his mountains and lose himself
again in the fog where I found him; or rather, he found me!
Come sir" (to Coll) "you must surrender to this fair besieger."

An introduction followed. "Coll Dhu!" murmured Evleen
Blake, for she had heard the common tales about him; but
with a frank welcome she invited her father's preserver to taste
the hospitality of that father's house.

"I beg you to come in sir," she said, "but for you our gaiety must have been turned to mourning. A shadow will be
upon our mirth if our benefactor disdains to join in it."

With a sweet grace, mixed with a certain hauteur from
which she was never free, she extended her white hand to the
tall, looming figure outside the window; to have it grasped
and wrung in a way that made the proud girl's eyes flash their
amazement, and the same little hand clench itself in displeasure, when it hid itself like an outraged thing among the shining folds of her gown. Was this Coll Dhu mad, or rude?

The guest no longer refused to enter, but followed the
white figure into a little study where a lamp burned and the
gloomy stranger, the bluff colonel, and the young m stress of
the house, were fully discovered to each other's eyes. Evleen
glanced at the newcomer's dark face, and shuddered with a
feeling of indescribable dread and dislike, then to her father
accounted for the shudder in a popular fashion, saying lightly:
"There is someone walking over my grave."

So Coll Dhu was present at Evleen Blake's birthday ball.
Here he was, under a roof which ought to have been his own,

a stranger, known only by a nickname, shunned and solitary. Here he was, who had lived among the eagles and foxes, lying in wait with a fell purpose to be revenged on his father's foe for poverty and disgrace, for the broken heart of a dead mother, for the loss of a self-slaughtered father, for the dreary scattering of brothers and sisters. Here he stood, a Samson shorn of his strength; and all because a haughty girl had melting eyes, a winning mouth, and looked radiant in satin and roses.

Peerless where many were lovely, she moved among her friends, trying to be unconscious of the gloomy fire of those strange eyes which followed her unweariedly wherever she went. And when her father begged her to be gracious to the unsocial guest when he would fain conciliate, she courteously conducted him to see the new picture-gallery adjoining the drawing rooms, explained under what odd circumstances the colonel had picked up this little paining or that; using every delicate art her pride would allow to achieve her father's purpose, whilst entertaining at the same time her own personal reserve; trying to divert the guest's oppressive attention from herself to the objects for which she claimed his notice. Coll Dhu followed his conductress and listened to her voice, but what she said mattered nothing; nor did she wring many words of comment or reply from his lips, until they paused in a retired corner where the light was dim, before a window from which the curtain was withdrawn. The sashes were open and nothing was visible but water; the night Atlantic, with the full moon riding high above a bank of clouds, making silvery tracks outward towards the distance of infinite mystery dividing two worlds. Here the following g little scene is said to have been enacted.

"This window of my father's own planning, is it not creditable to his taste?" said the young hostess, as she stood, herself glittering like a dream of beauty, looking on the moonlight.

Coll Dhu made no answer, but suddenly, it is said, asked her for a rose from a cluster of flowers that nestled in the lace on her bosom.

For the second time that night Evleen Blake's eyes flashed with no gentle light. But this man was the saviour of her father. She broke off a blossom, and with such good grace, and also with such queen-like dignity as she might assume, presented it to him. Whereupon, not only was the rose seized, but also the hand that gave it, which was hastily covered with kisses.

Then her anger burst upon him.

"Sir," she cried, "if you are a gentleman you must be mad! If you are not mad, then you are not a gentleman!"

"Be merciful," said Coll Dhu. "I love you. My God, I never loved a woman before! Ah!" he cried, as a look of disgust crept over her face, "you hate me. You shuddered the first time your eyes met mine. I love you and you hate me!"

"I do," cried Evleen vehemently, forgetting everything but her indignation. "Your presence is like something evil to me. Love me?—your looks poison me. Pray sir, talk no more to me in this strain"

"I will trouble you no longer", said Coll Dhu. And, stalking to the window, he placed one powerful hand upon the sash and vaulted from it out of her sight.

Bare-headed as he was, Coll Dhu strode off to the mountains, but not towards his own home. All the remaining dark hours of that night he is believed to have walked the labyrinths of the hills, until dawn began to scatter the clouds with a high wind. Fasting, and on foot from sunrise the morning before, he was glad enough to see a cabin right in his way. Walking in, he asked for water to drink, and a corner where he might throw himself to rest.

There was a wake in the house, and the kitchen was full of people, all wearied out with the night's watch, old men were

218

A warrior hears strange news from a far land.

dozing over their pipes in the chimney-corner and here and there a woman was fast asleep with her head on a neighbour's knee. All who were awake crossed themselves when Coll Dhu's figure darkened the door, because of his evil name, but an old man of the house invited him in, and offering him milk, and promising him a toasted potato by-and-by, conducted him to a small room off the kitchen, one end of which was strewed with heather, and where there were only two women sitting gossiping over a fire.

"A thraveller", said the old man nodding his head at the women who nodded back as if to say 'he has the traveller's right'. And Coll Dhu flung himself on the heather, in the farthest corner of the narrow room.

The women suspended their talk for a while, but presently guessing the intruder to be asleep, resumed it in voices above a whisper. There was but a patch of window with the grey dawn behind it, but Coll could see the figures by the firelight over which they bent; an old woman sitting forward with her withered hands extended to the embers, and a girl reclining against the hearth wall, with her healthy face, bright eyes and crimson draperies, glowing by turns in the flickering blaze.

"I do know", said the girl, "but it's the quarest marriage iver I h'ard of. Sure it's not three weeks since he tould her right an' left that he hated her like poison!"

"Whist asthoreen!" said the colliagh, bending forward confidentially; "throth an' we all know that o' him. But what could he do the crature! When she put the burragh-bos on him!"

"The *what*?" asked the girl.

"Then the burragh-bos machree-o? That's the spancel o' death avourneen; an' well she has him tethered to her now; bad luck to her!"

The old woman rocked herself and stifled the Irish cry breaking from her wrinkled lips by burying her face in her cloak.

"But what is it?" asked the girl eagerly. "What's the burragh-bos, anyways an' where did she get it?"

Och, och! It's not fit for comin' over to young ears but cuggir (whisper) acushla! It's a shtrip o' the skin o' a corpse, peeled from the crown o' the head to the heel without a crack or split or the charm's broke; an' that rowled up, an' put on a sthring roun' the neck o' the wan that's cowl'd by the wan that wants to be loved. An' sure enough it puts the fire in their hearts, but an' sthrong. afore twenty-four hours is gone."

The girl had started from her lazy attitude and gazed at her companion with eyes dilated by horror.

"Merciful Saviour!" she cried. "Not a sowl on airth would bring the curse out o' heaven by sich a black doin'."

"Aisy, Biddeen alanna!, an' there's wan that does it, an isn't the divil. Arrah asthoreen, did ye niver hear tell o' Pexie na Pishrogie, that lives betune two hills o' Maam Turk?"

"I h'ard o' her", said the girl, breathlessly.

"Well sorra bit lie, but it's herself that does it. She'll do it for money any day. Sure they hunted her from the graveyard o' Salruck, where she had the dead raised; an' glory be to God!, they would ha' murthered her, only they missed her thracks, an' couldn't bring it home to her afther."

"Wist, a-wauher (my mother)" said the girl, "here's the thraveller getting' up to set off on the road again! Och, then, it's the short rest he tuk, the sowl."

It was enough for Coll, however. He had got up and now went back to the kitchen, where the old man had carried a dish of potatoes to be roasted, and earnestly pressed his visitor to sit down and eat them. This Coll did readily, having recruited his strength by a meal, he betook himself into the mountains again, just as the rising sun was flashing among the waterfalls, and sending the night mists drifting down the glens. By sundown the same evening, he was standing over the hills of Maam Turk. Asking of herds his way to the cabin of one Pexie na Pishrogie.

In a hovel on a brown, desolate heath, with scared-looking hills flying off into the distance on every side, he found Pexie— a yellow-faced hag, dressed in a dark red blanket, with elf-locks of coarse black hair protruding from under an orange kerchief swathed around her wrinkled jaws. She was bending over a pot upon her fire, where herbs were simmering and she looked up with an evil glance when Coll Dhu darkened her door.

The "burragh-bos is it her honour wants?" she asked when he had made known his errand. "Ay, ay: but the arighad, the arighad! (money) for Pexie. The burragh-bos is ill to get."

"I will pay," said Coll Dhu, laying a sovereign on the bench before her.

The witch sprang upon it, and chuckling bestowed on her visitor a glance, which made even Coll Dhu shudder.

"Her honour is a fine king" she said "an' her is fit to get the burragh-bos. Ha! Ha!, her will get the burragh-bos from Pexie. But the arighad is not enough. More, more!"

She stretched out her claw-like hand, and Coll dropped another sovereign into it. Whereupon she fell into more horrible convulsions of delight.

"Hark ye!" cried Coll. "I have paid you well but if your infernal charm does not work, I will have you hunted for a witch."

"Work!" cried Pexie rolling up her eyes "If Pexie's charrm not work, then her honour come back here an' carry these bits o' the mountain away on her back. Ay, her will work. If the colleen hate her honour like the old desuil hersel', still withal her love will love her honour like her own white sowl afore the sun sets or rises. That (with a furtive leer) or the colleen dhas go wild mad afore wan hour."

"Hag!" snapped Coll Dhu "that last part is a hellish invention of your own. I heard nothing of madness. If you want more money, speak out, but play none of your hideous tricks on me."

The witch fixed her cunning eyes on him and took her cue at once from his passion.

"Her honour guess true" she simpered; "it is only the little bit more arighad poor Pexie want."

Again the skinny hand was extended. Coll Dhu shrank from touching it, and threw his gold upon the table.

"King, king!" chuckled Pexie. "Her honour is a grand king. Her honour is fit to get the burragh-bos. The colleen dhas sall love her like her own white sowl. Ha, ha!"

"When shall I get it?" asked Coll Dhu, impatiently.

"Her honour sall come back to Pexie in so many days, dodeag (twelve), so many days, for that the burragh-bos is hard to get. The lonely graveyard is far away, the dead man is hard to raise—"

"Silence!" cried Coll Dhu, "not a word more. I will have your hideous charm, but what it is, or where you get it, I will not know."

Then, promising to come back in twelve days, he took his departure. Turning to look back when a little way across the heath, he saw Pexie gazing after him, standing on her black hill in relief against the lurid flames of the dawn, seeming to his dark imagination like a fury with all hell at her back.

At the appointed time Coll Dhu got the promised charm. He sewed it with perfumes into a cover of cloth of gold and hung it on a fine wrought chain. Lying in a casket which had once held the jewels of Coll's broken-hearted mother, it looked a glittering bauble enough. Meantime the people of the mountains were cursing over their cabin fires, because there had been another unholy raid upon their graveyard and were banding themselves to hunt the criminal down.

A fortnight passed. How or where could Coll Dhu find an opportunity to put the charm round the neck of the colonel's proud daughter? More gold was dropped into Pexie's greedy claw, and then she promised to assist him in his dilemma.

Next morning the witch dressed herself in decent garb, smoothed her elf-locks under a snowy cap, smoothed the evil wrinkles out of her face, and with a basket on her arm, locked the door of the hovel and took her way to the lowlands. Pexie seemed to have given up her disreputable calling for that of a simple mushroom-gatherer. The housekeeper at the grey house bought poor Muireade's mushrooms of her every morning. Every morning g she left unfailingly a nosegay of wild flowers for Miss Evleen Blake, God bless her! She had never seen the darling young lady with her own two longing eyes, but sure hadn't she heard tell of her sweet purty face, miles away! And at last one morning, whom should she meet but Miss Evleen herself returning alone from a ramble. Whereupon poor Muireade 'made bold' to present the flowers in person.

"Ah," said Evleen, "it is you who leave me the flowers every morning? They are very sweet."

Muireade had sought her only for a look at her beautiful face. And now that she had seen it, bright as the sun, and as fair as the lily, she would take up her basket and go away contented. Yet she lingered a little longer.

"My lady never walk up big mountain?" said Pexie.

"No," said Evleen, laughing; she feared she could not walk up a mountain.

"Ah yes; my lady ought to go, with more gran' ladies an' gentlemen, ridin' on purty little donkeys, up the big mountains. Oh, gran' things up big mountains for my lady to see!"

Thus she set to work, and kept her listener enchanted for an hour, while she related wonderful stories of those upper regions. And as Evleen looked up to the burly crowns of the hills, perhaps she thought there might be sense in this wild old woman's suggestion. It ought to be a grand world up yonder.

Be that as it may, it was not longer after this that Coll Dhu got notice that a party from the grey house would explore the mountains the next day; that Evleen Blake would be one of the number; and that he, Coll, must prepare to house and refresh a crowd of weary people, who in the evening would be brought, hungry and faint, to his door. The simple mushroom gatherer should be discovered in laying in her humble stock among the green hills, should volunteer to act as guide to the party, should lead them far out of their way through the mountains and up and down the most toilsome ascents and across dangerous places; to escape safely from which the servants should be told to throw away the baskets of provisions which they carried.

Coll Dhu was not idle. Such a feast was set forth, as had never been spread so near the clouds before. We are told of wonderful dishes furnished by unwholesome agency, and from a place believed much hotter than is necessary for the purposes of cookery. We are told how Coll Dhu's barren chambers were suddenly hung with curtains of velvet and with fringes of gold; how the blank, white walls glowed with delicate colours and gilding; how gems of pictures sprang into sight between the panels; how tables blazed with plate and gold, and glittered with rarest glass; how rich wines flowed, as the guests had ever tasted; how servants in the richest livery, amongst whom the wizen-faced old man was a mere nonentity appeared and stood ready to carry in wonderful dishes, at whose extraordinary fragrance the eagles came pecking at the windows and the foxes drew near the walls, snuffing. Sure enough, in all good time, the weary party came within sight of the Devil's Inn and Coll Dhu sallied forth to invite them across his lonely threshold. Colonel Blake (to whom Evleen in her delicacy, had said no word of the solitary's strange behaviour towards herself)

225

hailed his appearance with delight, and the whole party sat down to Coll's banquet in high good humour. Also, it is said, in much amazement at the magnificence of the mountain recluse.

All went in to Coll's feast, save Evleen Blake, who remained standing on the threshold of the outer door; weary, but unwilling to rest there; hungry, but unwilling to eat there. Her white cambric dress was gathered on her arms, crushed and sullied with the toils of the day; but her bright cheek was a little sunburned; her small dark head with its braids a little tossed, was bared to the mountain air and the glory of the sinking sun; her hands were loosely tangled in the strings of her hat; and her foot sometimes tapped the threshold-stone. So she was seen.

The peasants tell that Coll Dhu and her father came praying her to enter, and the magnificent servants brought viands to the threshold, but no step would she move in ward, no morsel would she taste.

"Poison, poison!" she murmured and threw the food in handfuls to the foxes who were snuffing on the heath.

But it was different when Muireade, the kindly old woman, the simple mushroom-gatherer, with all the wicked wrinkles smoothed out of her face, came to the side of the hungry girl, and coaxingly presented a savoury mess of her own sweet mushrooms, served on a common earthen platter.

"An' darlin' my lady, poor Muireasde her cook them hersel' an' no thing o' this house touch them or look at poor Muireade's mushrooms."

Then Evleen took the platter and ate a delicious meal. Scarcely was it finished when a heavy drowsiness fell upon her, and unable to sustain herself on her feet, she presently sat down upon the doorstone. Leaning her head against the framework of the door, she was soon in a deep sleep, or trance. So she was found.

"Whimsical, obstinate little girl!" said the colonel, putting his hand on the beautiful, slumbering head. And, taking her in his arms, he carried her into a chamber which had been (say the story-tellers) nothing but a bare and sorry closet in the morning but which was now fitted up with Oriental splendour. And here on a luxurious couch she was laid, with a crimson coverlet wrapping her feet. And here in the tempered light coming through the jewelled glass, where yesterday had been a rough hung window, her father looked his last upon her lovely face.

The colonel returned to his host and friends and by-and-by the whole party sallied forth to see the after-glare of a fierce sun-set swathing the hills in flames. It was not until they had gone some distance that Coll Dhu remembered to go back and fetch his telescope. He was not long absent. But he was absent long enough to enter that glowing chamber with a stealthy step, to throw a light chain around the neck of the sleeping girl, and to slip among the folds of her dress the hideous glittering burragh-bos.

After he had gone away again, Pexie came stealing to the door and, opening it a little sat down on the mat outside, with her cloak wrapped around her. An hour passed and Evleen Blake still slept, her breathing scarcely stirring the deadly bauble on her breast. After that, she began to murmur and moan, and Pexie pricked up her ears. Presently a sound in the room told that the victim was awake and had risen. Then Pexie put her face in the aperture of the door and looked in, gave a howl of dismay, and fled from the house, to be seen in the country no more.

The light was fading among the hills, and the ramblers were returning towards the Devil's Inn, when a group of ladies who were considerably in advance of the rest, met Evleen Blake advancing towards them on the heath, with her hair disordered as by sleep, and no covering on her head. They noticed something bright, like gold, shifting and glancing with the motion of her figure. There had been some jesting among them about Evleen's fancy for falling asleep on the door-step instead of coming in to dinner, and they advanced laughing, to rally her on the subject. But she stared at them in a strange way, as if she did not know them, and passed on. Her friends were rather offended and commented on her fantastic humour, only one looked after her, and got laughed at by her companions for expressing uneasiness on the wilful young lady's account.

So they kept their way, and the solitary figure went fluttering on, the white robe blushing, and the fatal burragh-bos glittering in the reflection from the sky. A hare crossed her path, and she laughed out loudly, and clapping her hands, sprang after it. Then she stopped and asked questions of the stones, striking them with her open palm because they would not answer. (An amazed little herd sitting behind a rock, witnessed these strange proceedings). By-and-by she began to call after the birds, in a wild, shrill way, startling g the echoes of the hills as she went along. A party of gentlemen returning by a dangerous path, heard the unusual sound and stopped to listen.

"What is that?" asked one.

"A young eagle" said Coll Dhu, whose face had become livid, "they often give such cries."

"It was uncommonly like a woman's voice" was the reply; and immediately another wild note rang towards them from the rocks above, a bare saw-like ridge, shelving away to some distance ahead, and projecting one hungry tooth over an abyss. A few more moments and they saw Evleen Blake's light figure fluttering out towards this dizzy point.

"My Evleen!" cried the colonel, recognizing his daughter, "she is mad to venture on such a spot!"

"Mad!" repeated Coll Dhu. And then dashed off to the rescue with all the might and swiftness of his powerful limbs.

When he drew near her, Evleen had almost reached the verge of the terrible rock. Very cautiously he approached her, his object being to seize her in his strong arms before she was aware of his presence, and carry her many yards away from the spot of danger. But in a fatal moment, Evleen turned her head and saw him. One wild ringing cry of hate and horror, which startled the very eagles and scattered a flight of curlews above her head, broke from her lips. A step backward brought her within a foot of death.

One desperate though wary stride and she was struggling in Coll's embrace. One glance in her eyes, and he saw that he was striving with a mad woman. Back, back, she dragged him and he had nothing to grasp by. The rock was slippery and his shod feet would not cling to it. Back, back! A hoarse panting, a dire swinging to and fro; and then the rock was standing naked against the sky, no-one was there, and Coll Dhu and Evleen Blake lay shattered far below.

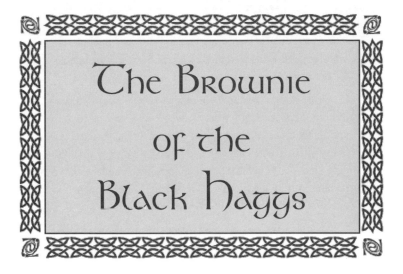

The Brownie
of the
Black Haggs

Relationships between the fairies and their human neighbors were always problematic. For the ancient Celts, fairies were everywhere. They were the embodiment of the natural forces that were in the landscape all around. But, even though they were supernatural beings, they often exhibited qualities that were recognizably human: They could be flattered, appealed to, angered, and irritated. They could also show displeasure, anger, or downright cruelty if they so chose. And it was also said that they could show love and hate, just as humans can. In fact, many Celtic seers stated that experienced such emotions far more keenly than any human.

Living cheek by jowl with such unpredictable beings was often difficult for their human neighbors. An old tale from Rathlin Island off the north Irish coast tells of how the fairies came and cursed a family for teeming (washing) potatoes too close to a fairy mound and for allowing the water to seep into their hall. The family never enjoyed any success after

231

that, and several of them were said to have died prematurely, whilst several others remained childless. Such was the penalty for annoying the fairies.

One had to be careful in other ways. In many parts of Ireland, Scotland, and Wales it was considered ill luck to speak to a fairy, even when one of them spoke first. Everywhere it was believed that accepting money from the fairy kind was to invite disaster. In fact, it was better to have nothing to do with the fairies at all and to keep oneself to one's own kind.

Scottish writer and poet James Hogg (1770–1835), widely known as the "Ettrick Shepherd," was well aware of the powers and forces that dwelt in the landscape all around him and of how capricious they could be. Born and raised in the Ettrick Forest on the Scottish Borders, much of Hogg's writings and poetry, "The Mountain Bard" (1807), "The Forest Minstrel" (1810), "Mador of the Moor" (1816), and his celebrated "Private Memoirs and Confessions of a Justified Sinner" (1824), reflect his rural background and the perspectives of the country people. He also wrote several supernatural tales, of which "The Brownie of the Black Haggs" is one: a tale of eerie retribution and justice that ably reflects the relationship between humans and the fairy kind.

"The Brownie of the Black Haggs"

by James Hogg

When the Spotts were lairds of Wheelhope, which is now a long time ago, there was one of the ladies who was very badly spoken of in the country. People did not openly assert that Lady Wheelhope was a witch but everyone had an aversion to hearing her named, and when by chance she happened to be mentioned, old men would shake their heads and say "ach, let us alane o' her! The less ye meddle wi' her the better!" Auld wives would give over spinning, and, as a pretence for hearing what might be said about her, poke in the fire with the tongs, cocking up their ears all the while; and then after some meaning coughs, hems and haws, would haply say, "Hech-wow sirs! An' a' be true that's said!" or something equally wise and decisive as that.

In short, Lady Wheelhope was accounted a very bad woman. She was an inexorable tyrant to her family, quarrelled with the servants. Often cursing them, and turning them away, especially if they were religious, for these she could not endure, but she suspected them of everything bad. Whenever she found out any of the servant men of the laird's establishment for religious characters, she soon gave them up to the military and got them shot [*Editor's Note*: During the late 1600s and part of the 1700s, the only form of worship that was tolerated in the British Isles was the Anglican Church. This was meant to disadvantage the Catholics, but it also disadvantaged Presbyterians, particularly the Covenanting Presbyterians, many of whom lived on the Borders. Presbyterianism was treated largely as treason, and those who worshipped in this manner were liable to be executed.], and several girls that were regular in their devotions, she was supposed to have popped off with poison. She was certainly a wicked woman, else many good people were mistaken in her character, and the poor persecuted Covenanters were obliged to unite in their prayers against her.

As for the laird, he was a stump. A big, dun-faced, pluffy body, that cared neither for good nor evil and did not know the one from the other. He laughed at his lady's tantrums and barley-hoods (outbursts), and the greater the rage she got into; the laird thought it the better sport. One day when two servant maids came running to him, and told him that his lady had felled one of their companions, the laird laughed heartily at them, and said he did not doubt it.

233

"Why sir, how can you laugh?" said they. "The poor girl is killed."

"Very likely, very likely" said the laird. "Well, it will teach her to take care who she angers again."

"And, sir, your lady will be hanged."

"Very likely; well it will learn her how to strike so rashly again—Ha ha ha! Will it not Jessy?"

But when that same Jessy died suddenly one morning, the laird was great confounded and seemed dimly to comprehend that there had been unfair play going on. There was little doubt that she was taken off by poison, but whether the lady did it through jealousy or not, was never divulged; but it greatly bamboozled and astonished the poor laird, for his nerves failed him, and his whole frame became paralytic. He seems to have been exactly in the same frame of mind with a colley I once had. He was extremely fond of the gun as long as I did not kill anything with her (there being no game laws in Ettrick Forest in those days) and he got a grand chase after the hares when I missed them. But there was one day I chanced for a marvel to shoot one dead, a few paces before his nose. I'll never forget the astonishment that the poor beast manifested. He stared for a while at the gun, and another while at the dead hare, and seemed to be drawing the conclusion that if the case stood thus, there was no creature sure of its life. Finally, he took his tail between his legs, and ran away home, and never again would face a gun in all his life.

So it was precisely with Laird Sprot of Wheelhope. As long as the lady's wrath produced only noise and splutter among the servants, he thought it fine sport, but when he saw what he believed the dreadful effects of it, her became like a barrel organ out of tune, and could only discourse one note which he did to everyone he met. "I wish she munna hae gotten something she has been the waur of". This note he repeated early and late, sleeping and waking, alone and in company, from the moment that Jessy died till she was buried; and on going to the churchyard as chief mourner, he whispered it to her relations by the way. When they came to the grave, he took his stand at the head, nor would he give place to the girl's father, but there he stood like a huge post, as though he neither saw or heard, and when he had lowered her late comely head into the grave and dropped the cord, he slowly lifted his hat with one hand, wiped his dim eyes with the back of the other, and said in a deep tremulous tone: "Poor lassie! I wish she dinna get something she had been the waur of."

This death made a great noise among the common people; but there was no protection for the life of the subject in those days, and provided a man or woman was a true loyal subject, and a real Anti-Covenanter, any of them might kill as they liked. So there was no-one to take cognisance of the circumstances relating to the death of poor Jessy.

After this, the lady walked softly for the space of two or three years. She saw that she had rendered herself odious, and had entirely lost her husband's countenance, which she liked worst of all. But the evil propensity could not be overcome, and a poor boy, whom the laird out of compassion had taken into his service, being found dead one morning, the country people could no longer be restrained, so they went in a body to the Sheriff, and insisted on an investigation. It was proved that she detested the boy and had often threatened him and had given him brose (meal) and butter the afternoon before he died, but the cause was ultimately dismissed, and the pursuers fined.

No-one can tell to what height of wickedness she might now have proceeded, had not a check of a very singular kind been laid upon her. Among the servants that came home at the next term, was one who called himself Merodach; and a strange person he was. He had the form of a boy, but the features of one a hundred years old, save that his eyes had a brilliancy and restlessness, which was very extraordinary, bearing a strong resemblance to the eyes of a well-known species of monkey. He was forward and perverse in all his actions, and disregarded the pleasure and displeasure of any person, but he performed his work well and with apparent ease. From the moment that he entered the house, the lady conceived a mortal antipathy against him, and besought the laird to turn him away. But the laird, of himself, never turned away any body, and moreover he had hired him for a trivial wage, and the fellow neither wanted activity or perseverance. The natural consequence of this arrangement was that the lady instantly set herself to make Merodach's life as bitter as it was possible, in order to get early quit of a domestic, every way so disgusting. Her hatred of him was not like a common antipathy, entertained by one human being against another—she hated him, as one might hate a toad or an adder; and his occupation of jotteryman (as the laird termed his servant of all work) keeping him always about her hand, it must have proved highly disagreeable.

She scolded him, she raged at him, but he only mocked her wrath, and giggled and laughed at her, with the most provoking derision. She tried to fell him again and again, but never, with all her address, could she hit him, and never did she make a blow at him that she did not repent it. She was heavy and unwieldy, and he as quick in his motions as a monkey; besides, he usually had her in such an ungovernable rage, that when she flew at him, she hardly knew what she was doing. At one time, she guided her blow towards him, and he at the same instant, avoided it with such dexterity, that she knocked down the chief hind or foreman; and then Merodach giggled so heartily that, lifting the kitchen poker, she threw it at him with a full design of knocking out his brains, but the missile only broken every plate and ashet on the kitchen dresser.

She then hasted to the laird, crying bitterly and telling him she would not suffer that wretch Merodach, as she called him, to stay another night in the family.

236

"Why then put him away and trouble me no more about him," said the laird.

"Put him away!" exclaimed she; "I have already ordered him away a hundred times; and charged him never to let me see his horrible face again; but he only flouts me, and tells me he'll see me at the devil first."

The pertinacity of the fellow amused the laird exceedingly, his dim eyes turned upwards into his head with delight; he then looked two ways at once, turned round his back on her, and laughed till the tears ran down his dun cheeks, but he could only articulate: "You're fitted now."

The lady's cry of rage still increasing from this derision, she flew on the laird, and said he was not worthy of the name of a man, if he did not turn away that pestilence, after the way he had abused her.

"Why Shusy, my dear, what has he done to you?"

"What has he done to me! Has he not caused me to knock down John Thomson and I do not know if he will come to life again?"

"Have you felled your favourite John Thomson?" said the laird, laughing more heartily than before, "you might have done a worse deed than that. But what evil has John done?"

"And has he not broken every plate and dish on the whole dresser?" continued the lad lady, disregarding the laird's question, "and for all that devastation he only mocks my displeasure— absolutely mocks me—and if you do not have him turned away, and hanged and shot for his deeds, you are not worthy of the name of man."

"O alack! What a devastation among the china metal", said the laird and calling on Merodach he said. "Tell me thou evil Merodach of Babylon, how thou dared to knock down thy lady's favourite, John Thomson."

"Not I your honour. It was my lady herself, who got into such a furious rage at me, that she mistook her man, and felled Mr. Thomson; and the good man's skull is fractured."

"That was very odd", said the laird, chuckling, "I do not comprehend it. But then, what the devil set you smashing all my lady's delft and china ware?—That was a most infamous and provoking action."

"It was she herself, your honour. Sorry would I have been to have broken one dish belonging to the house. I take all the house servants to witness, that my lady smashed all the dishes with a poker, and now lays the blame on me."

The laid turned his dim and delighted eyes on his lady who was crying with vexation and rage, and seemed meditating another attack on the culprit, which he did not at all appear to shun, but rather encourage. She, however, vented her wrath in threatenings of the most deep and desperate revenge, the creature all the while assuring her that she would be foiled, and that in all her encounters and contests with him, she would ultimately come to the worst. He was resolved to do his duty, and therefore before his master he defied her.

The laird thought more than he considered it prudent to reveal, but he had little doubt that his wife would wreak vengeance on his jotteryman which she avowed, and as little of her capability. He almost shuddered when he recollected one who had taken something *that she had been the waur of.*

In a word, the Lady of Wheelhope's inveterate malignity against this one object, was like the rod of Moses, that swallowed up the rest of the serpents. All her wickedness and evil propensities seemed to be superseded by it, if not utterly absorbed in its virtues. The rest of the family now lived in comparative peace and quietness; for early and late her malevolence was venting itself against the jotteryman, and him alone. It was a delirium of hatred and vengeance, on which the whole bent and bias of her inclination was set. She could not stay away from the creature's presence, for in the intervals when absent from him, she spent her breath in curses and execrations, and then, not being able to rest, she ran again to seek him, her eyes gleaming with the anticipated delights of vengeance, while, ever and anon, all the scaith, the ridicule and the harm rebounded on herself.

Was it not strange that she could not get quit of this sole annoyance of her life? One would have thought that she easily might. But by this time, there was nothing further from her intention, she wanted vengeance, full, adequate, and delicious vengeance on her audacious opponent. But he was a strange and terrible creature, and the means of retaliation came always, as it were, to his hand.

Bread and sweet milk was the only fare that Merodach cared for, and he, having bargained for that, would not want it, though he often got it with a curse and with ill will. The lady, having kept back his wonted allowance for some days, on the Sabbath morning following, she set him down a bowl of rich sweet milk, well drugged with a deadly poison, and then she lingered in a little anteroom to watch the success of her grand plot, and prevent any other creature from tasting of the poison. Merodach came in, and the house-maid says to him, "Here is your breakfast, creature."

"Oho! My lady has been liberal this morning", said he, "but I am beforehand with her—Here little Missie, you seem very hungry today—take you my breakfast." And with that he set the beverage down to the lady's favourite spaniel. It so happened that the lady's only son came at that moment into the anteroom, seeking her and teazing his mamma about something which took her attention from the hall-table for a space. When she looked again, and saw Missie lapping up the sweet milk, she burst from her lobby like a dragon, screaming as if her head had been on fire, kicked the bowl and the remainder of its contents against the wall, and lifting Missie in her bosom, she retreated hastily, crying all the way.

"Ha, ha, ha—I have you now," cried Merodach, as she vanished from the hall.

Poor Missie died immediately, and very privately; indeed she would have died and been buried, and never one have seen her, save her mistress, had not Merodach, by a luck that never failed him, popped his nose over the flower garden wall, just as his lady was laying her favourite in a grave of her own digging. She, not perceiving her tormentor, plied on at her task, apostrophising the insensate little carcass,—"Ah! Poor dear little creature, thou hast had a hard fortune, and has drank of the bitter potion that was not intended for thee, but he shall drink it three times double for thy sake."

"Is that little Missie?" said the eldritch voice of the jotteryman, close at the lady's ear. She uttered a loud scream and sank down on the bank. "Alack for poor little Missie!" continued the creature in a tone of mockery. "My heart is sorry for Missie. What has befallen her—whose breakfast cup did she drink?"

"Hence with thee, thou fiend!" cried the lady. "What right hast thou to interfere upon thy mistress's privacy? Thy turn is coming yet, or may the nature of woman change within me."

"It is changed already," said the creature, grinning with delight; "I have thee now, I have thee now! And were it not to shew my superiority over thee, which I do every hour, I would sooner see thee strapped like a mad cat, or a worrying bratch. What wilt thou try next?"

"I will cut thy throat, and if I die for it, will rejoice in the deed, a deed of charity to all who dwell on the face of the earth. Go about thy business."

"I have warned thee before, dame, and I now warn thee again that all thy mischief meditated against me will fall double on thine own head."

"I want none of your warning, and none of your instructions, fiendish cur. Hence with your elvish face, and take care of yourself!"

240

It would be too disgusting and horrible to relate or read all the incidents that fell out between this unaccountable couple. Their enmity against each other had no end, and no mitigation, and scarcely a single day passed over on which her acts and malevolent ingenuity did not terminate fatally for some favourite thing of the lady's, while all these doings never failed to appear as her own act. Scarcely was there a thing, animate or inanimate, on which she set a value, left to her, that was not destroyed, and yet scarcely one hour or minute could she remain absent from her tormentor, and yet all the while it seems, solely for the purpose of tormenting him.

But while all the rest of the establishment enjoyed peace and quietness from the fury of their termagant dame, matters grew worse and worse between the fascinated pair. The lady haunted the menial, in the same manner as the raven haunts the eagle, for a perpetual quarrel, though the former knows that in every encounter she is to come off the loser. But now noises were heard on the stairs by night, and it was whispered among the menials, that the lady had been seeking Merodach's bed by night, on some horrible intent. Several of them would have sworn that they had seen her passing and repassing on the stair after midnight, when all was quiet; but then it was likewise well known that Merodach slept with well fastened doors, and a companion in another bed in the same room, whose bed, too, was nearest the door. Nobody cared much what became of the jotteryman, for he was an unsocial and disagreeable person; but some one told him what they had seen, and hinted a suspicion of the lady's intent. But the creature only bit his upper lip, winked with his eyes and said, "She had better let alone; she will be the first to rue that."

Not long after this, to the horror of the family and the whole countryside, the laird's only son was found murdered in his bed one morning, under circumstances that manifested the most fiendish cruelty and inveteracy on the part of his destroyer. As soon as the atrocious act was divulged, the lady fell into convulsions, and lost her reason, and happy had it been for her had she never recovered either the use of her reason, or her corporeal functions any more, for there was blood upon her hand, which she took no care to conceal, and there was too little doubt that it was the blood of her own innocent and beloved boy, the sole heir and hope of the family.

The blow deprived the laird of all power of action; but the lady had a brother, a man of the law, who came and instantly proceeded to an investigation of this unaccountable murder, but before the Sheriff arrived, the housekeeper took the lady's brother aside, and told him he had better not go on with the scrutiny, for she was sure that the crime would be brought home to her unfortunate mistress; and after examining into several corroborative circumstances, and viewing the state of the raving maniac, with the blood on her hand and arm, he made the investigation a very short one, declaring the domestics all exculpated.

The laird attended his boy's funeral and laid his head in the grave, but appeared exactly like a man walking in a trance, an automaton, without feelings or sensations, oftentimes gazing at the funeral procession, as on something he could not comprehend. And when the death-bell of the parish church fell a-tolling, as the corpse approached the kirk-stile, he cast a dim eye up towards the belfry and said hastily, "What, what's that? Och ay, we're just in time, just in time". And often was he hammering over the name of "Evil Merodach, King of Babylon" to himself. [*Editor's Note*: This is probably a reference to the Persian monarch, Amel-Marduk, a son and successor of Nebuchadnezzer II, who ruled Babylonia from 562 to 560 B.C. He is also referred to, amongst other sources, in the biblical Books of 2nd Kings and Jeremiah where his name is translated, in the King James version, as "Evil-Merodach."] He seemed to have some far-fetched conception that his unaccountable jotteryman had a hand in the death of his only son, and other lesser calamities, although the evidence in favour of Merodach's innocence was as usual quite decisive.

The grievous mistake of Lady Wheelhope (for every landward laird's wife was then styled Lady) can only be accounted for, by supposing her in a state of derangement, or rather under some evil influence over which she had no control, and to a person in such a state, the mistake was not so very unnatural. The mansion-house of Wheelhope was old and irregular. The stair had four acute turns, all the same, and four landing-places, all the same. In the uppermost chamber slept the two domestics—Merodach, in the bed farthest in, and in the chamber immediately below that, which was exactly similar, slept the young laird and his tutor, the former in the bed furthest in, and this, in the turmoil of raging passions, her own hand made herself childless.

Merodach was expelled from the family forthwith, but refused to accept any of his wages, which the man of law pressed upon him, for fear of further mischief, but he went away in apparent sullenness and discontent, no-one knowing whither.

When his dismissal was announced to the lady, who was watched day and night in her chamber, the news had such an effect on her, that her whole frame seemed electrified; the horrors of remorse vanished, and another passion, which I can neither comprehend nor define, took sole possession of her distempered spirit. "He *must* not go!..... He *shall* not go!" she exclaimed. "No, no, no—he shall not—he shall not—he shall not!" and she instantly set herself about making ready to follow him, uttering all the while, the most diabolical expressions, indicative of anticipated vengeance—"Oh, could I but snap his nerves one by one, and birl (spin) among his vitals! Could I but slice his heart off piecemeal in small messes and see his blood lopper and bubble, and spin away in purple slays, and then see him grin, and grin, and grin! Oh-oh-oh

243

How grand and beautiful a sight it would be to see him grin, and grin, and grin!" And in such a style she would run on for hours together.

She thought of nothing, she spoke of nothing, but the discarded jotteryman, whom most people now began to regard as a creature that was not canny (natural or human). They had seen him eat, and drink, and work like other people; still he had that about him that was not like other men. He was a boy in form, and an antediluvian in feature. Some thought he was a mule, between a Jew and an ape, some a wizard, some a kelpie, or a fairy, but most of all that he was really and truly a Brownie. What he was, I do not know, and therefore will not pretend to say, but be that as it may, in spite of locks and keys, watching and waking, the Lady of Wheelhope soon made her escape and eloped after him. The attendants indeed would have made oath that she was carried away by some invisible hand, for that it was impossible that she could have escaped on foot like other people; and this edition of the story took in the country, but sensible people viewed the matter in another light.

As, for instance, when Wattie Blythe, the laird's old shepherd came in from the hill one morning, his wife Bessie, accosted him thus:—"His presence be about us Wattie Blythe! Have ye heard what has happened at the ha'? Things are aye turnin' waur an' waur there, and it looks like as if Providence had gi'en up our laird's house to destruction. This grand estate maun now gang frae the Sprots, for it has finished them."

"Na, na Bessie, it isna the estate that has finished the Sprots but the Sprots that hae finished it, an' themsells into the boot. They hae been a wicked and degenerate race an' aye the langer the waur, till they reached the utmost bounds o' earthly wickedness an' it's time the de'il were looking after his ain."

"Ah Wattie Blythe, ye never said a truer say. An' that's just the very point where your story ends and mine commences; for hanna the deil, or the fairies, or the brownies, ta'en our lady away bodily, an' the haill country is running an' riding in search o' her and there is twenty hunder merks offered to the first that can find her an' bring her safe back. They hae ta'en her away, skin an' bane, body an' soul an' a' Wattie!"

"Hech-wow! but that is awesome! And where is thought they have ta'en her to Bessie?"

"O, they hae some guess at that frae her ain hints afore. It is thought they hae carried her after that Satan of a creature. Wha wrought sae muckle wae about the house. It is for him they are a' looking, for they ken weel that where they get the tane they will get the tither."

"Whew! Is that the gate o't Bessie? Why then, the awfu' story is nouther mair nor less than this, that the leddy made a lopement (elopement), as they ca't and run away after a black-guard jotteryman. Hech-wow! wae's me fro human frailty! But that's just the gate! When aince the deil gets in the point o' his finger, he will soon have in his haill hand. Ay, he wants but a hair to make a tether of, ony day. I hae seen her, a braw sonsy lass, but even then I feared she was devoted to destruction, for she aye mockit at religion. Bessie, an' that's no a good mark of a young body. An' she made a' its servants her enemies; an' think you those good men's prayers were a' to blaw away i' the wind, and be nae mair regarded? Na, na Bessie, my woman, take ye this mark baith o' our ain bairns and aither folks—If ever ye see a young body that disregards the Sabbath, and makes a mock at the ordinances o' religion, ye will never see that body come to muckle good. A braw hand she has made o' her gibes an' jeers at religion, an' her mockeries o' the poor persecuted hill-folk!—sunk down by degrees into the very dregs o' sin and misery! run away after a scullion!"

"Fy, fy Wattie, how can ye say sae? It was well kenned that she hatit him wi' a perfect an' mortal hatred an' tried to make away wi' him mair ways nor ane."

"Aha Bessie; but nipping and scarting are Scots folk's wooing; an' though it is but right that we suspend our judgements, there will naebody persuade me, if she be found alang wi' the creature, but that she has run away after him in the natural way, on her twa shanks, without help either frae fairy or brownie."

"I'll never believe sic a thing of any woman born, let be a lady weel up in years."

"Od help ye Bessie! ye dinna ken the stretch o' corrupt nature. The best o' us when left to oursel's are nae better than strayed sheep, that will never find their way back to their ain pastures, an' of a' things made o' mortal flesh, a wicked woman is the warst."

"Alack a-day! we get the blame o' muckle that we little deserve. But, Wattie, keep a gayan sharp look-out about the cleuchs [*Editor's Note*: ravines] and caves o' our glen, or hope, as ye ca't, for the lady kens them a' gayan weel, an' gin the twenty hunder merks wad come our way, it might gang a waur gate. It wad tocher o' our bonny lasses."

"Ay, weel I wat, Bessie, that's nae lee. And now, when ye bring me amind, o't the L—forgie me gin, I didna hear a creature up in the Brock-holes [*Editor's Note*: badger-holes] this morning, skirling [*Editor's Note*: screaming] as if something war cutting its throat. It gars a' the hairs stand on my head when I think it may hae been our leddy, an' the droich [*Editor's Note*: wretch] of a creature murdering her. I took it for a battle of wulcats [*Editor's Note*: wildcats] an' wished they might pu' out one another's thrapples [*Editor's Note*: throats], but when I think on it again they were unco' like some o' our leddy's unearthly screams."

"His presence be about us Wattie! Haste ye. Pit on your bonnet—take your staff in your hand, and gang an' see what it is."

"Shame fa' me, if I daur gang Bessie."

"Hout, Wattie, trust in the Lord."

"Aweel sae I do. But ane's no to throw himself ower a linn, an' trust that the Lord's to keep him in a blanket, nor hing himsell up in a raip, an' expect the Lord to come and cut him down. And it's nae muckle safer for an auld stiff man to gang away out to a remote wild place, where there is ae body murdering another—What is that I hear Bessie? Haud the long tongue o' you and rin to the door, an' see what noise that is."

Bessie ran to the door, but soon returned an altered creature, with her mouth wide open, and her eyes set in her head.

"It is them, Wattie! it is them! His presence be about us! What will we do!"

"Them? Whaten them?"

"Why, that blackguard creature, coming here, leading our leddy be the hair o' her head, an' yerking her wi' a stick. I am terrified out o' my wits. What will we do?"

"We'll see what they say" said Wattie, manifestly in as great a terror as his wife, and by a natural impulse or a last resource, he opened the Bible, not knowing what he did, and then hurried on his spectacles; but before he got two leaves turned over, the two entered, a frightful-looking couple indeed. Merodach, with his old, withered face, and ferret eyes, leading the Lady of Wheelhope by the long hair which was mixed with grey, and whose face was all bloated with wounds and bruises and having stripes of blood on her garments.

"How's this!—How's this, sirs," said Wattie Blythe.

"Close the book and I will tell you goodman," said Merodach.

"I can hear what you hae to say wi' the book open sir," said Wattie, turning over the leaves as if looking for some particular passage, but apparently not knowing what he was doing. "It is a shamefu' business this, but some will hae to answer for't. My leddy I am unco grieved to see you in sic a plight. Ye hae surely been dooms sair left to yoursell."

The lady shook her head, uttered a feeble, hollow laugh, and fixed her eyes on Merodach. But such a look! It almost frightened the simple, aged couple out of their senses. It was not a look of love, nor of hatred exclusively, neither was it desire or disgust, but it was a combination of them all. It was such a look as one fiend would cast on another, in whose everlasting destruction he rejoiced. Wattie was glad to take his eyes from such countenances and look into the Bible, that firm foundation of all his hopes, and all his joy.

"I request that you will shut that book sir," said the horrible creature, "or if you do not, I will shut it for you with a vengeance" and with that he seized it, and flung it against the wall. Bessie uttered a scream and Wattiie was quite paralysed; and although he seemed disposed to run after his best friend, as he called it, the hellish looks of the Brownie interposed and glued him to his seat.

"Hear what I have to say first", said the creature, "and then pore your fill on that precious book of yours. One concern at a time is enough. I came to do you a service. Here, take this cursed, wretched woman, whom you style your lady, and deliver her up to the lawful authorities, to be restored to her husband and her place in society. She is come upon one that hates her, and never said one kind word to her in her life, and though I have beat her like a dog, still she clings to me, and will not depart, so enchanted is she with the laudable purpose of cutting my throat. Tell your master, and her brother, that I am not to be burdened with their maniac. I have scourged, I have spurned and kicked her, afflicting her night and day, and yet from my side she will not depart. Take her. Claim the reward in full, and your fortune is made, and so farewell."

The creature bowed and went away, but the moment his back was turned, the lady fell a-screaming and struggling like one in an agony, and, in spite of all the old couple's exertions, she forced herself out of their hands and ran after the retreating Merodach. When he saw better would not be, he turned upon her, and. By one blow with his stick, struck her down, and, not content with that, he continued to kick and baste her in such a manner as to all appearances would have killed twenty ordinary persons. The poor devoted dame could do nothing, but now and then utter a squeak like a half-worried cat, and writhe and grovel on the sward until Wattie and his wife came up and withheld her tormentor from further violence. He then bound her hands behind her back with a strong cord, and delivered her once more into the charge of the old couple, who contrived to hold her by that means and take her home.

Wattie had not the face to take her into the hall, but into one of the outhouses, where he brought her brother to receive her. The man of law was manifestly vexed at her reappearance, and scrupled not to testify his dissatisfaction, for when Wattie told him how the wretch had abused his sister and that, had it not been for Bessie's interference and his own, the lady would have been killed outright.

"Why, Walter, it is a great pity that he did not kill her outright", said he, "What good can her life now do to her, or of what value is her life to any creature living? After one has lived to disgrace all connected with them, the sooner they are taken off, the better."

The man, however, paid old Walter down his two thousand merks, a great fortune for one like him in those days, and not to dwell longer on this unnatural story, I shall only add, very shortly, that the Lady of Wheelhope soon made her escape once more and flew, as by an irresistible charm to her tormentor. Her friends looked no more after her, and the last time that she was seen alive, it was following the uncouth creature up the water of Daur, weary, wounded and lame, while he was all the way beating he, as a piece of excellent amusement. A few days after that, her body was found among some wild haggs, in a place called Crook-burn, by a party of persecuted Covenanters that were in hiding there, some of the very men whom she had exerted herself to destroy, and who had been driven, like David of old, to pray for a curse and earthly punishment upon her. They buried her like a dog at the Yetts of Keppel, and rolled three huge stone upon the grave, which are lying there to this day. When they found her corpse, it was mangled and wounded in a most shocking manner, the fiendish creature having manifestly tormented her to death. He was never more seen or heard of, in this kingdom, though all the countryside was kept in terror for him many years afterwards; and to this day they will tell you of *The Brownie of the Black Haggs*, which title he seems to have acquired after his disappearance.

This story was told to me by an old man, named Adam Halliday, whose great grandfather, Thomas Halliday, was one of those that found the corpse and buried it. It is many years since I heard it; but, however ridiculous it might appear, I remember it made a dreadful impression on my young mind. I never heard any story like it, save one of an old foxhound that pursued a fox through the Grampians for a fortnight, and when at last discovered by the Duke of Athole's people, neither of them could run, but the hound was still continuing to walk after the fox, and when the latter lay down beside him, and looked at him steadfastly all the while, though unable to do him the least harm. The passion of inveterate malice seems to have influenced these two exactly alike. But, upon the whole, I scarcely believe the tale can be true.

Thrawn Janet

For the Celts, the dead were never far away. They watched the affairs of the living from their place in the Otherworld, always ready to intervene in the lives of their descendants or in the communities that they'd left. Nowadays, when we speak of ghosts we imagine ethereal creatures, phantom knights and monks who are almost transparent in form, walking about with their heads tucked under their arms or drifting through some forgotten graveyard as mist does. This was certainly not the Celtic idea of the dead. If they returned to the world of the living, the dead were extremely substantial, just as they had been in life. They could eat and drink and even carry on a conversation if need be. And they were the phantoms of friends and neighbors, those who were well known to those who saw them. They were, in Ireland and in some parts of Scotland, the 'marbh bheo,' the nightwalking dead, substantial and solid 'ghosts' who could sometimes do harm.

In the matter of the marbh bheo, the Church found itself in a strange position: it couldn't condone a widespread belief in such phantoms, but it couldn't deny them either, because they were proof of the Afterlife that was to come. So it taught that these ghosts were malignant and evil, only wishing to do Mankind ill. They were the agents of the Devil. Nowhere was this belief more firmly held than in Scotland.

Celebrated Edinburgh writer Robert Louis Stevenson (1850-1894), author of such literary classics as *Treasure Island, Kidnapped,* and *The Strange Case of Dr. Jeckyll and Mr. Hyde,* well knew many of these traditions. He may have learned of them at the knee of his beloved nurse, Alison Cunningham, or 'Cummy,' who told him terrible tales of the Covenanters (strict Scottish Presbyterians) and of the Devil raising the dead to walk about at night in the fashion of the marbh bheo. This rather obscure tale of ghosts and witchcraft, 'Thrawn Janet' ('thrawn' meaning 'twisted') is thought to have been written around the same time as *Dr. Jeckyll and Mr. Hyde* and reflects the tangible and malignant Celtic ghostly presence, lurking in the shadows just beyond the wan glow of the lamp.

"Thrawn Janet"

by Robert Louis Stevenson

The Reverend Murdoch Soulis was long the minister in the moorland parish of Balweary in the vale of Dule. A severe, bleak-faced old man, dreadful to his hearers, he dwelt in the last years of his life, without relative or servant or any human company; in the small and lonely manse under the Hanging Shaw. In spite of the iron composure of his features, his eye was wild, scared and uncertain; and when he dwelt, in private admonition on the future of the impenitent, it seemed as though his eye pierced through the storms of time to the terrors of eternity. Many young persons, coming to prepare themselves against the season of Holy Communion, were dreadfully affected by his talk. He had a sermon on 1st Peter v and 8th: "The devil as a roaring lion" on the Sunday after every seventeenth of August, and he was accustomed to surpass himself upon that text both by the appalling nature of the matter and the terror of his bearing in the pulpit. The children were frightened into fits ands the old looked more than usually oracular, and were, all that day, full of those hints that Hamlet deprecated. The manse itself, where it stood by the water of the Dule among some thick trees, with the Shaw overhanging it on one side, and on the other many cold, moorish hill-tops rising toward the sky, had begun, at a very early period of Mr. Soulis's ministry to be avoided in the dark hours by all who valued themselves upon their prudence and guidmen sitting at the clachan (small village) alehouse shook their heads together at the thought of passing late by that uncanny neighbourhood. There was one spot, to be more particular, which was regarded with especial awe. The manse stood between the highroad and the water of the Dule, with a gable to each, its back towards the kirktown of Balweary, nearly half a mile away; in front of it, a bare garden hedges with thorn, occupied between the river and the road. The house was two stories high, with two large rooms on each. It opened not directly on the garden, but on a causewayed path, or passage, giving on the road on one hand and closed on the other by the tall willows and elders that bordered on the stream. And it was this strip of causeway that enjoyed among the younger parishioners of Balweary, so infamous a reputation. The minister walked there often after dark, sometimes groaning aloud in the insistency of his unspoken prayers, and when he was from the house, and the manse door was locked, the more daring schoolboys ventured with beating hearts, to "follow my leader" across that legendary spot.

The atmosphere of terror, surrounding, as it did, a man of God of spotless character and orthodoxy, was a common cause of wonder and subject of inquiry among the few strangers who were led by chance or business into that unknown, outlying country. But many even of the people of the parish were ignorant of the strange events which had marked the first year of Mr. Soulis's ministrations; and among those who were better informed, some were naturally reticent, and others shy of that particular topic. Now and again, only, one of the older folk would warm into courage over his third tumbler and recount the cause of the minister's strange looks and solitary life.

Fifty years sine [*Editor's Note*: since], when Mr. Soulis cam' first into Ba'weary, he was still a young man—a callant, the folk said—fu' o' the book learnin' an' grand at the exposition, but, as was natural in sae young a man, wi' nae leevin' experience in religion. The younger sort were greatly taken wi' his gifts and his gab, but auld, concerned, serious men and women were moved even to prayer for the young man, whom they took to be a self-deceiver, and the parish that was like to be sae ill-supplied. It was before the days o' the moderates—weary fa' them but ill things are like guid—they baith come bit by bit, a pickle [*Editor's Note*: a little] at a time, and there were folk even then that said that the Lord had left the college professors to their ain devices, an' the lads that went to study wi' them was hae done mair an' better sittin' in a peatbog, like their forebears of the persecution, wi' a Bible under their oxter [*Editor's Note*: armpit] an' a speerit o' prayer in their hearts. There was nae doubt onyway, but that Mr. Soulis had been ower long at the college. He was careful and troubled for mony things besides the ae thing needful. He had a feck o' books wi' him—mair than had ever been seen in a' that presbytery and said worked the carrier had wi' them, for they were a' like to have smoored in the De'il's Hag between this and Kilmackorlie. They were books o' divinity to be sure, or so they ca'ed them, but the serious were o' opinion there was little service for sae mony, when the hail o' God's Word would gang in the neuk o' a plaid. There he wad sit half the day an' half the nicht forbye, which was scant decent—writin' nae less an' first they were feared he wad read his sermons an' syne it proved, he was writin' a book himsel', which was surely no fittin' for ane o' his years an' sma' experience.

Onyway, it behoved him to get an auld, decent wife [*Editor's Note*: housekeeper] to keep the manse for him an' see to his bit denners, an' he was recommended to an auld limmer [*Editor's Note*: hussy]—Janet McClour they ca'd her—an' sae far left tae himsel' so to be ower persuaded. There was mony advised him to the contrae, for Janet was mair than suspeckit by the best o' folk in Ba'weary. Lang or that, she had a wean [*Editor's Note*: child] to a dragoon, she hadna come forrit [*Editor's Note*: come to church] for maybe thretty [*Editor's Note*: thirty] year and bairns had seen her mumblin' to hersel' up on Kelly's Loan in the gloamin', whilk it was an unco' time an' place for a Godfearn' woman. Howsoever, it was the laird himsel' that had first tould the minister o' Janet, an' in thae days he wad hae gone a fair gate [*Editor's Note*: a long way] tae please the laird. When folk tould him that Janet was sib to the de'il [*Editor's Note*: sold to the Devil], it was a superstition by his way o' it, when they cast up the Bible to him an; the witch of Endor, he would threep it down their thrapples [*Editor's Note*: put it down their throats] that thir days were a' gone by, an' the de'il was mercifully restrained.

Weel, when it got about the clachan that Janet McClour was to be servant at the manse, the folk were fair mad wi' her an' him thegither [*Editor's Note*: together]; an' some o' the guidwives had nae better to dae than get round her door cheeks an' charge her wi' a' that was kenn'd against her, frae the sodger's [*Editor's Note*: soldier's] bairn to John Tamson's taw kye [*Editor's Note*: two cows]. She was nae great speaker, folk usually let her gang her ain gate, and she let them gang theirs, wi' neither Fair-guid-een nor Fair-guid-day, but when she bucked to [*Editor's Note*: when she got worked up], she had a tongue to deeve [*Editor's Note*: deafen] the miller. Up she got, and there wasna an auld story in Ba'weary but she gart somebody lawp for it that day [*Editor's Note*: she ridiculed their own short-comings]; they couldna say ae thing but she could say twa to it, till at the hinder end, the guidwives up an' claught haud of her, clawed the coats of her back and pu'd her doun the clachan to the water o' the Dule to see if she were a witch or no, soom or droun [*Editor's Note*: swim or drown]. The carline [*Editor's Note*: evil old woman] skirled [*Editor's Note*: screamed] till ye could hear her at the Hangin' Shaw an' she focht like ten, there was mony a guidwife bure the merk o' her neist day [*Editor's Note*: next day] an' mony a lang day after, an' just in the hettest o' the collieshangie (uproar) what suld come up (for his sins) but the new minister!

"Women," said he had a grand voice, "I charge you in the Lord's name to let her go."

Janet ran to him—she was fair wud wi' terror—an' clang to him an' prayed him for Christ's sake, save her frae the cummers [*Editor's Note*: women], an' they for their pairt, tauld him a' that was ken't an' maybe mair.

"Woman", says he to Janet "is this true?"

"As the Lord sees me" says she, "as the Lord made me, no a word o't. Forbye the barn" says she, "I've been a decent woman a' my days."

"Will you," says Mr. Soulis, "in the name of God and before me, His unworthy minister, renounce the devil and his works?"

Weel, it wad appear that when he askit that, she gave a girn [*Editor's Note*: scream] that fairly frichit [*Editor's Note*: frightened] them that saw her an' they could hear the teeth play dirl [*Editor's Note*: grinding] the girther in her chafts [*Editor's Note*: cheeks], but there was naething for it but the ae way or the ither; an' Janet lifted up her hand an' renounced the de'il before them a'.

"And now", says Mr. Soulis to the guidwives, "home with ye, one and all, and pray to God for His forgiveness."

An' he gied Janet his arm, though she had little on her but a sark [*Editor's Note*: smock or chemise], and took her up the clachan to her ain door like a leddy o' the land and her screighin' [*Editor's Note*: shrieking] an' laughin' as was a scandal to be heard.

There were mony grave folk lang ower their prayers that nicht but when the morn cam' there was sic a fear that fell upon Ba'weary that the bairns hid theirsel's, an' even the men-folk stood an' keekit [*Editor's Note*: peeped] frae their doors. For there was Janet comin' doun the clachan—her or her like-ness, nane could tell—wi' her neck thrawn [*Editor's Note*: twisted], an' her heid on ae side, like a body that has been hangit, an a girn [*Editor's Note*: grimace] on her face like an unstreakit corp. By an' by they got used wi' it, an' even speered at her [*Editor's Note*: questioned her] to ken what was wrang, but frae that day forth she couldna speak like a Christian woman, but slavered and played click wi' her teeth like a pair o' shears; an' frae that day forth, the name o' God cam' never on her lips. Whiles she was try to say it, but it michtna be. Them that kenned best said least; but they never geid that Thing the name o' Janet McClour, for the auld Janet, by their way o't, was in muckle hell that day. But the minister was neither to haud nor to bind; he preached about naething but the folk's cruelty that had gi'en her the stroke of the palsy, he skelpit [*Editor's Note*: smacked] the bairns that meddled her, an' had her up to the manse that same nicht and dwalled there his lain [*Editor's Note*: lived alone] wi' her under the Hangin' Shaw.

Weel, time ga'ed by; an' the idler sort commenced to think mair lichtly o' that black business. The minister was weel thoct o'; he was aye late at the writin', folk was see his can'le doon by the Dule water after twal' at e'en [*Editor's Note*: midnight] an' he seemed pleased wi' himsel' an; upsittin' at first though a body could see that he was dwining [*Editor's Note*: pining away or growing weaker]. As for Janet, she cam' an' she gaed, if she didna speak muckle afore, it was reason she should speak less then; she meddled naebody, but she was an eldritch thing to see an' nane wud hae mistrysted wi' her for Ba'weary's glebe.

About the end o' July there cam a spell o' weather, the like o't never was in that countryside; it was lown an' het an' heartless [*Editor's Note*: extremely warm]; the herds couldna win up the Black Hill; the bairns were ower weariet to play; an' yet it was gousty [*Editor's Note*: windy] too, wi' cleps o' het wund that rumm'led in the glens and bits o' showers that slockened [*Editor's Note*: wetted] naething. We aye thocht it but to thun'er on the morn but the morn cam', an' the morn's morning, an' it was aye the same uncanny weather, sair on folks and bestial. O' them that were the waur, nane suffered like Mr. Soulis, he could neither sleep nor eat, he tauld his elders; an' when he wasna writin' in his weary book, he wad be stravaguin [*Editor's Note*: wandering] ower a' the country-side like a man possessed, when a'body-else was blithe to keep caller ben the house [*Editor's Note*: stay indoors].

Aboun [*Editor's Note*: above] the Hangin' Shaw, in the bield [*Editor's Note*: shelter] o' the Black Hills, there's a bit enclosed ground wi' an iron yett [*Editor's Note*: gate], an' it seems in the auld days, that was the kirkyaird o' Ba'weary, an' consecrated by the Papists before the blessed licht shone on the kingdom. It was a great howff [*Editor's Note*: haunt] o' Mr. Soulis's onyway, there he wad sit an' consider his sermons; an' indeed it's a bieldy bit [*Editor's Note*: tranquil spot]. Weel, as he cam' ower the wast end o' the Black Hill, ae day, he saw first twa, sine fower, syne seeven corbie craws [*Editor's Note*: hooded crows] fleein' roond an' roond abune the auld kirkyaird. They flew laigh [*Editor's Note*: low] an' heavy, an' squawked to ither as the gaed, an' it was clear to Mr.. Soulis that something had put them frae their ordinar. He wasna easy fleyed [*Editor's Note*: frightened], an' geyed straught [*Editor's Note*: straight] up tae the wa's [*Editor's Note*: walls] an' what should he find there but a man or the appearance o' a man, sittin' on the inside upon a

258

grave. He was great of stature and black as hell and his e'en were singular to see. Mr. Soulis had heard tell o' black men mony's the time but there was somethin' unco [*Editor's Note*: uncanny] about this black man that daunted him. [*Editor's Note*: There was a common belief in many parts of Scotland, especially amongst Presbyterians, that the Devil often took the shape of a black man in order to work his evil in the world. References to a black man, sometimes with cloven feet, are made in several Scottish witch trials, where he is described as the Master of the Sabbat or Coven.] Het as he was, he took a kind o' cold grue [*Editor's Note*: chill] in the marrow o' his bones, but up he spake for a' that; an' says he, "My friend, are you a stranger in this place?" The black man answered never a word; he got upon his feet an' begoud on to the hirsle [*Editor's Note*: moved in the direction of the sheepyard] in the wa' on the far side; but he aye lookit at the minister, an' the minister stood an' lookit back; till a' in a meenit the black man was ower the wa' an' rinnin' for the bield o' the trees. Mr. Soulis, he hardly kenned why, but he was fair forjeakit [*Editor's Note*: exhausted] wi' his walk an' the het, unhalesome weather; an' rin as he likit, he got nae mair than a glisk [*Editor's Note*: glance] o' the black man amang the birks [*Editor's Note*: trees], till he won doun to the foot o' the hillside an' there he saw him ance mair, gaun, hap-step-an'- lowp, ower the Dule water to the manse.

Mr. Soulis wasna weel pleased that this fearsome gangrel [*Editor's Note*: vagrant or beggar] suld mak' sae free wi' Ba'weary manse an' he ran the harder, an' wet shoon [*Editor's Note*: his shoes] ower the burn an' up the walk; but the de'il a black man was there to see. He stepped out upon the road but there was naebody there; he gaed ower the gairden, but na, nae black man. At the hinder end, an' a bit feared as was but natural, he lifted the hasp [*Editor's Note*: latch] an' into the manse; an' there was Janet McClour before his e'en [*Editor's Note*: eyes] wi' her thrawn craig [*Editor's Note*: twisted neck], an' nane sae pleased to see him. An' he aye minded sinsyne [*Editor's Note*:

in the past], when he first set his e'en upon her, he had the same cauld and deidly grue.

"Janet", says he, "have you seen a black man?"

"A black man!" quo' she. "Save us a'! Ye're no wise minister! There's nae black man in Ba'weary."

But she didna' speak plain, ye maun understan', but yam-yammered, like a powny wi' the bit in its moo.

"Weel," says he, "Janet if there was nae black man, I have spoken with the Accuser of the Brethren."

An' he sat doun like ane wi' a fever, an' his teeth chattered in his heid.

"Hoots", says she, "think shame to yoursel', minister", an' gied him a drap o' brandy that she keepit aye by her.

Syne, Mr. Soulis gaed into his study amang his books It's a lang, laigh, mirk [*Editor's Note*: gloomy] chalmer [*Editor's Note*: chamber], perishin' cauld in winter, an no' very dry even at the top o' the simmer, for the manse stands near the burn [*Editor's Note*: stream, river]. Sae doun he sat, and thoct of a' that had come an' gone since he was in Ba'weary an' his hame, an' the days when he was a bairn an' ran daffin' on the braes [*Editor's Note*: playing on the hillside], an' that black man aye ran in his like the owercome o' a sang [*Editor's Note*: melody of a song]. Aye the mair he thoct, the mair he thoct o' the black man. He tried the prayer, an' the words wouldna come to him, an', they say, he tried to write at his book, but he couldna make nae mair o' that. There was whiles that he thoct the black man was at, his oxter, an' the swat stood on him cauld as well-water; an' there were ither whiles when he cam' to himsel' like a christen bairn and minded naething.

The upshot was that he gaed to the window an' stood glowerin ' at the Dule water. The trees were unco thick, an' the water lies deep an' black under the manse, an' there was Janet washin' the cla'es wi' her coats kilted. She had her back to the minister an' he, for his pairt, hardly kenned what he was lookin' at. Syne she turned round an' shawed her face. Mr. Soulis had the same cauld grue as twice that day afore, an' it was borne upon him what folk said, that Janet was died lang syne, an' this was a bogle [*Editor's Note*: ghost] in her clay-cauld flesh. He drew back a pickle and scanned her narrowly. She was tramp-trampin' the cla'es, croonin' tae hersel', and eh! God guide us, but it was a fearsome face. Whiles she sang louder, but there was nae man born o' woman that could tell the words o' her sang, an' whiles she lookit side-lang doun but there was naething there for her to look at. There gaed a scunner [*Editor's Note*: loathing] through the flesh upon his banes an' that was Heeven's advertisement. But Mr. Soulis just blamed himsel', he said, to think sae ill o' a puir, auld afflicted wife that hadna a freend forby himsel'; an' he put up a bit prayer for him an' her an' drank a little caller water—for his heart rose again' the meat—an' he gaed up to his naked bed in the gloamin' [*Editor's Note*: twilight].

That was a nicht that has never been forgotten in Ba'weary, the nicht o' the seeventeenth o' August, seeventeen hun'er an' twal'. It had been het afore, as I hae said, but that nicht was hetter than ever. The sun gaed doun amang unco-lookin' clouds, it fell as mirk [*Editor's Note*: dark] as the pit, no' a star, no' a breath o' wund, ye couldna see your hand' afore your face; an' even the auld folk cuist the covers frae their beds an' lay pechin' [*Editor's Note*: panting] for their breath. Wi' a' that he had upon his mind, it was gey and unlikely that Mr. Soulis was get muckle sleep. He lay an' he tumbled; the guide caller bed that he got into brunt [*Editor's Note*: bruised] his very banes, whiles he slept an' whiles he wakened; whiles he heard the time o' nicht an' whiles a tyke yowlin' up the muir, as if somebody was deid, whiles he thoct he heard bogles claverin' in his lug [*Editor's Note*: specters whispering in his ear] an' whiles he saw spunkies [*Editor's Note*: will-o'-the-wisps] in the room. He behoved, he judged, to be sick, an' sick he was— little he jaloused the sickness.

At the hinder end, he got a clearness in his mind, sat up in his ark on the bed-side an' fell thinkin' ance mair o' the black man an' Janet. He couldna' weel tell how—maybe it was the cauld to his feet—but it cam' in upon him wi' a' spate that there was some connection between the twa an' that either or baith o' them were bogles. An' just at that moment, in Janet's room, which was neist to his, there came a stamp o' feet, an' then a loud bang, an' then a wund gaed reishing round the fower quarters o' the house; an' then a' was ance mair as seelent as the grave.

Mr. Soulis was feared for neither man nor de'il. He got his tinder-box an' lit a can'le, an' made three steps ower to Janet's door. It was on the hasp an' he pushed it open an' keeked bauldly in. It was a big room, as big as the minister's ain, an' plenished [*Editor's Note*: furnished] wi' grand auld solid gear, for he had naething else. There was a fower-posted bed wi' auld tapestry; a braw cabinet o' aik [*Editor's Note*: oak], that was fu' o' the minister's divinity books and put there to be out o' the gate [*Editor's Note*: out of the way]; an' a wheen o' duds [*Editor's Note*: a few belongings] o' Janet's, lyin' here an' there about the floor. But nae Janet could Mr. Soulis see nor any sign o' a contention [*Editor's Note*: argument, fight]. In he gaed (an' there's few that wud hae followed him) an' lookit a'round an' listened. But there was naething to be heard, neither inside the manse or in a' Ba'weary parish, an' naething to be seen but the muckle shadows turnin' round the can'le. An' then, a' at aince, the minister's heart played dunt an' stood stock-still, an' a cauld wund blew amang the hairs o' his heid. Whaten a weary sicht was that for the puir man's e'en! For there was Janet hangin' frae a nail beside the auld aik cabinet, her heid aye lay on her shoulther, her e'en were steerkit [*Editor's Note*: blank], the tongue projected frae her mouth, an her heels were twa feet clear abune the floor.

"God forgive us all!" thoct Mr. Soulis, "poor Janet's dead."

He cam' a step nearer to the corp, an' then his heart fair whammiled [*Editor's Note*: beat furiously] in his inside. For by what cantrip [*Editor's Note*: spell] it wad ill beseem a man to judge, she was hangin' frae a single nail an' by a single wursted thread for darnin' hose.

It's an awfu' thing to be your lane [*Editor's Note*: alone] at nicht wi' siccan prodigies o' darkness but Mr. Soulis was strong in the Lord. He turned an' gaed his ways oot o' that room and lockit the door ahint him; an' step by step doun the stairs, as heavy as leed [*Editor's Note*: lead], an' set doun the can'le on the table at the stairfoot. He couldna pray, he couldna think, he was dreepin' wi' caul' sweat an' naething could he hear but the dunt-dunting o' his ain heart. He micht maybe hae stood there an hour or maybe twa, he minded sae little; when a' o' a sudden he heard a laigh, un canny steer [*Editor's Note*: commotion] upstairs; a foot gaed to an' fro in the chalmer where the corp was hangin'; syne the door opened, though he minded weel that he had lockit it; an' syne there was a step upon the landin', an' it seemed to him as if the corp was lookin' ower the rail an' doun upon him whaur he stood.

He took up the can'le again (for he couldna want the licht); an' as saftly as ever he could, gaed straucht out o' the manse an ' to the far end o' the causeway. It was aye pit-mirk [*Editor's Note*: very dark], the flame o' the can'le when he set it on the grund, burnt steedy and clear as in a room; naethin' moved but the Dule water seepin' an' sabbin' doun the glen, an' yon unhaly footstep that cam' ploddin' doun the stairs inside the manse. He kenned the foot ower weel, for it was Janet's, an' at ilka step it cam' a wee thing nearer, the cauld got deeper in his vitals. He commended his soul to Him that made an keepit him, "and Oh Lord", said he, "give me strength this night to war against the powers of evil."

By this time, the foot was comin' through the passage for the door; he could hear a hand skirt alang the wa' [*Editor's*

Note: wall] as if the fearsome thing was feelin' for its way. The saughs tossed and mained thegither [*Editor's Note*: the tree branches tossed and blew together], a long sigh cam' ower the hills, the flame o' the can'le was blawn aboot; an there stood the corp of Thrawn Janet wi' her grogram goun an' her black mutch [*Editor's Note*: nightdress and comforter], wi' the heid aye upon the shoulther, an' the girn [*Editor's Note*: leer] still upon the face o't—leevin' ye wad hae said—died, as Mr. Soulis weel kenned—upon the threshold o' the manse.

It's a strange thing that the soul of man should be that thirled [*Editor's Note*: driven] into his perishable body, but the minister saw that an' his heart didna break.

She didna stand there lang; she began to move again an' cam' slowly towards Mr. Soulis where he stood under the saughs [*Editor's Note*: branches]. A' the life o' his body, the strength o' his speerit, were glowerin' frae his e'en. It seemed she was gaun to speak, but wanted words, an' made a sign wi' the left hand. There cam' a clap o' wund, like a cat's fuff, oot gaed the can'le, the saughs skreighed like folk [*Editor's Note*: the branches screeched together like people] an' Mr. Soulis kenned, live or die, this was the end o't.

"Witch, beldame [*Editor's Note*: hag], devil!" he cried. "I charge you, by the power of God, begone—if you be dead, to the grave—if you be damned, to hell!"

An' at that moment the Lord's ain hand out o' the Heevens struck the Horror whaur it stood, the auld, deid, desecrated corp o' the witch-wife, sae lang keepit frae the grave an' hirtled round' by de'ils [*Editor's Note*: tormented by devils] lowed up like a braunstane spunk [*Editor's Note*: blazed like tinder] an' fell in ashes to the grund, the thunder followed, peal on dirlin' peal, the rairin' rain upon the back o' that, an' Mr. Soulis lowped [*Editor's Note*: leapt] through the garden hedge, an' ran, skelloch upon skelloch (yell upon yell) for the clachan.

That same mornin', John Christie saw the Black Man pass the Muckle Cairn as it was chappin' [*Editor's Note*: striking] six; afore eicht, he ged by the change-house at Knockdow; an' no lang after, Sandy McLellan saw him gaun linkin' down the braes frae Kilmackerlie. There is little doubt but that it was him that dwalled sae lang in Janet's body, but he was awa' at last an' sinsyne the de'il has never fashed [*Editor's Note*: troubled] us in Ba'weary.

But it was a sair dispensation for the minister; lang, lang, he lay ravin' in his bed an' frae that hour tae this, he was the man ye ken the day.

The Botathen Ghost

Many of us today consider the idea of ghosts in an almost stereotypical fashion. For us, the phantoms are those of grand lords and ladies (sometimes with their heads under their arms) or of ethereal monks, drifting aimlessly in some crumbling mansion or fallen abbey, their sole purpose seeming simply to terrify the unwary. These are of Victorian English origin and bear little resemblance to the phantoms of Celtic antiquity. Here, the phantoms were not necessarily those of spectral aristocracy or disembodied clergymen who wailed and acted in an eerie fashion; rather they were the recognizable revenants of their friends and relatives returned from the Otherworld for a period and behaving very much as they had done when alive. In a famous tale from County Tyrone in Ireland, the ghost of a local 'character,' Frank McKenna, becomes something of an even greater character itself, appearing at midnight to tell jokes and stories to an assembled company pretty much in the style of a nightclub entertainer. In some cases, ghosts were not necessarily to be feared.

However, as the Church began to take an interest in such phantoms they took on a slightly more menacing aspect in light of religious teaching. Churchmen found themselves in an awkward position: they couldn't really deny the existence of ghosts, because that would be to deny the supernatural upon which their basic beliefs were founded, but they couldn't really approve of them either, as this challenged the finality of death and the cessation of involvement in the world, in which the Church also believed. Ghosts, therefore, became in the eyes of the righteous threatening and terrifying things, ready to do harm. And yet, in a sense, the Christian churchmen themselves were not all that far removed from the early Celtic druids in that they were interpreters of supernatural phenomena and that they were often called upon to deal with it. This perspective entered Celtic-based folklore and writing, particularly in Cornwall, where tales of the 'parsons' (local churchmen) either calling up or combating ghosts and spirits are numerous.

The Reverend Robert Stephen Hawker (1803–1875) was vicar of Morwenstow in Cornwall and is credited for penning what is widely regarded as the Cornish National Anthem: 'Men of the West.' He was also an antiquarian and folklorist with an interest in collecting traditional Cornish ghost and fairy stories. Occasionally Hawker also wrote fictional stories based around folktales and ghostlore. 'The Botathen Ghost' is one of them, and it reflects the struggles of the Cornish Church against the ghosts of the past, during the 17th century. Much of the writing, one suspects, is derived from folktales that Hawker himself collected throughout Cornwall.

"The Botathen Ghost"

by R.S. Hawker

There was something very painful and peculiar in the position of the clergy in the West of England throughout the seventeenth century. The Church of those days was in a transitory state, and her ministers, like her formularies, embodied a strange mixture of the old belief with the new interpretation. [*Editor's Note*: In certain parts of Cornwall, some pagan Celtic practices lingered on into the 16th and 17th centuries and beyond, some even being incorporated into the ritual of the Christian Church. The Celtic Church had been particularly strong in Cornwall, and it is not surprising therefore that ancient ways lingered on there. However about the mid-1600s, attempts were made to do away with any religious practice that might have pagan connotations, and so the Cornish Church found itself in a state of transition.] Their wide severance also from the great metropolis of life and manners, the city of London (which in those times was civilised England, much as the Paris of our own day is France) divested the Cornish clergy in particular of all personal access to the masterminds of their age and body. Then, too, the barrier interposed by the rude, rough roads of their country, and by their abode in the wilds that were almost inaccessible, rendered the existence of a bishop rather a doctrine suggested to their belief than a fact revealed to the actual vision of each in his generation. Hence it came to pass that the Cornish clergyman, insulated within his own limited sphere, often without even the presence of a country squire (and unchecked by the influence of the Fourth Estate—for until the beginning of the nineteenth century, *Flindell's Weekly Miscellany* distributed from house to house from the pannier of a mule, was the only light of the West), became developed about middle life into an original mind and man, sole and absolute within the parish boundary, eccentric when compared to his brethren within civilised

269

regions, and yet, in German phrase, "a whole and seldom man" in his dominion of souls. He was "the parson" in canonical phrase—that is to say, The Parson, somebody of consequence among his own people. These men were not, however, smoothed down into a monotonous aspect of life and manners by this remote and secluded existence. They imbibed, each in his own particular circle, the hue of surrounding objects and were tinged into a distinctive colouring and character by many a contrast of scenery and people. There was "the light of other days", the curate by the sea-shore, who professed to check the turbulence of the "smugglers landing" by his presence on the sands, and who "held the lantern" for the guidance of his flock when the nights were dark, as the only proper ecclesiastical part he could take in the proceedings. He was soothed and silenced by the gift of a keg of hollands or a chest of tea. There was the merry minister of the mines, whose cure was honeycombed by the underground men. He must needs have been artist and poet in his way, for he had to enliven his people three or four times a year, by mastering the arrangements of a "guary" or religious mystery which was performed in the topmost hollow of a green barrow or hill of which many survive, scooped out into vast amphitheatres and surrounded by benches of turf which held two thousand spectators. Such were the historic plays "The Creation" or "Noe's Flood" which still exist in the original Celtic as well as the English text and suggest what critics and antiquaries these Cornish curates, masters of such revels, must have been—for the native language of Cornwall did not lapse into silence until the end of the seventeenth century. [*Editor's Note*: This may not be strictly true, as the last Cornish speaker is traditionally given as Dolly Pentreath, the fish-wife of Mousehole, the date of whose death is given as 1777. Dolly may not actually be the last such speaker, because, at the time of her death, mention is made of another native Cornish speaker, John Nancarrow of Marazion, then aged 45. However, he may also have only spoken Cornish as a secondary language to English. The Cornish language therefore survived past the end of the 17th century.] Then, moreover, here and there, would be one parson more learned than his kind in the mysteries of a deep and thrilling lore of peculiar fascination. He was a man so highly honoured at college for natural gifts and knowledge of learned books which nobody else could read, that when he took his "second orders", the bishop gave him a mantle of scarlet silk to wear upon his shoulders in church, and his lordship put such power into that when the parson had it rightly on, he could "govern any ghost or evil spirit" and even "stop an earthquake".

Such a powerful minister, in combat with supernatural visitations, was one Parson Rudall of Launcetown, whose existence and exploits we gather from the local traditions of the time, from surviving letters and other memorials, and indeed from his own 'diaurnal' (diary) which fell by chance into the hands of the present writer. Indeed the legend of Parson Rudall and the Botathen Ghost will be recognised by many Cornish people as a local remembrance of their boyhood.

It appears then, from the diary of this learned master of the grammar school—for such was his office as well as perpetual curate of the parish—'that a pestilential disease did break forth in our town in the beginning of the year 1665; yea, and it likewise invaded my school, insomuch that therewithal certain of the chief scholars sickened and died'. 'Among those who yielded to the malign influence was Master John Eliot, the eldest son of the worshipful heir of Edward Eliot, Esquire of Trebursey, a stripling of sixteen years of age, but of uncommon parts and hopeful ingenuity. At his own especial motion and earnest desire, I did consent to preach his funeral sermon'. It should be remembered here that, howsoever strange and singular it may sound to us that a mere lad should formally solicit such a performance at the hands of his master, it was in consonance with the habitual usage of those times. The old services for the dead had been abolished by law, and in the

271

stead of sacrament and ceremony, moth's mind and year's mind, the sole substitute which survived was the general desire 'to partake' as they called it, of a posthumous discourse, replete with lofty eulogy and flattering remembrance of the living and the dead. The diary proceeds:

"I fulfilled my undertaking and preached over the coffin in the presence of a full assemblage of mourners and lachrymose friends. An ancient gentleman, who was then and there in the church, a Mr. Bligh of Botathen, was very much affected by my discourse, and he was heard to repeat to himself certain parenthesis therefrom, especially a phrase from Maro Vigilius which I had applied to the deceased youth: *"Et peur ipse fuit cantari dignus."*

The cause whereby the old gentleman was moved by my applications, was this: He had a firstborn and only son—a child who, but a very few months before, had been not unworthy the character I drew of young Master Eliot but who, by some strange accident, had of late quite fallen away from his parents' hopes and become moody, and sullen, and distraught. When the funeral obsequies were over, I had no sooner come out of church than I was accosted by this aged parent, and he besought me incontinently, with a singular energy, that I would resort with him forthwith to his abode at Botathen that very night, nor could I have delivered myself from his importunity, had not Mr. Eliot urged his claim to enjoy my company at his own house. Hereupon I got loose, but not until I had pledged a fast assurance that I would pay him, faithfully, an early visit the next day".

"The Place" as it was called, of Botathen, where old Mr. Bligh resided, was a low-roofed gabled manor-house of the fifteenth century, walled and mullioned, with clustered chimneys of dark-grey stone from the neighbouring quarries of Ventor-gan. The manor was flanked by a pleasance or enclosure in one space, of garden and lawn, and it was surrounded by a solemn grove of stag-horned trees. It had the sombre aspect of age and of solitude, and looked the very scene of strange and supernatural events. A legend might well belong to every gloomy glade around, and there must surely be a haunted room somewhere within its walls. Hither, according to his appointment on the morrow, Parson Ruddal betook himself. Another clergyman, as it appeared, had been invited to meet him, who very soon after his arrival, proposed a walk together in the pleasance on the pretext of showing him, as a stranger, the walks, and trees, until the dinner-bell should strike. There, with much prolixity, and with many a solemn pause, his brother minister proceeded to "unfold the mystery".

A singular infelicity, he declared, had befallen young Master Bligh, once the hopeful heir of his parents and of the lands of Botathen. Whereas he had been from childhood a blithe and marry boy, "the gladness", like Isaac of old, of his father's age, he had suddenly, and of late, become morose and silent—nay, even austere and stern—dwelling apart, always solemn, often in tears. The lad had at first repulsed all questions as to the origin of the great change, but of late he had yielded to the importune researches of his parents, and had disclosed the secret cause. It appeared that he resorted every day, by a pathway across the fields, to this very clergyman's house who had charge of his education and grounded him in the studies suitable to his age. In the course of his daily walk, he had to pass a certain heath or down where the road wound along through tall blocks of granite with open spaces of grassy sward between. There, in a certain spot, and always in one and the same place, the lad declared that he encountered every day, a woman with a pale and troubled face, clothed in a long loose garment of frieze, with one hand always stretched forth, and the other pressed against her side. Her name, he said, was Dorothy Dinglet, for he had known her well from his childhood, and she often used to come to his parents' house; but that which troubled him was that she had now been dead three years, and he himself had been with the neighbours at her burial; so that as the youth alleged, with great simplicity, since he had seen her body laid in the grave, this that he saw every day must needs be her soul or ghost.

"Questioned again and again", said the clergyman, "he never contradicts himself; but he relates the same and the simple tale as a thing that cannot be gainsaid. Indeed, the lad's observance is keen and calm for a boy of his age. The hair of the appearance, sayeth he, is not like anything alive, but is so soft and light that it seemeth to melt away while you look; but her eyes are set and never blink—no, not so when the sun shineth full upon her face. She maketh no steps, but seemeth to swim along the top of the grass, and her hand which is stretched out always, seemeth to point at something far away, out of sight. It is her continual coming, for she never faileth to meet him and to pass on, that hath quenched his spirits; and although he never seeth her by night, yet cannot he get his natural rest".

Thus far the clergyman; whereupon the dinner clock did sound, and we went into the house. After dinner, young Master Bligh had withdrawn with his tutor, under excuse of their books, his parents did forthwith beset me as to my thoughts about their son. So I said warily, "The case is strange but by no means impossible. It is one that I will study, and fear not to handle, if the lad will be free with me, and fulfil all that I desire". The mother was overjoyed, but I perceived that old Mr. Bligh turned pale, and was downcast with some thought which, however, he did not express. Then they bade that Master Bligh should be called to meet me in the pleasance forthwith. The boy came, and he rehearsed to me his tale with an open countenance, and, withal, a pretty modesty of speech. Verily, he seemed *ingenui vultis puer ingenuique pudoris*. Then I signified to him my purpose.

"Tomorrow", said I, "we will go together to the place; and if, as I doubt not, the woman shall appear, it will for me to proceed according to knowledge, and by rules laid down in my books".

274

The unaltered scenery of the legend still survives, and, like the field of the forty footsteps in another history, the place is still visited by those who take an interest in the supernatural tales of old. The pathway leads along a moorland waste, where large masses of rock stand up here and there from the grassy turf, and clumps of heath and gorse weave their tapestry of golden and purple garniture on every side. Amidst all these, and winding along between the rocks, is a natural footway, worn by the scant, rare tread of the village traveller. Just midway, a somewhat larger stretch than usual of green sod expands, which is skirted by the path, and which is still identified as the legendary haunt of the phantom, by the name of Parson Rudall's Ghost.

But we must draw the record of the first interview between the minister and Dorothy from his own words. "We met", thus he writes, "in the pleasance very early, before any others in the house were awake, and together the lad and myself proceeded towards the field. The youth was quite composed, and carried his Bible under his arm, from whence he read to me verses, which he said he had lately picked out, to have always in his mind. These were Job vii. 14, "Thou scarest me with dreams, and terrfiest me through visions" and Deuteronomy xxviii. 67, "In the morning thou shalt say Would to God it were evening and in the evening thou shalt say Would to God it were morning, for the fear of thine heart wherewith thou shalt fear, and for the sight of thine eyes which thou shalt see".

I was much pleased with the lad's ingenuity in these pious applications, but for mine own part, I was somewhat anxious and out of cheer. For aught I knew, this might be a *daemonium meridianum*, the most stubborn spirit to govern and guide that any man can meet, and the most perilous withal. We had hardly reached the accustomed spot, when we both saw her at once, gliding towards us, as punctually as the ancient writers describe the mention of their "lemures, which swoon along the ground, neither marking the sand nor bending the herbage". The aspect of the woman was exactly that which had been related by the lad. There was the pale and stony face, the strange and misty hair, the eyes firm and fixed that gazed, yet not on us, but on something that they saw, far, far away, one hand and arm stretched out, and the other grasping the girdle of her waist. She floated along the field like a sail upon a stream, and glided past the spot where we stood, pausingly. But so deep was the awe that overcame me, as I stood there in the light of day, face to face with a human soul, separate from her bones and flesh, that my heart and purpose both failed me. I had resolved to speak to the spectre in the appointed form of words, but I did not. I stood like one amazed and speechless, until she had passed clean out of sight. One thing remarkable came to pass. A spaniel dog, the favourite of young Master Bligh, had followed us, and lo! when the woman drew nigh, the poor creature began to yell and bark piteously, and ran backward and away, like a thing dismayed and appalled. We returned to the house, and after I had said all that I could to pacify the lad, and to soothe the aged people, I took my leave for that time, with a promise that when I had fulfilled certain business elsewhere which I then alleged, I would return and take orders to assuage these disturbances and their cause.

January 7, 1665—At my own house, I find, by my books, what is expedient to be done; and then Apage, Sathanas!

January 9, 1665—This day I took leave of my wife and family, under the pretext of engagements elsewhere, and made my secret journey to our diocesan city, wherein the good and venerable bishop then abode.

January 10—*Deo gratias*, in safe arrival in Exeter; craved and obtained immediate audience with his lordship, pleading it was for counsel and admonition on a weighty and pressing cause; called to the presence; made obeisance; then and by command stated my case—the Botathen perplexity—which I moved with strong and earnest instances and solemn asseverations

276

of that which I had myself seen and heard. Demanded by his lordship, what was the succour that I had come to entreat at his hands. Replied, licence for my exorcism, that so I might ministerially, allay this spiritual visitant, and thus render to the living and the dead, release from this surprise.

"But", said our bishop, "on what authority do you allege that I am entrusted with the faculty so to do? Our Church, as is well known, hath abjured certain branches of her ancient power on the grounds of perversion and abuse".

"Nay, my lord" I humbly answered, ""under favour, the seventy-second of the canons ratified and rejoined on us, the clergy, anno Domini 1604, doth expressly provide, that no minister, *unless he hath* the licence of his diocesan bishop, shall essay to exorcise a spirit, evil or good". Therefore it was. I did here mildly allege, "that I did not presume to enter on such a work without lawful privilege under your lordship's hand and seal". Hereupon did out wise and learned bishop, sitting in his chair, condescend upon the theme at some length, with many gracious interpretations from ancient writers and from Holy Scriptures, and I did humbly rejoin and reply, till the upshot was that he did call in his secretary and command him to draw the aforesaid faculty, forthwith and without further delay, assigning him a form, insomuch that the matter was incontinently done, and after I had disbursed into the secretary's hands certain monies for signatory purposes, as the manner of such officers hath always been, the bishop did himself affix his signature under the *sigellum* of his see, and deliver the document into my hands. When I knelt to receive his benediction, he softly said: "Let it be secret, Mr. R. Weak brethren! Weak brethren!"

This interview with the bishop, and the success with which he vanquished his lordship's scruples, would seem to have confirmed Parson Rudall very strongly in his own esteem, and to have invested him with that courage which he evidently lacked at his first encounter with the ghost.

277

The entries proceed:

January 11, 1665—'Therewithal did I hasten home and prepare my instruments, and cast my figures for the onset of the next day Took out my ring of brass, and put it on the index finger of my right hand, with the *scutum Davidix* traced thereon."

January 12, 1665—Rode into the gateway at Botathen, armed at all points, but not with Saul's armour, and ready. There is danger from demons but so there is in the surrounding air every day. At early morning then, and alone—for so the usage ordains—I betook me towards the field. It was void and I therefore had due time to prepare. First, I paced and measured out my circle on the grass. Then did I mark my pentacle in the very midst, and at the intersection of the five angles, I did set up and fix my crutch of raun (rowan). Lastly, I took my station south, at the true line of the meridian, and stood facing due north. I watched and watched for a long time. At last there was a kind of trouble in the air, a soft and rippling sound, and all at once a shape appeared, and came on towards me gradually. I opened my parchment-scroll and read aloud the command. She paused and seemed to waver and doubt; stood still, then I rehearsed the sentence again, sounding out every syllable like a chant. She drew near my ring but halted at first outside; on the brink. I sounded again, and at the third time I gave the signal in Syriac—the speech which is used, they say, where such ones dwell and converse in thoughts that glide.

"She was at last obedient, and swam into the midst of the circle, and there stood still, suddenly I saw moreover that she drew back her pointing hand. All this while I do confess that my knees shook under me, and the drops of sweat ran down my flesh like rain. But now, although face to face with the spirit, my heart grew calm and my mind was composed. I knew that the pentacle would govern her, and the ring must bind, until I gave the word. Then I called to mind the rule

A strange tale is written down.

laid down of old, that no angel or fiend, no spirit, good or evil, will ever speak until they have been first spoken to. NB—This is the great law of prayer. God will not yield reply until man hath made vocal entreaty, once and again. So I went on to demand, as the books advise, and the phantom made answer, willingly Questioned wherefore not at rest. Unquiet because of a certain sin. Asked what, and by whom. Revealed it, but it is *sub sigillo*, and therefore *nafas dictu* [*Editor's Note*: It was given to him under the seal of a confessional and cannot be directly spoken about.]; more anon. Enquired what sign she could give that she was a true spirit and not a false fiend. Stated, before next Yule-tide, a fearful pestilence would lay waste the land and myriads of souls would be loosened from their flesh, until as she piteously said: "all our valleys will be full". Asked again why she so terrified the lad. Replied: "It is the law; we must seek a youth or a maiden of clean life, and under age, to receive messages and admonitions". We conversed with many more words, but it is not lawful for me to set them down. Pen and ink would degrade and defile the thoughts she uttered and which my mind received that day. I broke the ring and she passed, but to return once more next day. At evensong, a long discourse with that ancient transgressor Mr. B. Great horror and remorse; entire atonement and penance; whatsoever I enjoin; full acknowledgement before pardon."

January 13, 1665—"At sunrise, I was again in the field. She came in at once, as it seemed with freedom. Enquired if she knew my thoughts, and what I was going to relate? Answered, "Nay we only know what we perceive and hear, we cannot see the heart". Then I rehearsed the penitent words of the man she had come to denounce, and the satisfaction he would perform. Then said she: "Peace in our midst". I went through the proper forms of dismissal, and fulfilled all as it was set down and written in my memoranda and then, with fixed rites, I did dismiss that troubled ghost, until she peacefully withdrew, gliding towards the west. Neither did she ever afterward appear, but was allayed until she shall come in her second flesh in the valley of Armageddon on the last day".

These quaint and curious details from the 'diurnal' of a simple-hearted clergyman of the seventeenth century appear to betoken his personal persuasion of the truth of what he saw and said, although the statements are strongly tinged with what some may term the superstition, and others, the excessive beliefs of those times. It is a singular fact, however, that the canon which authorises exorcism under episcopal licence is still a part of the ecclesiastical law of the Anglican Church, although it might have a singular effect on the nerves of certain of our bishops if their clergy were to resort to them for the faculty which Parson Rudall obtained. The general facts stated in his diary are to this day matters of belief in that neighbourhood; and it has been always accounted a strong proof of the veracity of the Parson and the Ghost that the plague, fatal to so many thousands, did break out in London at the close of that very same year. We may well excuse a triumphant entry, on a subsequent page of the 'diurnal' with the date of July 10, 1665.

"How sorely must the infidels and heretics of this generation be dismayed when they know that this Black Death, which is now swallowing its thousands in the streets of the great city, was foretold six months agone, under the exorcisms of the country minister, by a visible and suppliant ghost! And what pleasures and improvements do such deny themselves who scorn and avoid all opportunity of intercourse with souls separate and the spirits, glad and sorrowful, which inhabit the unseen world."

Index

283

About the Author

Dr. Bob Curran was born in a rural area of County Down, Northern Ireland. On leaving school he worked at many jobs, including journalism, music, truck driving, and grave digging. He travelled in America, North Africa, and Holland before returning to Northern Ireland to settle down and obtain degrees in history and education and a doctorate in Educational Psychology. From his early years, he has been interested in folktales and legends and has made a study of these, writing widely in books and magazines. His work has been printed in his native Ireland, Great Britain, France, Germany, and Japan. Still lecturing and teaching, he lives in County Derry with his wife and young family.